FEB - - 2022

WATCH HER

WATCH HER

EDWIN HILL

THORNDIKE PRESS

A part of Gale, a Cengage Company

GALE

A Cengage Company

LIBRARY OF CONGRESS CIP DATA ON FILE.
CATALOGUING IN PUBLICATION FOR THIS BOOK
IS AVAILABLE FROM THE LIBRARY OF CONGRESS.

ISBN-13: 978-1-4328-9387-3 (hardcover alk. paper)

Published in 2022 by arrangement with Kensington Books, an imprint of Kensington Publishing Corp.

Printed in Mexico
Print Number: 01   Print Year: 2022

To Michael

To Michael

■ ■ ■ ■

1997

■ ■ ■ ■

MAXINE

Eighty-seven stairs, straight up from the sidewalk to the front door of her brand-new condo, and Maxine Pawlikowski adored every single one of them. Her brother, Stan, had his own thoughts.

"A walk-up?" he said. "In Roslindale?"

"What's wrong with Roslindale?" Maxine asked.

"Nothing. If you like getting shot."

"Don't ruin my day."

Stan was a cop, a detective with the Boston police, and Maxine suspected that no neighborhood in the city would have been good enough for his little sister. At thirty-two, he was five years older than Maxine and always — always — would be. He protected her. Or he thought he did. But what Stan didn't know about Maxine's life could have filled twenty of the U-Haul vans they'd driven here today. Besides, she loved her new street with its trees and children and dogs and houses filled with friends, or friends she'd meet soon enough. More importantly, she'd finally made it out of her mother's house in Stoughton. And she had no plans to return.

"You have Mace, right?" Stan asked.

Oh, Jesus.

"I drove through here last night," he continued, "and the streetlighting sucks. There's a blind spot about halfway down the block, in front of that yellow house. When you get home, park right here. And carry your keys . . ."

Maxine tuned him out. At six-foot-two, with a blocky build, Stan had size and strength on his side, but Maxine wasn't much smaller than her brother. She could take care of herself. She *had* taken care of herself, in the back of cars, during college, at work, those secrets she packed away and kept from her brother. Stan couldn't understand those dangers, or that real danger *was* everywhere, and that parking in a well-lit spot was her baseline. But Maxine was twenty-seven years old, single, and owned her own home as of today. Tonight, August 30, 1997, would be the first night Maxine could do whatever she wanted without having to report her whereabouts to anyone, and she'd do it in an eight-hundred-square-foot walk-up (eighty-seven stairs) with laundry in the basement and on-street parking.

"I know," she said, cutting Stan off. "Use keys as a weapon. Shut up and get moving."

She balanced a box on her hip. She stopped with one foot on the first stair because she wanted to remember this moment. She wanted it to be hers, and hers alone.

"Wait up!"

The moment evaporated.

Down the street, Nathan hurried toward them. Nate. Her boyfriend, in a way.

She'd forgotten about him.

Nate taught chemistry at Boston Latin and lived in Stoughton with his own parents, two blocks from her mother's house. He was a year older than Maxine. "Facing the big three-o!" he said at least once a day, along with everything it implied. He'd say it at parties, over dinner, while they lay in bed. And he'd wait for Maxine to fill in the excruciating gap that followed. What Nate — Nathan — didn't understand was that her gap was so different than his.

Nathan wore Dockers and a beige shirt that matched the color of his face and hair and eyes. Everything about him was beige. He jogged toward them and kissed Maxine

11

on the cheek. "Hey, Max," he said.

She hated being called "Max."

Maxine had stunned Nathan when she'd told him she'd bought this condo, that she planned to move here on her own. And waiting till two days ago had been cowardly, she admitted. She'd listened to him cry and beg her to stay in Stoughton. Finally, she'd told him to meet her here after she'd finished signing the papers. Because she needed the help moving.

Soon, Nate would have to go, and not in the temporary way. In a way that hurt, sometimes for months, sometimes forever. Or so Maxine had heard. No one had broken Maxine's heart; not yet. She almost looked forward to the feeling.

"Grab a box!" she said, leading the way up the first flight of stairs, through tiered gardens overflowing with perennials, to a porch suspended twenty feet above the sidewalk. A woman let herself out the front door. She had braids cascading down her back, and a bag slung over one shoulder.

"I'm on the second floor," she said. "Brandy," she added. "Like the singer."

Maxine introduced herself and Stan and forgot to mention Nathan.

"She's on the third floor," Stan said. "Once you get to know her, she'll talk your ear off."

"Be careful to close this door," Brandy said. "It doesn't latch on its own."

"We'll get that fixed," Stan said.

Brandy left them on the porch, heading down the stairs to a red Geo Metro. Later, Maxine promised herself, she'd ask Brandy over for drinks and make sure they became friends. Maybe she'd invite her over to watch *Friends* with her friend Jennifer on Thursday night. Maybe they'd drink Chardonnay.

Maxine led the way up the remaining two flights, over orange and brown shag that had to be twenty years old. On the landing outside her apartment, she balanced the box on her knee while fishing out the key.

"We'll get that door replaced," Stan said, tapping the opaque glass on the top pane. "We'll put in a dead bolt and make an appointment with the alarm company."

The door glided open. Inside, the walls were covered in pink and gold wallpaper. The kitchen had yellowed linoleum tiles and chipped Formica counters and a refrigerator that jutted into the center of the room like an afterthought, but all Maxine saw was the promise of gleaming hardwood floors and windows in every wall and stunning views of the Boston skyline. She saw the future.

"What a dump!" Nathan said.

He dropped his boxes by the door even though she'd labeled them KITCHEN in thick, black Sharpie, but she forgave him. He'd be gone soon enough.

"That van won't unload itself," she said.

They spent the next two hours going up and down those stairs till cardboard boxes lined the walls in each room and sweat soaked their T-shirts. When they finished, Maxine ordered pizza using the wall phone and cracked open three bottles of Rolling Rock. Outside, on her front deck, she toasted her new home while the sun set.

"I'm proud of you," Stan said.

"We can spend weekdays here and weekends in Stoughton," Nathan said. "This'll make my commute so much easier."

"Sure," Maxine said.

Stan's phone rang, one of those cell phones, the ones that had taken over coffee shops, the ones that people yammered on in loud voices. Stan wanted Maxine to get one so that he could "check on her," but she couldn't imagine a phone following her wherever she went.

He took the call inside. Nate lifted his beer and smiled, his mind seeming to churn as he tried to think of something to talk about. "Great place," he said.

"Do you go by Nathan or Nate?"

Shouldn't Maxine know this? They'd dated off and on for years. Since high school!

"Either's fine," Nathan said. "It's like you. Maxine or Max. It's all the same."

Stan leaned through the doorway. "Duty calls," he said. "Over by Ruggles."

"The pizza isn't even here," Maxine said.

"I'll grab something later."

She listened as he thundered down the stairs. Out on the street, he waved before driving off in his sedan.

"Good guy," Nate said.

"He's a pain in the ass," Maxine said. "What should we do now?"

Nate sat on a pile of cardboard boxes that matched his khakis. He shielded his face from the setting sun as an attempt at the salacious touched his beige eyes. Sometimes, Maxine slept with him because they had nothing better to do. She even considered it now.

"You should go," she said, surprising even herself.

"But . . . the pizza."

Nate was nice. Too nice. Maxine was done with nice.

"And I'm facing the big three-o," he said.

"Find someone who wants to face it with you."

To his credit, Nathan got angry. His beige face even turned red. "Are you dumping me?"

Maxine hadn't dumped anyone before, but she knew to take the blame herself. "It's not you," she said. "It's me."

When the pizza arrived, Maxine learned that the buzzer to the front door didn't work, so she trotted all the way down two flights and back up. She dug her clock radio from one of the boxes and turned the station to NPR, but the news was all about a car crash in Paris, endless updates, speculation on who would survive, and it was too sad, too depressing to imagine that beautiful body mangled in a highway tunnel. Maxine turned to WBCN and danced through the apartment.

Her apartment.

Fiona Apple felt like a criminal. So did Maxine. And like Fiona, she didn't mind. So, when the phone rang, she ignored it, assuming it was Nate, ready to beg.

She was happier than she'd ever been in her entire life. Right now.

The phone rang again, and when it rang a

third time, Maxine checked caller ID. It wasn't Nathan. It was Jennifer. Jennifer Matson. Maxine's best friend. She let the call go to voice mail. Tonight wasn't meant for sharing.

Maxine had met Jennifer when Maxine's boss, Tucker Matson, had asked her to the house for a barbecue to meet his family. She'd even brought Nathan with her. Like Maxine, Jennifer was twenty-seven years old, but the two of them had made such different life choices it was hard to believe they were the same age. Maxine still had one foot in adolescence, while Jennifer already had two children, a Newfoundland named Shadow, and, in Tucker, a thirty-seven-year-old husband with money to burn since he owned the art school where Maxine worked as the director of admissions. Jennifer and Tucker lived a few miles away in a Queen Anne–style mansion with a name — Pinebank. It was right on the shore of Jamaica Pond, and its renovation had been recorded all spring on *This Old House.* Most Thursdays, Jennifer would leave the girls with Tucker and come over so that the two of them could watch *Friends* and *Seinfeld,* with *Suddenly Susan* in between. Jennifer, who had long, straight blond hair, would say, "I'm like Phoebe and you're like

Monica," even though Jennifer, with her perfect life and perfect family, was nothing at all like any of the characters on *Friends*.

Still, it had surprised Maxine when, two years earlier, Jennifer had named her second daughter Rachel.

Maxine secretly yearned for alone time with Jennifer's girls, four-year-old Vanessa and two-year-old Rachel. She loved when she drove through the trees to their house, and they greeted her at the front door like children from a Victorian novel. They'd take her hand and lead her to their tiny table with its tiny teapot and cups, where the one choice, the one challenge, was graham crackers or saltines.

Maxine sat on her front porch. Night had settled over the city. The people who'd packed the street during the day had retreated for the evening. A car alarm went off. She checked to be sure it wasn't her own car, and then settled into her chair. See, she could get used to the city. She could get used to these noises. Once she had more than cardboard boxes as furniture and had covered the bare light bulbs with shades, she could call this place home.

A voice rose from the street.

Below, in a circle of light from a street

lamp, Brandy danced with a friend before kissing the friend goodbye and heading up the stairs. The sound of her new neighbor's shoes hitting the floor echoed through the walls. It was good to have someone close. Someone to rely on. Maxine's body was sore from moving. A good sore. It was Labor Day weekend, so she'd have Monday off to recover.

Cool air blew through her hair. And the phone rang.

Jennifer.

Again.

■ ■ ■ ■

Twenty-Four Years Later

Wednesday, March 31

■ ■ ■ ■

HESTER

Freezing rain splattered the windshield and heat poured from the vents as Hester Thursby's non-husband, Morgan, tried to parallel park their truck on an industrial street in Jamaica Plain. A week into spring, and winter still had a hold on Boston.

"Success," he said, after the third attempt, cutting the engine and leaning across the cab to kiss Hester on the cheek.

Tonight, he'd tamed his red hair and changed out of the scrubs he wore at the veterinary hospital and into a navy blue suit that fit perfectly, a suit that made its way out of his closet about once a year.

"Hello, Mrs.," he said, kissing her again.

"Yuck! Quit kissing."

Hester's five-year-old niece, Kate, glared at them from the rear cab. These days, the girl seemed to drink in everything and anything that happened around her and didn't think twice about voicing her opin-

23

ions. It was a good quality to have, though sometimes Hester had to remind herself to encourage it. Kate would finish kindergarten in a few months, and Hester knew she'd blink and soon enough the girl would be heading to college. She tried to make every moment with her niece special, even the ones that gave her a glimpse of the teenage years.

"How's this?" Morgan asked, kissing Hester with exaggerated smacks. He rolled over the seat and into the back, and kissed Kate, too, who shrieked and shoved him away. "Uncle Morgan, you are disgusting!"

"Guilty as charged," Morgan said.

"And saying no is your prerogative," Hester said.

"It is!" Morgan said, having the good sense not to go in for a final smooch.

"What's prerogative?" Kate asked.

"Your privilege. Your right. You're in control of your body," Hester said, quickly adding, "except when it comes to eating vegetables."

"None of us has a choice when it comes to vegetables," Morgan said.

"It's pouring out," Hester said. "We'll have to run between the raindrops."

"You can't run between raindrops," Kate said.

"And I can't fool you with anything these days," Hester said.

She opened the door to the truck and leapt to the asphalt below while yanking the hood up on her blue raincoat. When she stepped onto the running board, Kate had already undone her seat belt. "I can do it myself," the girl said, slipping right past Hester's outstretched arms and leaping to the ground.

Yes, you can.

Morgan dashed to their side, and the three of them hurried through the rain, down Amory Street, toward a long, brick building that took up most of the block. Banners for Prescott University, a local art school, spanned the building's street face, and lights blared from plate-glass windows. A prominent placard over the entrance read TUCKER MATSON STUDENT CENTER and beside it, their destination, THE MATSON GALLERY.

"Brand-new campus center," Hester said. "Big change. I haven't been to this neighborhood in a few years."

"I went to high school a few blocks from here," Morgan said.

Hester tensed at this tidbit of information. For most of their nine-year relationship, Hester and Morgan had had an unspoken rule: they didn't talk about their pasts, including dating history or family. It was like they'd both appeared on Earth fully formed on the day they'd met. Lately, though, Morgan had begun to dangle factoids like this one, tiny windows into his past. She could have asked follow-up questions — What school? Were you in the marching band? Did you date the head cheerleader? — but she let the statement hang between them.

Kate, however, did not.

"Can we see your school?" she asked.

"I don't think it's there anymore," Morgan said. "They tore it down."

"When?"

"Maybe ten years ago."

Kate considered the answer for a moment. "Before I was born," she said, her latest obsession being the time before her own existence.

"Long before," Morgan said.

Hester yanked open the glass doors to the gallery and led the way into an atrium that spanned the length of two buildings. The noise from the crowd thankfully drowned out any more of Kate's questions.

"I didn't know this would be such a big deal," Hester shouted.

Banners fell from the soaring ceilings announcing BOSTON'S THIRTY UNDER 30 IN

GRAPHIC DESIGN while servers in black ties circulated among the crowd of women in cocktail dresses and men in expensive glasses. Hester recognized familiar faces from TV, local newscasters and politicians, even a state senator. She pointed to a photo on one of the banners. "There's Jamie," she said, grinning at the image of their friend's beaming face.

Kate took a step toward the banner, into the throngs surrounding them. Hester grabbed her hand. "Stick with me," she said.

Kate glared at her. "I'm not a baby," she said.

"I know, but stay where I can see you anyway."

Morgan checked their coats and offered an arm. "Should we dive in?"

Hester smoothed the fabric on her black cocktail dress and put a hand to her hair, which she'd tied into a bun. She'd even dug out contact lenses and makeup for this event. She occasionally attended cocktail parties at Harvard, where she worked as a research librarian, but most nights she spent at home with Morgan and Kate and their basset hound, Waffles, or, occasionally, out with a tight-knit group of friends, one of whom, Angela White, Sergeant Detective Angela White, walked toward her now.

"I'm like a fly in milk at this shindig," Angela said.

Usually, Angela wore tailored suits and practical shoes that made it easy to move on the job, but tonight she'd opted for a multicolored caftan and had wound a scarf around her thick, natural hair and tied it in an elaborate knot. She even wore heels. "I went for artistic," she said, when she caught Hester eyeing her getup. "Don't get used to it. These shoes are killing me."

Hester brushed a few dog hairs from Angela's dress. "George travels with you, even when you leave him home."

"Damn dog," Angela said, shooting Morgan a glare. "I still blame you for foisting that creature on us, Dr. Maguire."

Angela's wife, Cary, appeared and handed her a plastic cup of white wine. "She loves George," Cary said, in her soft, therapeutic voice. "Even when he slobbers."

"He's a pain in my ass."

Isaiah, Cary's seven-year-old son, tugged at Hester's sleeve. Unlike Kate, Isaiah was shy and avoided speaking unless Hester crouched to let him whisper in her ear. "I won the hundred-meter butterfly," he said.

"Like Michael Phelps," Hester said. "Show me the ribbon next time I'm over."

Just as Angela hated most dogs, Hester, as

a rule, wasn't a fan of most kids other than Kate. She made a few rare exceptions, and Isaiah was one of them.

Morgan sidled up to her. "Don't you want to know more about my high school?" he whispered.

A server swung by with a tray of well-timed hors d'oeuvres. "Lobster and corn empanada?"

Hester shoved one into her mouth to keep from answering, but Morgan waited patiently for her to finish chewing.

"You could tell me something too," he said. "It could be a game. One question a day. Ask me anything. We both have to answer, no matter what."

"That sounds like a terrible game," Hester said.

"Come on. Tell me something little. Did you play the clarinet?"

"Do I look like I played the clarinet?"

"A thespian?"

"Not even close."

Morgan tilted his head.

"You look like Waffles waiting for a treat," Hester said, and when he still wouldn't let it go, she added, "Tomorrow, at work, I'll find any answer I want. Maybe I'll figure out what Jamaica Plain schools were demolished. I'll find your yearbook, and I'll do it

29

all in secret. Happy?"

Morgan grinned. "You wouldn't do that. We trust each other too much."

She wouldn't. But it was nice to know she could.

"Mathlete?" he asked.

"Fine," Hester said. "Chess club."

"That, I should have guessed," Morgan said.

"Where did the kids go?" Angela asked.

Hester turned in the crowded room, but Kate had managed to slip away. So had Isaiah, though Hester would bet money that Kate had led the escape. "I'll find her. Get me a whisky. Neat."

Morgan saluted and headed toward the bar.

"You go that way," Angela said. "I'll go this way."

"Text if you find them."

Hester shoved her way into the crowd. She also shoved down the fear that still gripped at her heart whenever Kate was out of sight. They couldn't have gone far.

Not in thirty seconds.

BARRET

A little girl with curly, honey-colored hair pushed her way past Barret. "Where are the snacks?" she asked. Barret pointed toward the table of hors d'oeuvres on the other side of the room that he'd helped set up earlier, and the girl shoved her way into the crowd, tugging a boy behind her. A moment later, a tiny woman in a black dress flashing a photo asked if he'd seen the girl. "Wearing a light blue dress," she said. "Bossy."

"They were looking for food," Barret said.

"Figures," the woman said, jostling her way forward.

Barret had already filled his stomach with as many of the hors d'oeuvres as he could pilfer, even if he'd been told that staff should wait till the end of the evening to eat. He'd also stuffed the pockets of his rented suit with more to eat later. He'd make at least two meals out of the spoils, because he'd spent what he'd earn tonight on renting this getup — black suit, black shoes, thick-framed glasses with non-prescription lenses — to look like an artist. Someday soon, he'd be one of the Thirty Under 30 in something. He was convinced of it. Now, he had to convince the rest of the world.

He grabbed a crab cake from a passing tray as the woman in the black dress re-emerged, this time dragging the two glum-looking children behind her. "You can't run off like that," she said.

"We were hungry," the boy said.

"What if the fire alarm went off?"

Barret could practically feel the girl's eye roll through the stuffy air. "We'd find the helpers," she said.

The woman stopped in front of him. "Thanks," she said. "They were exactly where you said they'd be."

A waiter swung by, and the woman took two plastic cups. "Let me buy you a drink," she said, handing him a cup of red wine. "The finest box around."

Barret couldn't have picked box over bottle to save his life, but he took the cup anyway, even if he'd been warned — upon threat of immediate dismissal — not to drink tonight, especially since he was under-age. He swallowed the wine in one gulp and got rid of the evidence.

"Hester Thursby," the woman said.

Barret introduced himself.

"This place is a zoo," Hester said, before disappearing into the throngs again.

Barret surveyed the room. The woman in charge of the event, Maxine something, stood against the wall, probably taking notes. She had to be fifty, at least, and had a pouf of auburn hair that hovered over her sagging face. She worked at the school in an administrative role and had hired him as temporary staff for tonight's grand opening. All Barret knew was to stay out of her way.

Barret was nineteen and heading toward the end of his first semester at Prescott University. The one thing that had saved him from going completely broke was that he'd been in the drama club in high school and knew how to work a sound system. Somehow, he'd earned enough cash to scrape by in his first months in this new city. He pushed his way through the crowd to where the soundboard was set up and checked the mics and amplifier. The program would start in about ten minutes, but everything here seemed ready.

Someone tapped his arm.

"Are you in charge of sound?"

Gavin Dean appeared beside him, standing close in a way that made Barret's skin crawl. Gavin was the CFO of the college. He was probably around thirty and wore a houndstooth suit the color of the winter sky. "The mic rubs against my beard," he said. "Can you test it?"

Gavin's five o'clock shadow had probably taken a half hour to perfect.

"We'll use a lavalier instead of the head-piece," Barret said. "It'll be on your lapel."

"Great. Call when you need me," Gavin said, heading toward a small group of guests, where he laughed, his hand lingering on a woman's lower back.

Not a surprise. He was a certified creep.

Barret had met him before — alone, in Gavin's office — but since then, Barret had cut his blond hair and dyed it black. He'd also pierced his ears with flesh tunnels and tattooed a snake on his neck, all with the goal of transforming into someone new. Apparently, he'd succeeded. Gavin hadn't seemed to remember him.

Now, Barret watched as the man floated from one group to another, easily making his way through the crowd. Students stopped to talk to him, and Barret wondered how many of them had endured similar experiences behind closed doors.

He took out the headsets and lined them

up. Across the room, he noticed a swish of Botticelli curls and the wild eyes of Libby Thomas, Barret's girlfriend, at least the closest he'd been to having one since Alice, back home. What are you doing here? he texted.

Free wine! she wrote a second later.

Hang out till I'm done. We can leave together.

Everything about Libby was intense, from those tight curls and green eyes, to the way she tackled every project in her architecture program. Tonight, Tucker Matson, with his thick, white hair and eyebrows like caterpillars, stopped to talk to her, as though they knew each other. She leaned against the wall, chatting away.

"We should get set up. It's almost time to start."

Gavin was back.

Barret handed him one of the lavaliers.

Libby stood against the wall, watching them both. Barret gave her a little wave.

"Do I know you?" Gavin asked.

Barret focused on the soundboard and mumbled, "Perv," under his breath.

"What did you say?"

"Run this up your coat," Barret said. "Attach it to your lapel."

Gavin snatched the lavalier as a woman

with close-cropped blond hair and a sleeve of tattoos joined them.

"It's about that time," she said.

This was Vanessa Matson, the twenty-eight-year-old president of Prescott University. And Gavin Dean's wife. She was also the head curator at the Matson Gallery. In the few years since Vanessa had joined the family business, she'd discovered dozens of local artists. Barret would have given anything to have her notice him. He grabbed a headset for her and tripped.

"Steady there," Vanessa said, adding "it's okay," as she took the headset, looped it over her ear, and attached the transmitter to her dress. "I've put these on about a million times. But you'll have to help my dad out. He can barely turn on the TV. Dad, get over here," she added, waving Tucker Matson over.

When the lights dimmed, Barret took his place in the sound booth. He looked to where Libby had been standing earlier, but she was gone.

HESTER

"Don't run off again," Hester said to Kate as they returned to their small group, and Morgan handed her a drink.

"But . . ." Kate began.

"No buts. Make sure I can see you."

"The man of the hour!" Morgan said, as Jamie Williams joined them.

At six-foot-five and 250 pounds, Jamie towered over most people in the room, his dark complexion standing out, too, in a sea of white faces. "Causing trouble?" he asked Kate.

"No!" Kate said.

"Her?" Hester said. "Never."

Jamie gave Isaiah a high five and lifted Kate in the air while the girl shrieked in delight. "Trouble or not," he said, "glad you made it."

He lived in the first-floor apartment of Hester and Morgan's house along with his bichon frise, Butch. When Hester first met him, he'd had trouble speaking after suffering a head wound. Now, after years of speech therapy, he'd regained most of his speaking abilities, though he still stumbled over words.

"I wouldn't have missed this in a million years," Hester said. "None of us would."

"How much of this did you design?" Angela asked, waving a hand at the banners and awnings throughout the room.

"All of it," a middle-aged woman said as she joined them. "At least all the good parts. We're trying to rebrand with the new campus opening, and Jamie's been the best design intern I've ever had. Anything terrible, you can blame on me."

"Maxine!" Angela said.

Hester remembered meeting Maxine Pawlikowski at Angela's Super Bowl party in February, where the woman had spent the entire evening texting on her phone. Tonight, she'd teased her auburn hair into a cloud and wore an eggplant-colored pantsuit that somehow worked.

"Ms. Pawlikowski," Morgan said.

"Dr. Maguire," Maxine said. "And don't call an old broad *Ms.* It makes us feel decrepit."

"Maxine, then," Morgan said. "Maxine brings her dogs to my practice."

"I forgot I'd hooked the two of you up," Angela said. "Maxine hired Jamie, too. She's the general manager of Prescott University."

Maxine banged out a text on her phone. "Excuse me. I have to deal with something," she said, as she disappeared into the crowd.

Hester drank down her whisky and grabbed a glass of champagne from a passing tray. The lights dimmed. "Time for toasts," she said, checking to be sure that Kate hadn't used the darkness to stage another escape.

To be safe, she rested a hand on the girl's shoulder as, all around them, screens descended from the ceiling, and then a video began playing, featuring snippets of each of the thirty artists being honored tonight. In Jamie's snippet, he focused on the importance of friends and family, and Hester punched him in the arm. "All true," he whispered.

When the video stopped, a young woman stood at the podium, a spotlight shining on her short blond hair. Two men flanked her, one older with a thatch of white hair that rivaled Albert Einstein's, the other younger and styled within an inch of his life. "Welcome, everyone!" the woman said. "We're livecasting this on Twitter," she added, "so keep the applause coming!"

"That's Vanessa Matson," Angela whispered. "The president of the college."

"How old is she?" Hester asked. "Twelve? She looks more like a club kid than a college president."

After fifteen years at Harvard University, Hester was used to a more austere leadership team.

"Her family owns the school," Angela said. "That's her father on the left. The one with the eyebrows. He stepped aside a year or two ago, and Vanessa replaced him as president. Vanessa's husband is the other one. Gavin Dean. He's the CFO."

"They keep it in the family," Hester said. "This is one of those for-profit colleges, right?"

"And all the profit goes to the Matsons," Angela said. "It's a privately held company. No investors. No stockholders. And sometimes it seems like they own half of Boston."

Most of what Hester knew about the school she'd learned on TV, from the ads that ran for it during late-night television. As she checked out the well-heeled and connected crowd here tonight, she doubted many of them would shell out tens of thousands of dollars for a school like this one.

"Maxine's worked here for decades,"

Angela said. "She runs the show, but don't tell that to Vanessa or Tucker."

Hester tuned in as the applause around her faded, and a black-and-white image of the building they were in appeared on the screen.

"If you came to this building a hundred years ago," Vanessa Matson began, "you'd be standing at the center of a thriving sugar factory, one that processed cane shipped all the way from the Caribbean and employed hundreds of people. Twenty years ago, you'd have been lucky if rats didn't run over your toes as buildings like this one all over the city were left to the elements. Prescott University acquired this site when my father" — Vanessa paused, turning to Tucker Matson and applauding softly — "envisioned a new future for our college. And tonight is the culmination of that vision!"

Vanessa led a more rapturous applause as Tucker raised a hand to wave.

"Tomorrow, the new campus opens with state-of-the-art classrooms, the latest equipment, and a faculty consisting of the leading thinkers from around the world! But first, let's pause — and I can tell you, I could use a pause, because the last six months have been exhausting. Let's pause to celebrate my own dream, the Matson

41

Gallery, this beautiful, modern atrium where we stand tonight. The Matson Gallery will be used to showcase up-and-coming artists, and the very best students and faculty at Prescott University. We hope that it becomes a center for Boston's creatives!"

Hester couldn't help but be impressed by the space, with its steel frame and gleaming windows. She'd sat on enough committees at Harvard to know how much planning and negotiation went into the smallest decision, let alone a whole new campus.

"Now, for the main show," Vanessa said, introducing Tucker. "He'll present tonight's Thirty Under Thirty, a series we hope to launch across many mediums. He's not only my father," she added, "he's the chairman of the board, and my boss."

Tucker took Vanessa's place at the podium. His voice boomed from the speaker. "And I can still fire you," he said, to a smattering of chuckles while Vanessa offered a practiced smile.

For the next few moments, Tucker read off the names of the men and women being honored, while Vanessa and her husband, Gavin, handed out plaques. When Tucker reached Jamie's name, Hester's small group cheered as loudly as they could. Morgan lifted Kate on his shoulders while she clapped her hands over her head. Even from halfway across the room, Hester could see Jamie blushing as he beamed into the cameras.

At the end of the ceremony, Vanessa took to the podium again to thank everyone for coming. "And I might as well tell you now, this opening couldn't have been delayed much longer," she said, touching her belly. "Because there'll be a new Matson in about six months."

Gavin Dean leaned across her. "She means a new Dean," he said.

"We can talk later, dear," Vanessa said. "Did you hear that, Mommy? You have a grandchild on the way!"

Vanessa waved into the camera and blew a kiss before stepping away from the podium and out of the light.

As the ceremony ended, a young woman shoved her way through the crowd toward the exit, her eyes wild, her tightly curled hair trailing behind her.

"What do you think happened there?" Angela asked.

"Who knows?" Hester said. "Maybe they forgot her plaque."

MAXINE

Maxine mouthed along as Vanessa worked her way through the speech. Maxine knew every joke, every emphasis, and every pause, because she'd written the whole thing. The vision for the school — the one Vanessa credited to her father — had been Maxine's too. She'd found this building and this neighborhood over a decade ago, when Vanessa was still in high school, and had immediately seen where she could take the school. Tucker probably believed he'd done the work, labored over the ideas, fought for the funding, and Maxine was happy to let him bask in the glory. Tonight was her night, even if no one else knew it.

She'd also known about Vanessa's surprise announcement — the baby. Vanessa told her these things before she released them to the world. She trusted Maxine, and knew that when it came to secrets, Maxine was a steel vault.

As Tucker launched into the list of artists, Maxine tuned out. Even Tucker Matson couldn't mess up reading a list, and she had her own to-do list to worry about. On Monday, she was launching a new outreach program to current students and alums. It was part of the whole rebranding of the school, and her goal was to connect Prescott University to longtime career success. Tonight, when she got home, she'd review the student data Gavin had pulled together for her — late, as usual — and figure out what he'd missed.

She checked her e-mail with a sense of dread. Earlier today, she'd fired some of the adjunct faculty. Via e-mail. She hadn't exactly fired them, but she'd let them know that their contracts wouldn't be renewed come the end of the term, and for adjunct faculty, no contract meant no job. Thankfully, none of the fired instructors had responded yet.

Her phone pinged.

She read through the message and banged in a response. A pipe had burst in Van Gough, one of the dormitories over by Forest Hills, and shit was dripping from the twelfth floor. Actual shit. Students were on the verge of rioting, and if the maintenance team didn't show up soon, Maxine would head over there herself with a wrench and plunger. She carried both in the trunk of her car.

People began to applaud. The program was over. She put away her mental list for later. At the podium, a crowd surrounded Vanessa, congratulating her on the opening of the gallery and the news of her pregnancy. When Maxine approached, Vanessa pulled her in for a hug, letting go long after Maxine would have ended the embrace herself.

"She already knew," Gavin said to Vanessa. "Didn't she?"

"Only I knew," Vanessa said, keeping their truth going.

"Tucker," Maxine said, wondering why the man couldn't invest in a pair of tweezers.

"Maxine," Tucker said, with a curt nod before excusing himself and disappearing into the crowd.

"He's pissed off," Vanessa whispered. "Now he's stuck with Gavin, whether he likes it or not. You are too."

"I love Gavin," Maxine whispered.

"Keep telling yourself that."

"Don't stay too late tonight," Maxine said. "We have the video shoot in the morning."

"How could I forget?"

The sound guy took Vanessa's headset.

"Do you need anything else tonight?" he asked.

His name tag read BARRET. *HE/HIM* as Maxine's read MAXINE. *SHE/HER.* You couldn't take anything for granted these days. "Make sure the equipment is packed away," Maxine said.

She left Vanessa to her fans, floating through the guests, checking details. The charcuterie station was mobbed. So was the dessert buffet. In the prep area, the catering staff worked in an intense silence. As she piled a half-dozen hors d'oeuvres on a cocktail napkin, Dr. Maguire — Morgan — watched her. He seemed so out of context here, away from his office. Morgan was attractive. And, with at least a decade on him, flirting was safe. "I thought you lived at the animal hospital," she said, sidling up to him. "And I'm ravenous," she added, stuffing a crab cake into her mouth.

"They let me out from time to time," he said.

"I'd forgotten our small world," she said. "My brother, Stan, works with Angela at the police department, so I guess she's the cog in this wheel. I'm glad you made it tonight."

"Me too."

"Where's that wife of yours?"

"She's around here somewhere. Non-wife, though. We've been non-spouses for nine years now."

"You should take care of that," Maxine said.

"I would if I could," Morgan said, in a way that made Maxine realize she'd overstepped. Still, at age fifty, she hardly cared.

"Life'll pass you by before you know it," she added.

"I've heard," Morgan said.

To Maxine, cocktail parties were like an endless journey from island to island. As soon as she found one island, she wanted to swim out in search of a new one. She excused herself. By the entrance, she stopped by the coat check. A swirl of raw air swept through the open door, lifting skirts and hair, sending cocktail napkins flitting across the floor. A moment later, she slid in front of Morgan's non-wife in the line at the bar and ordered a Manhattan. "What do you want?" she asked. "It's on me."

"Whisky, neat," Hester said. "And a white wine spritzer."

"Lightweight."

"That one's for Angela. I can drink anyone under the table."

"I'll take you up on that one of these days."

"Challenge accepted," Hester said. "Great party, by the way."

"It's been in the works for about ten years," Maxine said. "I hope the empanadas live up to the hype."

"I've had about a dozen of them," Hester said.

Maxine fished the cherry from the cup and tasted the alcoholic sweetness on it. "You're that woman who finds missing people," she said. "I remember now. I read about you."

"Guilty," Hester said. "Or I used to before I found out what assholes people can be."

"It's an important lesson," Maxine said. "However painful."

Maxine's phone pinged again.

"That thing's relentless," Hester said. "You on call?"

"It seems like it, most days," Maxine said, reading through a text from Jennifer Matson, and feeling her blood pressure skyrocket. "Where's Angela?"

"This way," Hester said, leading them across the room, to where Angela stood with Cary. "I barely recognize you in that getup," Maxine said.

"I don't recognize me either," Angela said.

"I need your help."

"As in, you need help from the police?" Angela asked.

"Not yet. I'll tell you about it in the car." Maxine turned to Hester. "You're a librarian, right?" she asked.

"You know a lot about me," Hester said.

"I know a lot about many people," Maxine said. "You should come too."

BARRET

Barret wheeled the soundboard through a dark hallway and into a storage closet. He texted Libby one more time to see where she'd gone, though she didn't respond. As he hung the headsets in a cabinet, he sensed someone approaching, and a shadow stretched across the floor beside him.

"Dude."

Barret spun around to face Gavin Dean, who leaned into the doorjamb, blocking any retreat.

"What kind of name is Barret, anyway?" Gavin asked.

"Mine," Barret said.

Gavin took out a billfold and counted five twenties. "Great job with the sound tonight. No feedback," he said, folding the money into quarters and tucking it into Barret's shirt pocket. "The way I like it. Quiet."

The cash burned through Barret's shirt.

"You're a student here. We've met, right?"

51

Gavin asked.

"I don't know."

"You don't know if you're a student, or you don't know if we've met?"

Barret didn't answer.

"It doesn't matter. I have your name. I'll look you up in the morning."

As Barret tried to maneuver around him, Gavin put an arm across the doorway. "We're good, right?" he asked.

The party seemed far away, the rumble of voices distant. Barret let his gaze fall to the floor and nodded. It was best not to engage.

"Good boy," Gavin said, before returning to the party.

Barret wanted to take a bath. He remembered sitting in Gavin's office in January, when he'd stopped in to talk about his housing situation. Gavin had listened, leaning forward, his blue eyes intent. At one point, he rested his dimpled chin on a fist.

"I hoped I might get a different room," Barret said. "My roommates are . . . We don't get along that well. They'd be happier with someone else."

"I can't imagine that!" Gavin said.

"It'd be easier if I had a single."

Gavin stood suddenly and came around the desk. He had the lean body of a runner, and the confidence of someone who knew people looked at him. "Tell me where you're from," he said.

"Illinois," Barret said.

"And your major?"

"Painting."

"I can't believe your roommates wouldn't want you around. Someone like you." Gavin leaned across Barret and tapped the office door closed. "We don't usually move students around once the semester is under way," he said. "Unless there's a motivation."

"It's tight quarters," Barret said. "Four of us in one room."

Gavin was close, too close. His breath reeked of coffee. "Tight quarters," he said. "I bet. We all have secrets we'd like to hide."

Barret knew where the conversation could have gone. For a price he'd have gotten what he wanted. But even at nineteen, he had too much practice fending off threats far more dangerous than Gavin Dean. He excused himself and left before the suggestions turned real, before he allowed himself to become the hunted. Since then, he hadn't returned to the housing office or reported the incident. And he still lived in the quad. What proof did he have, anyway?

Fuck you, Gavin Dean.

Barret finished putting the equipment away. Outside, he turned his gaze toward

53

the sky and let the rain wash his face clean. Then he ripped his name tag off and threw it on the wet ground. He took out the five twenties and thought about tossing those too, but it was too much money to give up, too many art supplies to buy, and the only person he'd hurt would be himself. He tucked the wad into his wallet and headed toward Centre Street in downtown Jamaica Plain, toward Libby's house.

Barret had met Libby Thomas the day he arrived at the school in January, after he'd left home for the first time ever, and had taken a bus to a train to a subway, and then walked through the ice-encased city toward freedom. On campus, he headed straight to the studios as soon as he could.

There, he found Libby.

She sat at a drafting table working through a design. Not till Barret dropped his bag on the floor did she look at him.

"Today's my first day," he said.

"This is my last semester," Libby said. "I transferred here in the fall."

"From where?"

Libby drew a line across the drafting paper. "Somewhere else," she said.

"I'm a painter."

"I'm an architect. Pull up a chair. Get to

54

work. That's why we're here."

At the end of that first day, when all Barret wanted was to heave his travel-worn body into the bottom bunk in his dorm room, he already called Libby a friend.

"Let's hit the town," she said, dragging him to her apartment to get ready.

"I don't have an ID," Barret said.

Libby had her back to him, wearing nothing but a pair of white, high-waisted underwear. Masses of curls spilled over her shoulders. "You won't need one," she said, as she squeezed a halter top over her head. "Not when I'm there to watch out for you."

Since then, they'd spent nearly every free moment together. Recently, right before Spring Break, it had turned to something more.

Libby lived on the second floor of a rundown triple-decker with two roommates. Sasha and Emma. Emma and Sasha. Semma? Emasha? Barret couldn't tell them apart. They walked through the long, railroad-style apartment in tandem, finishing each other's sentences, wearing each other's clothes. If they didn't talk about boys one hundred percent of the time, Barret would have assumed they were a couple.

Libby didn't like him to come over without an invitation. Even so, he found himself on her street, staring up through the rain at her darkened window. He must have stood there for a half hour before the bedroom light went on, and Libby walked into the room, laptop balanced on one arm. By then, Barret was soaked to the skin. He scaled the trellis that ran up the side of the house to the window. Through the rain-streaked glass, Libby worked feverishly on a design while simultaneously polishing off a family-sized bag of Cheetos. He texted her again. She checked the phone without picking it up, which could have fueled his insecurity, but one of the things he loved about Libby was the way she disappeared into her work. It was the same passion he brought to his own painting.

Eventually, she glanced up and jumped when she focused on him sitting outside. She opened the window and returned to work. Inside, he found a towel to dry off with, and sat, knowing enough not to say anything, not to disturb her thoughts. She changed out a window for a doorway in the design, and then clacked some notes into the file before scooching over in the twin bed, half an inch, but it was as much of an offer as Barret ever got. He lay beside her. She didn't close the laptop or stop working.

He touched her arm, and she recoiled and returned the touch at the same time, something he still hadn't gotten used to, something that made him question what to do next. She was so different from Alice, his high school girlfriend, who'd been all stolen kisses and furtive touches in the hidden alcoves of the church. Alice was Father Todd's daughter. She sat in the very first pew next to her sisters and brothers, hands folded in her lap, her skirts nearly falling to the floor, an example to be held up for the rest of the congregation. Barret wondered if Alice's parents, with their guitars and homemade clothes, ever guessed that their little girl cornered him in a storage closet after the church coffee and kissed him till his lips felt raw. With Alice, he hadn't wondered where he stood, not even at the end.

"Fine," Libby said, kissing him, her eyes still on the screen.

Her mouth tasted of Cheetos. He pressed against her, and she gave in before shoving him away.

"With you," she said, "it's like I ordered French fries and got onion rings. You're a lot to get used to."

So was she.

"So are you."

Barret rolled over and closed his eyes. He could fall asleep, wake up, and start a new day. He could spend the hundred bucks in his wallet and then pretend Gavin Dean didn't exist.

"What were you doing there tonight?" he asked.

"What's it matter?"

"You didn't tell me you'd be there. You didn't even talk to *me.* You only talked to Tucker Matson. How do you even know him?"

"You were working," Libby said. "And I thought I'd get buzzed. Like I said, the wine was free."

"Did I do something wrong?"

Barret hated the sound of those words as soon as they spilled from his mouth. Libby glared at him, put the laptop aside, and headed into the hallway. The sound of running water came from the bathroom as she brushed her teeth.

Her laptop sat on the bed, open and inviting. Libby hadn't locked it when she left. Barret could view her search history. He could open her e-mail. He closed the computer before giving in to temptation and walked through the room, searching her shelves, her desk. The room was sparse, free of photos or other memorabilia, though she'd framed that drawing he'd given her, the one of his dog, Rusty, and hung it by her closet. As the water in the bathroom shut off, his gaze landed on a box of matches from Craigie on Main in Cambridge. He struck one of the matches and let it burn till the flame nearly reached his flesh. He struck another one, and when the bedroom door opened, he flicked it toward Libby, and struck a third.

"Stop," she said.

"You went to Craigie."

Barret didn't talk about money with Libby. He didn't have any to talk about, anyway, but he did know that Craigie was expensive and not the type of restaurant you went to on your own. It was a place for a date. He struck another match.

"You'll start a fire," Libby said, snatching the box from him. "I went there with a friend, okay?"

"You don't have any friends. Not that I've ever met."

"I told you from the start that I didn't want anything serious. And things have changed, and I have something big to deal with, and it doesn't have anything to do with you. Go paint or do whatever you do. Go to the dorm. I don't care. But go someplace else."

"It's late. I'm tired."

Libby got in bed, her back to the wall, her knees pulled to her chest. "I'm tired too," she said. "Of you. Why do you think I ignored your texts? I forgot you were even working that event tonight. I wish I hadn't seen you."

Barret took a step toward Libby, to comfort her. But she scrambled away from him, pressing herself into the corner in a way that made him turn to the mirror and see his own face, twisted with rage.

In the hallway, one of the roommates made a noise.

"I love you," Barret said.

"Get out," Libby said, and when he didn't move, she added. "I mean it."

The roommate knocked. "Is everything okay in there?"

Barret wrenched open the door and passed Emma in the hall. Or maybe Sasha? She wore an oversized T-shirt and her dark cowlicked hair stood up in every direction. She watched silently till he'd left the apartment. He stood on the landing, long after the dead bolt slid into place.

Later, afterward, Barret wandered through Jamaica Plain, a densely populated, residential neighborhood in Boston with a thriving commercial area along Centre Street. He stopped by Dreamscapes, the café where he worked, where a poetry slam was finishing up and they were getting ready to close. He didn't want to return to the dorm, so he walked till he found himself on the asphalt path surrounding Jamaica Pond. Here, during the day, people with dogs and strollers clogged the walkways, but tonight, in the rain, he nearly had the place to himself. He followed the path, to a Victorian-era boathouse and bandstand that sat on the banks.

He remembered coming here on a February night, his feet crunching through ice-crusted snow, his shoulder glancing off Libby's. The winter air was so cold Barret could barely breathe. They stopped at the boathouse, and Libby spun him around, those curls streaming out from under her hat, her breath freezing in clouds. "So . . ." she said, her eyes shining in light from a street lamp.

"We're here," he said, anticipation building in his stomach.

The nylon edge of her glove brushed his jawline, the scratch burning cold-numbed skin. His lips parted. She ducked under his arm and dashed around the boathouse, and he closed his eyes, resting his forehead against the brick.

"Come," she called. "Find me."

He turned the corner, and she stood on the snow-covered ice, fifty yards from shore. Waiting. He slid toward her, across the frozen surface, his feet slipping as he reached her. They fell, together, their legs entangling, and yet he still didn't dare make a move, not after what had happened with Alice, who he remembered hovering beside Father Todd at the end of the service and nodding at Barret as though they barely knew each other. Later, when he'd found her paging frantically through the Bible, she'd put her hands over her ears and refused to listen when he pleaded with her, till she finally stood and moved as far from him as she could. "It won't work," she'd said. "Not here! Not ever."

Barret hadn't dared believe that anyone could ever want him again. He lay beside Libby and faced the night sky. With nothing but the full moon to bear witness, he handed her the package. "I made it for you," he said.

She ripped the paper and held it up to the light from her phone. It was the drawing of Rusty lying in the driveway, tail in midwag, the drawing she still had hanging on her wall, even now.

She rolled toward him, her elbow buried

in snow. "It's beautiful," she said. "Like you."

She reached across the ice. The glove was gone.

"You don't mind?" he asked.

She touched his lips and quieted his doubts.

"You wouldn't like me," she said, "if you knew my secrets."

That's how Barret had believed she'd feel about him, too.

He climbed the stairs to the bandstand and looked out over the pond. The ice was long gone, replaced by inky water. Across it, through a row of trees, lights in Pinebank Mansion shone through the night. The Matsons lived there, on the hill, overlooking the pond in that Queen Anne–style mansion straight from a fairy tale. Or a gothic novel.

What a difference a few weeks could make. What a difference a single night could make. He'd trusted Libby, like he'd trusted Alice. Now, Barret felt alone — abandoned — all over again. And he had no idea what to do next.

HESTER

Rain pelted the windshield as Angela maneuvered her sedan through the narrow streets of Jamaica Plain.

"Sorry to ruin your party," Maxine said.

"It was *your* party," Angela said.

"Once Jamie got his award, we were happy to skedaddle," Hester said, from the back seat.

"I hate those types of events," Angela said. "When you're a cop, you see danger in everything. There were too many people in that space and not enough exits. It can be crazymaking."

"Why did we leave anyway?" Hester asked. "What do you need from us?"

Maxine took a moment to answer. "I'd like your thoughts on something," she finally said.

"Do you mean something like a corn chowder recipe or something I should call in to the station?" Angela asked.

"I'm not sure yet," Maxine said.

Angela pulled onto the Jamaicaway, a narrow, winding parkway that snaked through the city. "I'm not on duty," she said, "I don't have my firearm, and I have two civilians with me. If the answer's maybe, then it's yes. And you already got me in plenty of trouble with Cary for leaving your shindig. Do you have any idea what it's like to fight with a therapist? Every time I think I advance in the game, she turns it around and checkmates me."

Maxine smiled for the first time since they'd left the gallery. "The last time I had a boyfriend was in another millennium. I can't remember what it's like to compromise. But you don't need to report this. It's between us. Jennifer said that someone broke into the house."

"Into her house?" Angela said.

"And who is Jennifer?" Hester asked.

"Jennifer Matson," Maxine said. "Vanessa's mother. Tucker's wife. And yes, someone broke into their house. Or she claims someone did."

"That sounds like something we'll be calling in," Angela said.

"Would you trust me on this?" Maxine asked. "Tell me what you think afterward."

Angela caught Hester's eye in the rearview

mirror. There was something going on here, something Maxine wasn't telling them.

"I see you . . . two, maybe three times a year," Angela said. "We don't know each other well enough for this kind of trust. I'm here because you're Stan's sister. And I'll remind you that Stan is a lieutenant and I'm a sergeant. He's my boss."

"Then do it for Stan."

"Should I call him?"

"Please don't."

"See."

Hester sat up and rested her head between them. "Then do it for me," she said. "I'm curious. Aren't you?"

"Oh, Lord," Angela said, as she skirted the shore of Jamaica Pond.

A hundred years earlier, Jamaica Plain had been a summer retreat for wealthy Boston families, with the pond at its center. The pond eventually became the crown jewel in an extensive network of parks designed by Frederick Olmsted called the Emerald Necklace. Angela pulled off the main road and onto a long driveway that wound through trees and ended at a gabled, red-and yellow-brick mansion ornamented with terra cotta and sandstone. The structure overlooked the pond, with two cottonwood trees framing it on each side.

"Fancy," Hester said.

"This is Pinebank," Maxine said, "the one house that Olmsted kept when the Boston Parks Department acquired this land. It was on the verge of being torn down in the nineties after a fire, when Tucker bought it and restored it. Technically, the Matsons only own the house. The land is public property."

"I wouldn't complain," Angela said. "And don't make me regret this," she added as the three of them dashed through the rain, across the pea-stone driveway to a side entrance, where Maxine let herself in with her own key.

"Who else has a key?" Angela asked.

"The family. And me."

"And the family is?"

"Tucker, Jennifer, Vanessa." Maxine sighed. "And Gavin."

"You don't like Gavin?" Angela asked.

"He's awesome," Maxine said, in a tone that said anything but.

"And they all live here?"

"For the time being."

Once inside, they passed through a narrow hallway, up a set of stairs, and out into a large, wood-paneled foyer. A darkly stained split staircase led to the second floor. The ornate, old-fashioned interior was offset with sophisticated, modern furniture and art that had been chosen by someone with both an eye for design and deep pockets. At Widener, Hester was the Americana expert, and researched American artists. Here, on a pedestal beneath the stairs, she recognized a Vincent Fecteau sculpture built of papier-mâché and walnut shells. "Is that an Elizabeth Peyton?" she asked, stepping toward a highly stylized portrait over the fireplace.

"I couldn't tell you," Maxine said.

Those two pieces alone had to be worth more than Hester's annual salary. And the whole house seemed to be filled with similarly valuable works.

"Well, I'd break in here if I knew they had all this art. They must have a staff with a house this big," she said, though Angela glared at her before the sentence had left her mouth.

"I'm the sergeant," Angela said. "I ask the questions."

"Go ahead," Hester said.

"Staff?" Angela asked.

"A house cleaner who comes in twice a week. That's it. But she doesn't have keys."

"How does she get in?" Angela asked.

"It's not a problem. Someone's always here," Maxine said, moving to the foot of the staircase, where she shouted Jennifer's name. "Where are you?"

Two cocker spaniels, one buff, the other black, appeared at the top of the staircase. They trotted to the landing and barked in tandem.

"Fred, Adele. Shut up," Maxine said as she scooped up the black dog, and a woman Hester assumed was Jennifer Matson materialized behind them. She wore a long, flowing blue dress, and had white hair that cascaded around her shoulders. When Angela stepped forward to join Maxine, Jennifer stopped, suspicion grounding her. "Who's this?" she asked, her voice sharp, but soft.

"Angela White," Maxine said. "She works with Stan. She's a cop. I thought you could tell her what happened here. This is her friend, Hester. She's Dr. Maguire's wife. The vet."

Non-wife, Hester thought to herself, though she didn't bother with the correction.

"You called the police?" Jennifer said, stumbling as she stepped forward.

"Maxine told us that someone broke into the house," Angela said.

"Upstairs," Jennifer said. "I heard footsteps. And the dogs were barking. But I didn't expect . . . I didn't expect you to bring anyone, Maxine. This wasn't what I wanted."

"Is anyone still in the house?" Angela asked.

"If someone was here, Fred and Adele would still be barking their heads off," Jennifer said, coming close enough that Hester could smell liquor on her breath. "I found a window open in my office. You can see for yourself."

"How many rooms are upstairs?" Angela asked.

Jennifer looked to Maxine.

"Six," Maxine said. "Plus bathrooms. Jennifer's office is in the northwest corner."

Angela handed her purse to Hester. "Hang on to that," she said. "And don't move. None of you. I'll take a quick look. If you hear anything at all, call nine-one-one."

ANGELA

Everything Angela was doing was against procedure, and she was doing it in heels. She edged up the wooden staircase, crouching one more time, to take in the trio of women huddled below, waiting. "Don't move," she whispered, meeting Hester's eye. "That means you."

At the top of the staircase, she flipped on recessed lighting that ran the length of the house. Unlike the first floor, this part of the house seemed to have been gutted and redesigned. She slipped off her heels and moved from room to room, opening closets and checking under beds, half expecting to have a cat leap out at her.

At the end of the hallway, she found a tiny, comfortable room with a small desk and walls lined with bookshelves. One of the windows had swung open, and rain pattered on the sill. Outside, branches from one of the ancient cottonwood trees brushed against the house. This was the type of access most homeowners didn't consider, but trees like this one helped originate the term *cat burglar.* Angela ran her finger along the windowsill. It was soaked, though that could easily be explained away by the rain. She felt the floor and carpet for footprints but didn't find any. Without an evidence tech, she wouldn't get much here, and unless something was missing from the house, the chances of getting a tech were next to nothing. Besides, one look at Jennifer Matson told Angela that the woman had spent the evening with a bottle.

Back on the ground floor, she slipped her feet into her shoes.

"Anything?" Hester asked.

"The open window," Angela said, taking her handbag. "But you have a lot of expensive-looking items in this house. I assume you have a security system?"

"There is one," Maxine said. "But it was off."

"Cameras?"

"Nope," Maxine said.

That was strange, especially for people this wealthy.

"It was kind of you to come all this way, Sergeant," Jennifer said.

"This is hardly an official visit. Call me

Angela."

"Can I get you some tea?" Maxine asked.

Angela glanced toward Hester, who nodded. "Sure, we'll have tea."

Maxine led them through a formal sitting room to a huge kitchen with state-of-the-art appliances. The dogs trotted along behind them, and then curled into each other on a velvet dog bed in the corner. A mostly empty bottle of vodka sat in the middle of the soapstone island. Maxine moved the bottle into a cabinet. French doors led outside, where the black surface of the pond shimmered through the trees with the lights of Jamaica Plain beyond it.

"You sit," Maxine said to Jennifer. "I'll take care of the tea."

Jennifer wobbled as she perched on a stool, and Hester caught her arm. "What did you find?" Jennifer asked.

"I don't know enough to know if I found anything," Angela said. "Is there anything missing?"

"Nothing so far," Jennifer said, "But I'll check again in the morning."

"You'll need to file an official police report for the insurance."

"That can wait," Jennifer said.

The kettle whistled, and Maxine poured water into a teapot. To Angela, this was all a bit too cozy. Victims of home invasions felt violated and frightened, and that could come out in anger or tears, or anything in between, but not in pots of tea. After fifteen years as a detective, Angela hadn't once experienced indifference like this. "You should have the branches on that tree trimmed at any rate," she said. "And check the locks on your windows."

"Yes, yes," Jennifer said. "I'll do all that, but Maxine, you made this into something it shouldn't have been. Now I'm embarrassed."

Maxine handed a cup of tea to Angela, who let it sit while an uncomfortable silence built around them. She wanted to see who would break it and how, but, to her annoyance, Hester spoke first. "Why don't you walk us through what happened?" she said. "You heard a noise upstairs. What did you do then?"

"It'll sound ridiculous," Jennifer said.

"Tell us anyway," Angela said.

"I took a fire poker and went to investigate. Like a heroine in a gothic novel."

"That's what I'd have done," Hester said.

"God forbid you call the police," Angela said. "What next?"

"I searched the second floor, kicking in doors, flipping on lights. I was convinced

I'd find a man wearing a ski mask. Finally, I heard the rain through the open window in my office. That's when I texted Maxine."

"Maybe you left the window open yourself," Hester said, as she added about a quarter of a cup of sugar to her tea.

"I could have," Jennifer said.

"But . . ." Angela said.

"He left this behind too," Jennifer said, laying a battered copy of a novel on the table.

"Now you know why I asked you to come too," Maxine said to Hester.

Hester picked up the book before Angela could stop her. "Fingerprints!" Angela said.

"Sorry," Hester said, letting the book drop to the counter.

"I'm afraid mine are all over it," Jennifer said.

"*Adam Bede.* By George Eliot," Hester said, turning her head to read the spine. "Why this book?"

Jennifer glanced toward Maxine.

"Don't look at me," Maxine said. "I don't have time to read. Why do you think I asked you here? You're the librarian."

"That room is filled with books," Angela said. "Maybe this is one of them?"

"I'd know if I owned that," Jennifer said.

"Did your husband buy it for you?"

"Who do you think the dogs were barking at? There was someone here," Jennifer said, her voice rising. "If you don't believe me, then go."

Finally, a reaction. It was the first time Angela had come close to believing the woman. "You'd have to tell me who they were barking at," she said.

Jennifer stood and took the bottle of vodka from where Maxine had stashed it.

"Jen, don't," Maxine said.

Jennifer topped off her tea, drank it down, and poured another. "Maybe Rachel left it," she said into the cup.

"Who's Rachel?" Angela asked.

"Ignore it," Maxine said.

"Do you have a good memory?" Jennifer asked Hester, who shrugged and said, "Mostly."

"How about you?" she said to Angela. "You have to have a good memory to be a cop. How far back do you remember? Do you remember being ten? Six? Even younger?"

Angela was the oldest of four sisters, all spaced a year and a half apart. She had vague flashes of the times they'd come home as babies, at least the two littlest ones, but couldn't guarantee the memories hadn't been constructed from years of her parents' stories.

"How about Pepper Anderson?" Jennifer asked. "Do you remember her?"

The name sparked a vague memory, but Angela couldn't place from where.

"*Police Woman,*" Hester piped in. "Angie Dickinson. One of my favorites."

"I thought you'd be too young to remember," Jennifer said.

"I watch a lot of crap," Hester said.

Jennifer drank her vodka and looked at Angela. "You remind me of Pepper."

Angela did remember now, though Jennifer was right, she was too young and had seen the show in reruns. "I don't know what about *me* reminds you of Angie Dickinson," she said.

"You're both tough. And you fight crime in high heels."

"This isn't my usual getup," Angela said. "Pepper's feet must have ached."

Maxine came to Jennifer's side and took the mug from her. "Jen, *Police Woman?* Who cares? Maybe it's time they left."

Jennifer ignored her. "I have this memory of sitting outside my mother's bedroom and listening to the TV through the door when she thought I was asleep. She was watching that show. I wanted to be Pepper. I think I was four years old, but I couldn't bet my life on it, because the show ran till I was eight. It could have been any of those years."

"That's how memory works," Angela said. "It can be hard to trust. That's one of the challenges of police work. People don't remember things in the same way, and we're all susceptible to suggestion."

One of the dogs stood, ran to the French doors, and barked. The other followed.

Angela drank down the last of her tea. She was ready for this night to be over. "Let me take a look around the house and see if there's anything to find." She nodded toward Hester. "Come with me."

Outside, the rain had slowed to a drizzle. "What do you think happened in there?" Angela asked. "You're good at reading people. Did anyone break into that house?"

"My gut says no."

"Mine too. But why tell us someone did? And what's up with that book? I don't know if I've ever read anything by George Eliot."

"I haven't read it in years," Hester said. "It's about a love triangle, but that's all I remember. Jennifer seemed pissed off that Maxine brought us with her. Maybe she wanted attention, but not from the police."

"At least they didn't file a false report. Give me a minute. With all this rain, if someone did climb that tree there might be footprints."

Angela lifted the hem of her caftan and skirted the house till she came to the cottonwood tree. It had a tall, smooth trunk, with branches high enough from the ground that anyone who wanted to climb it would need a ladder. Her own heels sank into the mud, but the flashlight on her phone showed undisturbed ground. No one had been back here, not tonight.

What a waste of time.

She retraced her steps across the lawn. In the trees, a twig snapped. "Did you follow me?" Angela said, into the darkness.

"Did you say something?" Hester shouted from where Angela had left her in the driveway.

Someone burst from the bushes, running straight at Angela and knocking her into the mud. Her phone flew from her hand. She sat up in time to see the person retreating down a set of stairs toward the pond. "Do *not* move!" she shouted at Hester.

Angela tore across the lawn and down the stairs, running into the dark without backup or defense beyond a handbag clutched in a fist, like the heroine in a bad TV show. Like Pepper Anderson herself. Or maybe Jackie Brown. This was the kind of decision-making that got rookie cops killed, and when Angela reached the paved pathway at the bottom of the staircase, her better sense and years of training finally kicked in. She leaned over, trying to catch her breath. She'd have to get to the gym one of these days.

Ahead, a couple with a dog strolled toward her.

"Did you see someone running?" she asked, and when the man eyed her with suspicion, she shoved her badge in his face. "Did you see anyone?" she asked again, this time in her Sergeant Voice.

"No," the man said.

"Was that so hard?"

Angela walked the couple around the next bend and waited till they'd climbed into their car and driven away. She peered into the darkness, across the pond, trying to see any sign of someone fleeing. But it was too late. Whoever had run into her was long gone. And it seemed that Jennifer's story may have had some truth to it after all.

HESTER

"What happened?" Hester asked, as Angela hobbled toward her.

"I broke a heel on these damn shoes. That's what happened. Help me find this phone."

Hester scanned the muddy ground with the light on her own phone till she spotted Angela's Red Sox–emblazoned case and retrieved it. Angela spoke to Dispatch and gave the address. "Send a cruiser here," she said. "There's a prowler in the yard."

When Angela clicked off the call, she pulled the scarf from her hair and looked irritated as she stuffed it into her bag. "I had to sit in front of a YouTube video for about an hour learning how to tie that damn thing right. Here's a tip," she added. "No matter how ludicrous a situation seems, take it seriously. They teach that on day one at the police academy. You'd think I'd have learned it myself. Tell me what you saw."

Hester hadn't seen anything. She'd been texting Morgan to fill him in on what had already happened.

"You saw the guy, right?" Angela said. "The one I chased. Or I assume it was a guy. Hell, what do I know? I saw him for all of two seconds."

"I didn't see anyone but you," Hester said. "Sorry."

"Do you think *I'm* making things up now?" Angela said, and Hester had the good sense not to answer. To Hester, Sergeant White was a different person from Angela, the woman who came to her house to watch football on Sunday afternoons, and Hester had no desire to face Sergeant White on a bad day. Or on a good day, for that matter.

"Sorry," Angela added. "Not you, me. I'm pissed off at myself for acting like an idiot. But keep your mouth shut when we get inside. And listen."

Lights shone through the trees as a car pulled toward the house. A black Lexus drove over the pea stone, and one of the garage doors groaned open. A moment later, Tucker Matson strode toward them, his white hair glowing under a floodlight. "This is private property," he said.

Angela already had her badge out.

"Officer," Tucker said.

"Sergeant," Angela said. "Do you get a lot of trespassers?"

Tucker stood even taller. His chest was broad, like a college football player who'd spent his middle years fighting an endless battle of the bulge. This was a person used to being heard, Hester realized, but then so was Angela.

"We're right next to the pond," Tucker said. "People assume the house is part of the park. But I can't imagine you're on duty in that outfit."

Angela gestured toward the front door.

Tucker stood his ground. "What is this about?" he asked, each word emphasized.

The door opened. "Cut the crap, Tucker," Maxine said. "I asked her to come. What did you find?"

"More than I expected," Angela said.

Tucker sighed and headed into the house. "Are you a sergeant too?" he asked Hester.

At just shy of five feet tall, Hester was used to having people try to dismiss her. She didn't give the man the satisfaction of an answer. As Tucker hung his coat, a cruiser pulled into the driveway, its lights flashing.

"Are you serious?" Maxine said to Angela.

"Someone hiding outside this house knocked me flat on my ass and took off."

"That could have been anyone," Maxine

said. "This isn't exactly a gated community."

"Or it could be the person who broke in," Angela said.

"Would someone please tell me what the hell happened?" Tucker asked, his deep voice reverberating through the house.

"Jennifer claims someone broke in and left a book behind," Maxine said.

As if on cue, Jennifer drifted into the foyer, the two dogs in her wake. Tucker draped an arm over her slim shoulders, pulling the slip of a woman to his large frame. "You must have been frightened," he said.

Maxine's eye roll would have put Kate to shame.

An officer knocked on the doorframe. Angela conferred with him for a moment. "Officer Rodriguez and I will have another look," she said. "Stay here, please."

She hobbled after the officer, leaving Hester alone with the Matsons. Tucker puffed his cheeks out. Maxine tapped a toe and shot glares at him. "Big news tonight," she said, breaking the silence. "With Vanessa's baby."

"You'd think she'd tell me first," Jennifer said.

"You know Vanessa," Maxine said. "Always the flair for the dramatic. Where is she anyway?"

"She stayed behind with Gavin to wind things down," Tucker said.

"Listen, Jen," Maxine said. "You didn't ask anyone into the house tonight, did you?"

"Of course I didn't," Jennifer said.

"Anyone want a drink?" Tucker asked.

"Please," Jennifer said.

"Let's wait," Maxine said. "There's been enough of that already."

"You can wait," Tucker said, stepping out of the foyer and returning with two glasses of amber liquor. He gave one to his wife.

Hester didn't have to be a police officer to know that it would take a whiteboard, string, and about a hundred hours of group therapy to figure out the dynamics going on among these people. "You're all so calm," she said. "Aren't you concerned? If someone broke into my house and left a random gift behind, I'd have the entire police force over for a keg party."

"But you don't live a public life," Tucker said.

"I live a life where I like to stay alive and not have my house invaded by strange people, but maybe that's me."

Tucker nodded toward the door. "We don't need this," he said. "You should wait outside."

Thankfully, Angela returned right then,

followed by the officer. "No one else out there," she said. "Not that we can find, but make sure the house is locked up and secure and if you hear anything tonight, anything at all, call nine-one-one. Officer Rodriguez will write up a report on this so that we have it on record."

"Just what we need," Tucker said.

"Does he have to do that?" Maxine asked.

"Procedure," Angela said.

"Thank you for coming," Maxine said. "I'm sorry I got you in trouble with Cary. Please tell her it was my fault."

The Matsons had closed ranks, and Hester and Angela were being dismissed.

"It's best to be cautious," Angela said.

As she and Hester headed outside, Maxine accompanied them into the cold air. Angela spoke with the officer by his cruiser.

"Sorry to have involved you in this," Maxine said to Hester. "They don't trust people outside their circle."

"Lots of tension in that room," Hester said.

"We're like any family," Maxine said. "We fight and make up."

"You're part of the family?" Angela asked, as the officer drove off and she joined them.

"An associate member, at least," Maxine said. "And what do you think happened, anyway?"

"Why don't I reflect that question right back on you," Angela said. "What do you think happened? Why leave something so random?"

Maxine considered the question for a moment. "The school is a big organization, with lots of people and personalities. We have students and faculty and staff, each with their own gripes. I mean, I let a bunch of part-time instructors go today. It could have been any one of them."

"Sounds like a motive to me," Angela said. "Send me their names tomorrow. Who else? Students?"

"We enroll about twenty thousand students a year in some sort of coursework. Some of them get in trouble with debt or flunk out or can't find jobs when they graduate. When it comes to blame, we're an easy target."

That sounded like every student Hester had ever worked with.

"That's another good theory," Angela said. "What else?"

"Sometimes Jen can . . . She doesn't leave the house much. She gets bored. And the house, it's public. It's exposed. People walk by. Sometimes she gets them talking. Sometimes she even invites them inside, though

87

she claims she didn't do it tonight."

The door opened behind them. "Are you coming in, Maxine?" Tucker asked. "Or heading home?"

"Just a second," Maxine said, but when Tucker stood his ground, she shook the concern from her face. "I'm letting my imagination get the better of me. Thank you both for coming tonight. I suspect this is a whole lot of nothing. Do me a favor, Angela? Don't tell Stan. He's my older brother, and he can be really, really annoying."

"I'm the oldest of four girls," Angela said. "I've probably annoyed them every day of their waking lives."

"Then you get it," Maxine said, as she went inside.

"Thanks again for coming, ladies," Tucker said.

"It's Sergeant," Angela said, as the front door slammed in their faces.

A moment later, Angela drove them along the Jamaicaway toward Somerville. Hester texted Morgan to tell him she'd be home soon, then filled Angela in on the conversation she'd witnessed in the foyer. "All I know," Hester said, "is that they hate each other's guts. Or some of them do."

"Also, Tucker is a pompous jerk," Angela said.

"And Jennifer is a lush."

"We know more than we thought," Angela said. "But if they don't want the police involved, I can't do much else. No matter what Maxine asks, tomorrow I plan to tell Stan every single detail about this wild-goose chase. Nothing destroys trust in a department more than secrets."

BARRET

The rain had turned to drizzle, and the raw air was cold enough to freeze Barret's breath, but he allowed the energy from the empty city to flow through him, to revitalize him, to replace numbness. Tonight, he needed distraction. He came to the Green Line tracks near the Longwood station and ran down the chain-link fence till he found the hole to crawl through, then he continued till he got to the bridge, where he climbed, starting with the fence and then leaping to the base of the bridge.

His canvas.

Street art in Boston was competitive, much more so than back home, and the best places to paint, the places that got the most exposure, were on the T trains that traveled throughout the city. Barret had snuck into a train yard one night when he first came to Boston, only to be caught in the act. The cop who'd found him made him dump all his paint — hundreds of dollars' worth of paint — over his head before letting him leave. The paint had found its way into his mouth and ears and the pockets of his winter coat, and he hadn't dared try again, so, instead, he found less exposed places to work, like this one.

The mural here was small, hidden in the shadows on the underside of the bridge. He'd begun this piece two weeks earlier, and tonight, he dug red paint from his bag — he'd learned to carry only a small amount — and started in on an image of a dog panting. As he worked, time disappeared. So did the cold and damp. But then, the feeling of Gavin's touch crept into his head, those fingers lingering, the scratch of a nail through cloth. His paint strokes got shorter, angrier. The images of Libby telling him to get out of her life returned too.

Earlier, he'd stood on the bandstand by the pond watching Pinebank for what seemed like hours. Yes, the Matsons lived there, their castle on the hill. Everyone at school knew that.

But Gavin lived there too.

Barret took the five twenties from his wallet. He could walk up to the front door of that mansion and demand to be seen, demand to be spoken to. He could toss the cash in Gavin's face and tell him he couldn't be bought, and then let Gavin face the consequences.

Barret gathered his courage. He left the boathouse and skirted the pond, leaving the traffic of the busy Jamaicaway behind. He found himself pulled toward the house, up a set of stairs, and into the Matsons' yard, where a huge stone veranda perched on the edge of the hill. He imagined what the Matsons' lives must be like, sitting out here in the summer, sipping cocktails while the sun went down, believing their idyllic existence was safe. He wanted to expose his piece of their truth.

He edged onto the veranda, peering through the French doors to where four women sat at a kitchen island over tea. He knew the one in purple, the woman who'd hired him to work the event tonight. Maxine. He remembered the little one in the black dress too, the one who'd lost her kids. Barret had also done enough running in his life to identify the one in the brightly colored caftan as a cop. When two cocker spaniels came to the glass and barked, he stepped away. He edged around the house and peered into the driveway where a single car was parked, a late-model sedan he couldn't imagine any of the Matsons driving. At the school, the reception was probably still going on, Vanessa and Gavin still working the room. Barret could wait here for them to come home, though the rain had soaked through to his rented suit, and he'd begun to shiver.

Right then, the front door opened. The cop came outside followed by the woman in the black dress. Barret knew how to disappear, how to blend in, how to be still and quiet.

He also knew when it was time to run.

When the cop came into the yard, he bowled right into her, before plunging down those stairs to the pond, his backpack bouncing behind him. He sped around a bend, across a baseball field, and onto Perkins Street, hoping that the cop's high heels would keep her from pursuing him. Horns blared. Cars barely missed him. A truck skidded to a stop. Barret had stumbled to the other side of the road, arms still pumping as he'd melted into the darkness of the forest.

A Green Line trolley blew its horn. Barret lifted himself into the recesses of the bridge long enough for the train to pass beneath him. This was one of the murals he wanted

Vanessa Matson to notice. It was called *Rusty,* and like all the murals Barret had painted around the city, it was about love. He stopped to assess, liking the way the short, angry brushstrokes had filled in the dog's coat. The mural was almost ready to sign.

"Hey!"

A shout echoed from above.

Barret froze. Then he lifted himself into the base of the bridge again, pressing himself to the girders and willing away the distinct odor of paint.

"I see what you're doing. Don't move."

A beam shined from above, searching. Again, it was time to run. Barret swung from the girders to the fence, not even trying to mask the sound of clanking metal as he dropped to the ground below. A transit officer waved his arms and shouted for him to stop. Barret dashed to the hole in the chain-link and slid through to the other side. The cop shouted again, his voice growing fainter and finally disappearing.

By tomorrow, that mural would be gone, washed away or painted over in gray. Even though it was one of his favorites, this was also part of the high, the chance of discovery. The ephemeral nature of art. At least he'd gotten away this time. He collapsed on a bench, grinning.

"If someone painted a mural on something I built, I'd be pissed too," Libby had once said to him.

"That's art," Barret had replied. "Once it's out there, it's not yours anymore. That goes for murals and buildings."

He pictured Libby's face, and for a moment, he forgot everything that had happened tonight. Then disappointment spread through him like a drop of ink in water. The grin faded. He texted Libby. Again. What happened? he wrote. Please. Then he called, not bothering to leave a voice mail. She rarely listened to them anyway.

HESTER

By the time Angela dropped Hester off in Somerville, eleven o'clock had come and gone. "Sorry to get you involved in this," Angela said. "Especially on a school night. And if you see Stan, don't mention that you were with me."

"What did you say earlier about secrets in the department?"

"Do as I say, not as I do," Angela said. "But any final thoughts?"

Hester pondered for a moment. "*Police Woman,* to start. Who even remembers Pepper Anderson?"

"You do," Angela said.

"But I'm a special case."

"In many ways. Anything in the show stand out?"

Hester shook her head. "It's your standard seventies cop show, but with a woman lead. She does carry a purse and wear heels, but she's tough, too. Students write papers on it once in a while, usually through the lens of second-wave feminism."

"Positive or negative?"

"A mix," Hester said. "It comes out ahead of *Charlie's Angels.*" She thought about the rest of the conversation, of the things she'd noted. "Jennifer said that Rachel might have left the book."

"You caught that too."

"I wonder if she's one of these strangers Jennifer asks into the house. Maybe there's a history there. That'd be the first question I'd want to answer."

"Me too," Angela said. "But that would mean giving this one more minute of my time."

"Maybe I'll try to answer it."

"Don't do that."

Sergeant White was back.

"No promises," Hester said, before dashing into the rain and to her front stoop, where she unlocked the door and waved.

"Stay out of this," Angela shouted through the window as she backed out of the driveway.

Upstairs at Morgan's apartment door, not one, but three wet noses welcomed Hester. She stopped to greet each of the attached dogs: Waffles, her own basset hound mix; O'Keefe, a greyhound; and Butch, Jamie's bichon frise. O'Keefe was staying for the week while her owners, Prachi and Jane, caught the final days of ski season in Aspen.

Jamie and Morgan hovered over a jigsaw puzzle spread across the rarely used dining room table, fitting pieces into the thousand-piecer. Beers and an open bag of Doritos sat between them. On the TV, race cars circled a track. Behind them, Ian, a six-foot-long green iguana, Morgan's latest stray, lay along the kitchen counter, his tongue flicking in and out of his mouth. "Kate's in bed?" Hester asked.

"Hours ago," Morgan said. "Where I'd be if I wasn't waiting for you."

Hester ran upstairs to check on the girl, who slept soundly, then poured herself two fingers of whisky before joining Morgan and Jamie at the puzzle. She snapped a blue puzzle piece into place. "What are we working on?" she asked.

Morgan didn't bother to answer. He was a firm believer that jigsaw puzzles should go together without any help or reference, including the picture on the box. It drove Hester crazy, but it didn't stop her from fitting three more pieces together while she told them about her strange visit to Pinebank.

"No Jennifer at the event tonight?" Jamie

said. "Spent tons of time with the family."

"That was one of the strangest parts," Hester said. "I'm not sure she even leaves the house. I mean ever. Maxine seems to do everything for her."

"Maxine is the one who brings the cocker spaniels in for their appointments," Morgan said. "Fred and Adele. I thought they were hers. And all this time I thought she was a sad old lady."

"She's hardly old," Hester said. "Fifty, maybe."

"You know what I mean," Morgan said. "Look at that hair. I wouldn't have guessed that she ran a huge operation like Prescott University. What's she like to work for?"

"Tough," Jamie said. "Like a drill sergeant. A fair one."

"What about the others?" Hester asked. "The Matsons?"

"Don't see much of them," Jamie said. "Nothing happens at that school without Maxine's sign-off."

"That's what Angela says too," Hester said.

On the TV, the race finished. "May be done for the night," Jamie said, cupping Butch under his arm and taking the beer bottles to the recycling bin.

Neither Hester nor Morgan bothered to

let him out. By now, Jamie was more like a roommate than a tenant. After the door closed, Morgan flipped the TV off and searched the puzzle pieces, sorting a pile into a plastic bowl. "Morning'll come quickly," he said. "Have you found info on my high school yet?"

"What are you working on?" Hester asked.

"Green."

She gave him a fistful of green pieces. With all the excitement, she'd forgotten their conversation from earlier, or Morgan's lame idea of a game. There was a lot she could ask about Morgan's past, big and small, and if she gave in to this game, all those questions she'd avoided would flood their lives. "Did it bother you when I left the party tonight?" she asked.

"Are we playing?" Morgan asked.

"I thought the game was about the past," Hester said. "Not what happened today."

"Still, you wouldn't normally ask a question like that. Usually we let things fester."

"You make us sound pathological."

"Aren't we?" Morgan asked. "And no, it didn't bother me."

"Because you trust Angela's judgment more than mine?"

"You said it, not me."

"See," Hester said. "We know each other

pretty well, even with our poor interpersonal communications skills. So, here's your question for the night: What was your first job?"

"That's an easy one. The shoe booth at Southie Bowl Candlepins. My uncle knew the owner."

"Spraying shoes? I love that smell."

"It paid $4.75 an hour. I've never been richer. How about you?"

"Babysitting for the couple who lived down the street. I used to snoop the minute the kids went to bed. The husband had a stash of *Playboy* magazines in his sock drawer that I read from cover to cover."

"More detail than I expected," Morgan said. "You're getting into this."

Hester sat and closed her eyes, as exhaustion from the evening finally hit her. It was nicer than she expected to have a broad stroke to fill in Morgan's history, and she imagined him, spraying bowling shoes with disinfectant and lining them up along the counter. In truth, she hadn't thought about that couple down the street from her mother's apartment in years — the Connors, she remembered now, who'd bought a cottage right on the water and replaced it with an enormous, view-blocking monstrosity — or the way she'd sat in the middle of the couple's bedroom floor with the *Playboy* magazines surrounding her as she listened to the waves crashing on the beach, unfolded the centerfolds, and imagined growing up to look like that month's Playmate. At the time, she'd wondered what Mr. Connor would do on the day Mrs. Connor discovered his secret. Now, here, tonight, she realized that Mrs. Connor had likely known the secret all along. Maybe the Connors had opened those centerfolds together.

"This wasn't too hard," Morgan said.

"I guess not," Hester said, though what Morgan didn't know was that she'd left out the good parts. The parts about her mother, who'd find ways to walk by the Connors' house when Mr. Connor was outside mowing the lawn. Or that Mrs. Connor, after Hester's mother came by one too many times, eventually stopped asking Hester to babysit.

Then again, Morgan probably knew that there was more to her story than a stack of *Playboy* magazines, like Hester knew there was more to his than spraying shoes. That's why he wanted to play this terrible game. She wondered how much of her truth he'd want to learn.

MAXINE

Maxine pulled her gold Trans Am onto the darkened street and parked with one tire creeping onto the curb. She paused, reflecting on the evening, and how strange it must have seemed for Angela and Hester, on the outside looking in. Every now and then, she examined her choices, the life she'd carved out with the Matsons at the center, with Jennifer at the center, and wondered how things could have been different. But, as her brother Stan often said, it wasn't worth dwelling on hypotheticals.

The car door groaned as she shoved it open, and her knees cracked as she hauled herself out from under the steering wheel. Everything seemed to be getting old these days.

From the trunk, she lifted a file folder of reports she'd have to review before tomorrow. So much for sleep.

She paused when she reached the house

to catch her breath. Eighty-seven steps, from the pavement to the front door of her third-floor walk-up. They hadn't seemed so bad when she'd bought this place as a twenty-seven-year-old. Now, she considered installing an elevator whenever she came home. Not that an elevator was even a possibility. Since she'd bought this condo, the neighborhood had come and gone a minimum of three times, and Maxine had yet to get her act together in time to sell at the top of the market. Besides, where would she go? And the idea of paying a mortgage again gave her the hives.

She hiked up the first set of stairs to the front porch, where Derek (was that his name?) maneuvered a baby carriage, a double-wide, out the door. He wore a wool coat over his pajamas and hadn't bothered to change shoes for slippers. Derek and his wife had bought the second-floor unit less than a year earlier, but now that the twins had arrived, the family would be gone within months. Maxine couldn't even remember most of the people who'd moved in and out over the years, single men and women, couples. Even one throuple whom she did remember, because they'd made so much noise that she'd kept a baseball bat by her bed to bang on the floor once they got going. She'd long ago given up on the idea of making friends.

Forty-two steps to go.

The stairway was still covered in the same worn shag carpet that had been there the day Maxine moved in. At the summit, the door to her apartment was ajar. The lights in the kitchen blazed, and ice clinked in a glass. She tapped the door open with her toe and dropped her bag and files to the floor.

"In the kitchen," Tucker called.

He'd already mixed drinks, a Manhattan for Maxine.

"I didn't think I'd see you," she said.

"I slipped away. She won't wake up, not after the night she had."

Maxine drank the cocktail and let Tucker pull her in for a kiss. At least one thing could go right tonight.

"Tuck me," Tucker groaned. "Tuck me hard."

Maxine wanted to shush him — she'd wanted to shush him since the first time he'd come up with that doozy — and besides, Derek and his wife had probably gotten the twins to sleep again. They didn't need to hear this. But Tucker was vocal, and it was one of the things she'd learned to accept about him. Like his eyebrows.

But technically, wasn't Maxine the one getting *tucked*? From behind. Standing on the cold linoleum floor. Staring out those windows that encircled the entire apartment and praying — *praying* — that the neighbors were fast asleep, that they wouldn't raise their blinds and see her pressed against the Formica countertop she'd promised herself to replace every day since she'd moved into this apartment. She pawed at the switch, relaxing as the track lighting faded to a warm glow.

Tucker turned her. At sixty, he still had grace.

Maxine closed her eyes. He kissed her neck. She thought about the first time she'd seen him, at St. Catherine's College in Stoughton, a dying Catholic school where Maxine had earned a B.A. with a double major in business administration and English, and then worked her way up to dean of the college by age twenty-five, all while living with her mother. Then, one day, Tucker swept into her office — six-four and so present in boxy jeans and a blousy white button-down that showed off his tanned face — that she'd gasped.

"I'm buying this dump," he announced, and Maxine hadn't thought twice about signing on for the ride. Tucker hired her to manage the new campus, and Maxine transformed St. Catherine's into one of the most successful and profitable satellite campuses in the Prescott University system. Tucker visited the campus as often as he could, and two years later, Stan, who'd met Tucker and seen the way she looked at him, cautioned her against moving to Boston. "Is this all you want?" he asked, always the older brother.

"It's what I want now," Maxine said.

Besides, her offer on this condo had already been accepted.

Back then, Jennifer and Tucker were still restoring Pinebank. They lived in a small portion of the mansion, with the Newfoundland Shadow.

And the girls.

Vanessa.

And Rachel.

Tucker kissed Maxine gently. "You're off somewhere," he said.

It was afterward, her favorite time. They lay in her bed — her enormous, soft, comfortable, all-white bed with feather pillows and a down throw, in a room with blinds. She ran her fingers through Tucker's white but still-thick hair. She was glad of the choices she'd made. Tucker was good and oddly faithful for a married man (God knows he hadn't *tucked* Jennifer in years, or at least he claimed that was true). And he'd taken to his new role as chairman of the board, out of the spotlight and on the sidelines. Tucker lived in a world where good things happened, where puppies had homes, where babies swam, where companies grew. When the slow boil began, when the school began to fail, he hadn't been able to make the changes needed to survive. He wouldn't have eliminated programs or fired adjuncts, and he certainly wouldn't have sold off the St. Catherine's campus when enrollments no longer supported it. He'd had to go, and Maxine, in her heart, believed he knew it.

"You're worried about something," he said. "I can tell."

"Shush," she said.

Having Tucker here helped her forget about the burst pipe and the angry instructors. Tucker even helped her forget about Jennifer and that stupid book. Maxine wondered if he even knew how much she relied on him.

"I'll be fine," she said.

"You're a sly fox."

"I haven't had any other choice."

Of course, Maxine had had plenty of choices. She could have stayed in Stoughton and married that boy, the one who'd taught at Boston Latin, the one who'd moved to Vermont after she dumped him. She could have said no to Tucker that night he'd shown up. Instead, she'd stood in the hallway while he banged on the door, her fingers on the latch, her cheek pressed to the cool, smooth molding. She waited till his voice softened before she turned the dead bolt. Who was the woman who'd lived on the second floor then? Belinda or Baily or Brandy? All Maxine could remember was her voice, disembodied and annoyed, echoing up the stairwell. "Are you serious?" she shouted. "It's after midnight."

"All set," Maxine said as she held the door open, and Tucker came in.

One option Maxine hadn't considered was regret. Jennifer was like a jigsaw puzzle with a few missing pieces, and sex, Maxine assumed, was one of those pieces.

"You need to go," she said now. "It's late. Jennifer will wonder where you are."

"Jennifer drank a quart of vodka. She'll sleep till noon."

Tucker fumbled on the bedside table with a bottle of blue pills. Maxine relented, nestling into the crook of his arm, her one safe place. "You're a pervert," she said.

"That I am."

Later, after Tucker did finally leave, Maxine opened the box of files from work and sat in bed along with another Manhattan and some cold pad Thai. She wondered if Jennifer even remembered that Maxine had set up all her online accounts, that she paid her credit card bills and tracked her spending. It took less than a minute to see that Jennifer had ordered the copy of *Adam Bede* herself. At St. Catherine's, Maxine had written her senior thesis on George Eliot, on the influences of agrarian society on nineteenth-century literature or some bullshit like that. She'd read that book, she knew the story it told, and Jennifer knew it, but maybe asking Angela to come by tonight would keep Jennifer from doing this type of thing again.

Maxine packed away that worry for another time and turned to the data Gavin had supplied. And later, as the sky outside began to turn gray, she knew she had another problem to deal with.

HESTER

It was late. Or early, really. The whole house was asleep, except for Hester. The time on her bedside clock glowed as the minutes and then the hours clicked by while Morgan snored softly beside her. When three o'clock arrived, she gave up, climbing out of bed and waiting for the satisfying thump as Waffles leapt from the bed to follow. In the hallway, Hester gave in to her instincts and nudged Kate's door open. The little girl lay in her queen-sized bed, asleep, light from a streetlamp pouring through the windows, which Hester checked to be sure were locked. She also checked to see if anyone was levitating outside the third-story window, a Peter Pan ready to snatch Kate away. Or worse.

Old habits die hard.

Where Kate once surrounded herself with a moat of stuffed animals, now most of the stuffed animals had been relegated to the toy chest and replaced with books. Hester was proud of Kate and how seriously she took learning. She also fiercely guarded the girl's childhood and would as long as she could.

Tonight, O'Keefe had curled up in a tight ball, worn out from wrestling with Waffles all day. Hester kissed Kate's forehead. Even in sleep, the little girl managed to swipe the kiss away with a defiant fist.

Hester left her to sleep and headed downstairs, where she almost screamed out when she stepped on a Lego piece with her bare foot. She hopped up and down till the pain subsided, then continued through Morgan's apartment, and out onto the landing, where she opened a small door in the wall and headed up a narrow set of attic stairs with Waffles at her heels.

Nine years earlier, when Hester had agreed to buy this house with Morgan, she'd insisted on finding a building where she could create her own space, however small. Her apartment, a tiny aerie high over Somerville, had its own tiny kitchen, bathroom, bedroom, and closet. For a while, Hester had given up on this apartment, telling herself she didn't need it anymore and that she'd be happy to live with Morgan and Kate and lead a normal life. But last year, she'd begun to reclaim it. She didn't need to be normal. And she didn't need to be likable. All she needed was to be her whole self, and part of that whole self was this space, one where she could be as messy and grumpy as she wanted.

She lay on the green love seat and patted the cushion. Waffles leapt up beside her. She flipped on the TV — a new, flat-screen TV — and added a disc to the DVD player. She used to come here to watch horror movies — *Friday the 13th, Halloween, The Shining* — but these days she turned to her box set of *The Waltons,* all nine seasons. She liked the simple story lines, the importance of family, and that, in the end, even the terrible people on Walton Mountain usually turned out to be mostly good. As a kid, she'd lost herself in this show, wondering if there could actually be a family as loving and whole as this one, and whether that family might find her and welcome her into their lives.

Plus, she loved the theme music.

As the episode began, Hester booted up her laptop, heading straight for the Prescott University website, where she found a time line of major events in the school's history. The school was founded right after World War II by Tucker Matson's grandfather as the Anthony Matson's Ladies' School of

Drawing, where, Hester suspected, newly unemployed housewives had gone to fill their days drawing still-lifes. For the next forty-five years, the school occupied a single floor in a warehouse in the Leather District while the city transformed around it, and Anthony Matson was replaced with his son as the head of the school. Tucker Matson took over as president in 1985 from his own father, when he was twenty-five years old, and a time of expansion began. Tucker changed the name of the school to Prescott College of Art, and then to Prescott University. He bought up dilapidated real estate in the city and refurbished it. He began to offer residential programs, and in the nineties expanded into graphic design, fashion, and architecture. He also targeted small, failing colleges around New England and bought them to create satellite campuses.

Hester left the school website and entered "Prescott University" in a search engine. One of the top suggestions was "Prescott University scandals," which led to a series of articles from over ten years ago that questioned recruiting tactics used by the school, including recruiting students who were unqualified to complete their degrees and defaulted on federal loans. One article profiled a student who'd enrolled and

114

dropped out after racking up over a hundred thousand dollars in debt after a single year of classes. The article quoted Maxine. "We take our role as educators seriously," she said. "That means we want students to attend college at the right time in their lives. It's how they can take full advantage of the multiple opportunities that Prescott University has to offer."

Another set of articles in the *Boston Globe* outlined conflicts the school had with the city of Boston, particularly around real estate. Tucker had bought up most of the school's property when businesses were ready to leave the city. The Matson family owned those properties outright and leased them to the school, and the articles questioned whether the family should benefit from revenue generated by federally funded grants and loans.

A series of more recent articles outlined the closing of many of the school's campuses, including most of the satellite campuses throughout New England. "Our student profile has changed," Maxine told the paper. "And those students impacted by the changes can either enroll at the main campus or take their courses online. We are working with each individual to ensure they receive a quality education."

Two years earlier, Tucker Matson stepped down as president with little fanfare, though Hester did find a puff piece featuring art-directed photos where Vanessa looked impossibly young and Tucker seemed annoyed. "I took over running this school at Vanessa's age," he was quoted as saying, and Hester could practically hear his teeth gritting through the PR-directed answers. "My father had the good sense to know it was time for new ideas. He helped me guide the school to incredible growth, and I'll do the same for my daughter."

"I like being able to pick up the phone and say, 'Dad, what would you do?' " Vanessa said.

"Besides," Tucker said, "I'm the chairman of the board. I can still fire you."

Vanessa must have been sick of that one by now.

Hester closed the laptop. Morning had almost come. *The Waltons* had ended. She turned off the TV and snuggled into the love seat, determined to get an hour of sleep before the day began. Waffles sighed and lay down beside her, and Hester was on the precipice of sleep when a thought made her sit up and open the laptop again, this time searching on Jennifer Matson's name. This last search brought more questions than answers.

■ ■ ■ ■

THURSDAY, APRIL 1

■ ■ ■ ■

ANGELA

George had engaged Angela in a staring contest from the moment she'd sat down to breakfast. He stood next to her stool at the kitchen counter eyeing her granola, while a long strand of drool stretched from his snout. George was huge, a mix of German shepherd and pit bull and whatever else had made it into his DNA, and occasionally Angela found room in her heart to admit he was lovable. But mostly he annoyed her. "You wouldn't even like this," she said to him, to no avail.

"I'll get Isaiah off to school," Cary said, "if you don't mind picking him up at swim practice. I have appointments till seven."

George nosed Angela's elbow. "I'll be there," she said, though she'd been up too late to deal with the daily to-do list. "Unless there's a murder."

"As excuses go, it's not a bad one," Cary said. "But if you can't make it, call Brenda."

Brenda.

Angela had gone on her first date with Cary four years earlier, and they'd gotten married a year later. They'd both brought the maturity and baggage of being in their mid-thirties to the relationship. For Cary, that came in the form of Isaiah, her son, and Brenda, her ex-wife. Angela couldn't help but hear the hint of a threat whenever Cary brought up her ex, and Isaiah's other mother, the one Cary still co-parented with and whose decisions about Isaiah trumped anything Angela had to say. Brenda lived in Charlestown in a brand-new condo that seemed to clean itself. Like Cary, she was a social worker and a therapist, which didn't stop her from spoiling Isaiah. Inevitably, when he came home from spending the weekend with her, Cary had to get on the phone and tell Brenda to return her latest lavish gifts. "She's jealous," Cary would say to Angela. "And let me handle it."

As a professional listener and empathizer, Cary could be infuriating. Angela rarely knew when she'd crossed a line, even if the nearly silent breakfast punctuated by the to-do list confirmed her suspicions about the night before. But when it came to home repair and relationships, Angela's two favorite words were *deferred maintenance.*

She chose to defer this conversation.

"Let's go, kiddo," she shouted up the stairs, as she pulled together Isaiah's backpack. "Mom's taking you to school."

Isaiah pounded down the stairs, while George danced around their tiny house, leaping onto Angela and leaving a trail of slobber and fur.

"By the way," Cary said. "One of my clients is going into hospice today. She has two cats and a dog. I told her we'd take them."

"More dogs! More cats! More dogs!" Isaiah yelled, jumping up and down and clapping his hands. "Please say yes, Angie!"

Suddenly, exhaustion from the night before hit Angela. She'd had enough with the dogs and children of other people. She turned on the pair of them, ready to put a stop to this.

"April Fool's Day!" they said in tandem.

"I'm going to kill you both," Angela said.

"Please don't," Cary said, giving her a quick hug. "Then you won't be able to pick up Isaiah at swim practice."

An hour later, Angela parked at police headquarters in Roxbury and finished up a call with her youngest sister, Annette. Angela rarely went a day without talking to each of her three sisters, Annette, Audrey, and Amelia, usually picking up exactly where they'd left off the last time. Annette was running the Boston Marathon in three weeks, something she'd wanted Angela to do with her. Angela hated to admit it, especially after last night, but she wondered if she could run a 5k, let alone a marathon.

"Next year," Annette said.

Annette worked a nine-to-five job that probably paid four times Angela's salary. She also didn't have kids to pick up at swim practice. "Gotta go," Angela said.

"See you," Annette said.

Upstairs, Angela checked Stan's empty office, where his laptop was open, a cold cup of coffee beside it. She jotted *See me* on a Post-it note and stuck it to his screen. At her desk, she checked e-mail and reviewed a report she'd drafted the day before. She also flipped through the photos she'd taken at Pinebank, of the open window and the water on the floor.

"Hey, Sarge!"

The voice cut through Angela. She closed her eyes and took a deep, relaxing breath before facing Zane Perez. As a sergeant detective, Angela oversaw a unit of two detectives, and Detective Zane Perez was the newest addition to her unit. Each year, the rookie detectives got younger, but Zane barely seemed old enough to drink, which made Angela wonder who he knew, and who'd pulled strings to get him the job. Of course, most of the detectives in the department had wondered the same thing of her when she'd joined Homicide. It wasn't a fair question to ask. Stan wanted Angela to mentor the kid, but so far, all she'd noticed was that, despite his lack of experience, Zane brought unbridled confidence to the job, the kind of confidence that led detectives to chase suspects down dark paths wearing heels and without backup. The kind of confidence that got cops killed.

"Where you been?" Zane asked.

"It's seven forty-five."

"Early bird catches the worm!"

Zane wore a brand-new suit that hugged his well-toned body. His hair never reached two millimeters in length, and his deep brown eyes hurt to look at. Only ears the size of dinner plates belied his confidence. "Working a case?" he asked, his hip resting on the side of Angela's desk.

She turned the phone off even as Zane's gaze followed the screen.

"If I had a case, you'd know about it," Angela said. "You're part of the unit. We work cases together."

"That looked like a case. Those photos. On your phone."

He'd caught Angela in a lie, and she didn't like it.

"We've been slow lately," she said. "No homicides in a few weeks. It can get boring, especially when you're new."

In a year or so, Zane would understand that death brought more than an adrenaline rush, and he'd stop wishing for tragedy.

"Take advantage," Angela continued. "Look at some cold cases. Tell me what you see. Before you know it, you'll be working a ninety-hour week and wondering whether you've changed clothes in the last month."

"Yes, ma'am," Zane said, adding in a salute.

"Quit it with the *ma'am* crap."

"I say it to bother you. And I made these," he said, leaving a bag behind as he trotted to his desk.

Angela peeked into the bag, which was filled with homemade chocolate chip scones. Maybe Zane wasn't completely terrible after all.

An IM popped onto her screen. She closed her laptop and headed to Stan's office, bag in hand.

Lieutenant Stanislaus Pawlikowski.

Fifteen years earlier, Stan had been Angela's mentor when she passed the detective exam, and he'd welcomed her to his unit. He watched her back when beat cops gave her attitude, to her face and otherwise, by using words like *affirmative action* as weapons. Stan hadn't fought her battles for her — not that she knew — but he'd believed she could stand up for herself even when she'd had her own doubts.

She hovered in the doorway as he worked. In his mid-fifties, Stan took pride in his physical fitness. He stood over six feet tall, with perfect posture, thinning white hair, a mustache, and a South Shore accent so thick with misplaced R's that Angela sometimes had to ask him to repeat whole sentences. Recently, he'd begun to hint at retirement and putting Angela's name forward as his replacement, but she couldn't imagine life on the force without him. She also couldn't imagine pushing paper all day long.

"Was I a pain in the ass when I started?" she asked.

Stan finished working on his computer. "This shit is endless," he said. "And yes. Every new detective is a pain in the ass. That's how they get to be detectives. Remember when you chased that goon into a warehouse in Southie without calling it in and nearly got killed? I bet there's still a paper trail about that in one of these filing cabinets."

"You're lucky I didn't shoot him. He ran a dogfighting ring."

"I thought you hated dogs," Stan said, waving Angela toward a chair.

"Want a scone?" she asked, holding the bag out so that Stan could help himself. "Your sister took me on an adventure last night."

"Maxine?"

"Do you have another sister?"

Stan took a bite of the scone. "Not bad," he said. "You make these?"

"Are you kidding?" Angela said, and then filled him in on the events from the night before, omitting the parts about bringing Hester along or chasing the suspect on her own. She expected a tongue-lashing, but when she finished, he asked to see the photos.

"What did you notice?" he asked, as he flipped through her phone. It was the same question he always asked.

"When you work a home invasion, how do the victims respond? Generally?" Angela asked.

"Not to be a sexist pig, but men usually get angry because someone invaded their castle. Women are usually terrified."

"That's my experience too. Last night, Jennifer Matson seemed thrilled, and Tucker seemed annoyed."

"And Maxine?" Stan asked.

"She seemed . . . concerned, maybe? Confused? Until I got bowled over in the backyard, I was convinced that Jennifer had made the whole thing up."

One thing Stan had emphasized with Angela since the first day they'd worked together was time management. "Get the wins," was one of his catchphrases, and, to Angela, this seemed like nothing but a time suck. So, it surprised her when he asked her to keep an eye on the case.

"I'll annoy Maxine if I play older brother," he said. "You can do it for me."

"What are you worried about?" Angela asked.

"That Maxine would step in front of a bullet for that family," he said. "Let's see if we can save her from herself."

MAXINE

Maxine rushed down the stairs at 8:07 a.m., about two hours later than she'd planned to leave the house to meet Vanessa for the video shoot. She'd stupidly decided to "rest her eyes" and had woken with a start eight minutes earlier. So much for that half hour on the elliptical.

The heels on her pumps barely caught the worn carpet. Below, the front door opened, and when she went to descend to the first floor, Derek had already begun to maneuver the baby carriage up the narrow stairwell. His eyes were as bleary with exhaustion as Maxine assumed hers were.

"Sorry," he mumbled, pushing the carriage to the side of the narrow passage.

Maxine squeezed along the wall, away from the banister. Derek shuffled to the side. Maxine's heel slipped. She reached out, grasping at Derek's pajama top, which tore as she toppled forward and somersaulted down the last five steps. Paper from files scattered around her, and her face hit the floor hard enough to see stars.

"Oh, shit," Derek said, trying to reach her while keeping the baby carriage from falling. "Sorry," he added, and Maxine couldn't tell if he was apologizing for the fall, or for swearing. But she said, "Fuck it," picked herself up, and ran out the door.

She'd have a shiner later. But, right now, she was late.

Today, the new campus center opened for use. Next week, they'd celebrate with a grand opening with all the faculty and students — even the mayor had committed to attending. Maxine couldn't begin to imagine what kinks she'd need to work out with the new building. Still, as she parked, she couldn't help but pause and soak in the achievement. Whereas the university used to be a hodgepodge of locations throughout the city that could take hours to travel between on public transportation, this building, with its six stories of high-ceilinged rooms, with its exposed beams, wooden floors, and enormous windows overlooking the Boston skyline, provided a center to the school, with the amenities students expected in college. They had dining options, a gym, a library. And the gallery. As part of the transformation, Maxine had also begun to expand the curriculum beyond the arts. In the fall, she'd launch a coding academy, and last year she'd created a UX/UI design program that had a one hundred percent job placement rate.

One hundred percent!

She dared any other local college to beat that statistic. She knew what people said about the school, but she was proud of what she'd done and proud of the students who graduated. One of her biggest goals with these changes was to instill a sense of pride in the student body and alumni so that Prescott University became an institution that students chose to attend, not a default.

Inside, the automatic lights popped on, bathing the sleek, modern lobby in a soft glow. The new branding, complete with the dolphins, adorned nearly every surface. Vanessa had taken on the interiors and had chosen reclaimed materials for most of the surfaces, along with a living wall of ivy as an ode to their much better-known competitor in Cambridge.

On the third floor, Maxine found Vanessa already fussing with her hair and makeup.

"You beat me," Maxine said.

Vanessa stood, barely missing a beat as

she took in Maxine's bruised face.

"Is it that bad?"

"You've seen better days," Vanessa said.

"I tripped this morning. It was a long night."

"My dad told me what happened when Gavin and I got home. Why'd you call the cops?"

There was an edge to Vanessa's voice that hinted at anger, anger Maxine wanted to head off. She was too tired to face it today. "Angela's a friend," Maxine said. "It'll be okay."

"A bunch of nothing, right?" Vanessa said, finishing her makeup. "I haven't read that book she found. Have you?"

It wasn't worth getting into. "Maybe I'll catch the movie," Maxine said.

At twenty-eight, Vanessa wasn't that far removed from her own college days. She'd attended Boston University and majored in art history, and her parents hadn't even considered having her enroll at Prescott. None of the Matsons had attended the school, but maybe that would change now with the new baby.

"Ready, babe?"

Hero, the videographer, hovered by the studio in his tight jeans and even tighter T-shirt. Vanessa had met Hero in college.

He made terrible documentaries and didn't have an actual job, and yet still managed to live in a palatial South End loft. Vanessa greeted him with an air kiss, and then went to her mark by a green screen while Maxine hovered. They'd taped half a dozen of these spots by now, and they all knew their roles. Hero adjusted a light and took a few preliminary shots. "You're a pro," he said. "This should be a breeze."

He wanted to get in and out as quickly as he could, but Maxine would make him earn his keep, like usual. He'd make four thousand dollars for this shoot (plus expenses!).

"Action!"

Vanessa looked straight into the camera. "That's not us!" she said.

One of her tattoos peeked out from under a sleeve. Her spiky blond hair shone in the lights. The Internet trolls would call her a dyke when this commercial ran.

"That's a wrap," Hero said.

Maxine hadn't dragged herself here for a two-minute shoot. "Another take."

The muscles along Hero's scrawny neck tensed. He took two long strides toward Maxine in a way, she suspected, he thought made him seem intimidating. He was skinny enough that she could have broken him over her knee.

"What do you want?" he asked.

"I don't know," Maxine said. "Do it again."

"I could use more guidance," Hero said. "More direction."

"Aren't you the director?"

Thirty seconds later, they were back to work.

"That's not us!" Vanessa said.

Closer, but not quite. "One more time," Maxine said.

These ads mostly ran in the middle of the night on local TV stations. After Hero finished here, he'd head out to the streets of Boston where he'd shoot random interviews asking people what they thought when they heard "Prescott University." Most people still said things like, "Can't you buy those diplomas online?" or "They sell visas to terrorists." Maxine's favorite so far had been when a man said, "Ph.D.s in lifelong debt?"

That's when Vanessa popped on screen saying, "That's not us!" followed by the statistics that refuted the claim.

"Again," Maxine said.

"That's not us!" Vanessa said.

This time, her eyes were wide, her hair stuck in every direction, and she jabbed at the camera with her index finger. She looked crazy. Super crazy. Lunatic-in-the-

135

attic crazy.

"That's a wrap," Maxine said.

"I guess," Hero said.

"When will it be ready?"

"Three weeks."

"Make it three days. We need to drive fall enrollments."

Maxine's original plan for these ads had backfired. When she'd developed the concept, she'd meant the ads to be a public relations ploy, a way to tell the Prescott University story on her own terms. But when the first ad aired, it went viral, making it into late-night monologues and onto cable news shows. Even now, that ad racked up a few thousand views a day, and strangers still stopped Vanessa on the street and asked her to say, "That's not us!"

And somehow, beyond all common sense, the ads increased enrollment by two percent, beating national trends, which were going nowhere but down.

"Did you get what you needed?" Vanessa asked.

"Always," Maxine said. "Now I need to find that husband of yours."

"What's he done now?" Vanessa asked.

Maxine thought about the reports in her bag, about the data Gavin had managed to screw up. But suddenly she knew what to do about it. Maybe resting her eyes had been a good idea after all. "Nothing," she said. "I have a quick question for him."

HESTER

The ivy had yet to leaf out for the spring, and the lawns were distinctly brown and muddy, but, to Hester, walking into Harvard Yard on her way to Widener Library — the Harry Elkins Widener Memorial Library, to be precise — had yet to grow old. The morning was crisp, but the rain had ended, for the time being. She scaled the broad steps to the building's imposing classical façade and passed through a set of wrought-iron doors into the vestibule, where she swiped her ID and greeted Burt at the security desk. The long front hall, lined with buttery Botticino marble, swept right to the Memorial Room, where Harry Widener's portrait hung overlooking his collection of rare books. The room housed Harry's collection, intact, including Hester's favorite volume, a set of drawings by George Cruikshank, Charles Dickens's illustrator. Harry's premature death on the *Titanic* had spurred his mother to donate the funds to build the library.

Hester gave Harry's portrait her morning salute and headed up one more flight of stairs, where she ducked through an unobtrusive door and into an office filled with gray cubicles. At her desk, she inserted her laptop into its docking station and booted up. A moment later, Kevin, her boss, popped his head over the cubicle wall. "The search committee meets at eleven," he said.

Kevin was a big man with a monk's ring of unnaturally dark hair that encircled an otherwise bald head. He had a penchant for colorful sweaters and held documents an inch from his face because he refused to submit to reading glasses. Now, he hovered long enough for Hester to guess that he needed a favor. Kevin had been nothing but kind to her since they'd met, but especially in the last two years, ever since Kate had come to live with her. But that didn't keep Hester from making him ask for the favor anyway.

"How's Kate?" he said.

"Same as yesterday," Hester said. "Still five years old. Still promising to be an architect when she grows up. And every time I step on one of those Legos, I have you to blame."

"Thank me by taking on the online catalog," Kevin said. "Margery has to be out for a few weeks. I need someone to replace her on the committee."

"Can she take teaching-design? I can't do both."

"If she can't, someone else will," Kevin said, retreating to his office before Hester could have second thoughts.

She opened her schedule for the day, reviewed appointments, and found one lingering e-mail from a middle school student researching St. Louis circuses. She wrote a query to find materials. Widener tradition meant that any request, no matter the source and no matter how obscure, got a response from one of the librarians. Hester looked forward to digging into this one.

Her phone rang.

"There's someone at Security for you," Burt said. "A cop."

Hester ran down the stairs to where Angela chatted with the security guard.

"You causing trouble again?" Burt asked.

"Don't start any rumors," Hester said.

"This badge'll usually get me in anywhere," Angela said, after Burt buzzed open the gate.

"Not here," Hester said. "Too many valuable documents to let in the riffraff."

"We didn't have buildings like this one where I went to college."

"Not many schools do," Hester said, as she led Angela to her desk. "I didn't think I'd see you so soon, after last night."

"There's a rookie detective named Zane who's driving me crazy. I needed to get away from him." Angela pulled up a chair. "What did you learn last night after I dropped you off?"

"I went to bed," Hester said.

"No, you didn't," Angela said. "You snooped. I can tell by the dark circles under your eyes."

"Okay, I read a little bit about the school."

"See, I'm a good detective. Some people would say I'm great. But what I could use help with is that book. Why *Adam Bede*?"

Hester didn't know the book that well, even if it was still assigned in an occasional class or used as part of a dissertation. She had read it, years earlier. "Go with the obvious, right?" she said.

"Always."

"Someone's sending a signal. Like any Eliot novel, *Adam Bede* is full of imagery and themes. It's about class, sex, motherhood. Look at the themes and connect one to something going on in the house."

"That's why I'm talking to you," Angela

141

said. "College was a long time ago and if I'm being honest, I spent a lot more time smoking dope than I did studying. Help me out and don't make me feel stupid."

"Sergeant White smoked dope?"

"Sergeant White has never smoked dope, but Angela might have. And it's legal now, so who cares."

Hester let that one go. "Start with class," she said. "The book spends a lot of time talking about illiterate country folk and how close they are to nature."

"Maxine mentioned students being pissed off."

"So, a student who feels that they aren't learning enough, maybe," Hester said.

"It's a stretch. And honestly, it rubs me the wrong way. You get what you give in school."

"You should spend more time with undergrads. They can make anything about themselves."

"Noted and annoyed. What's another theme?"

"I'll ask around to see if anyone's researching the book or George Eliot in general. English lit isn't one of my areas, but I do know the whole story is about a love triangle — or, actually, there may be four of them involved. Whatever you call that? There's lots of passion between the lines, without showing too much. It's a typical nineteenth-century novel. And everyone suffers."

"The Matsons are hardly suffering," Angela said. "They're loaded."

"Even rich people have their things. Again, talk to some of the students I work with. Some of the richest ones are the most messed up."

Angela's phone rang. She flashed the screen toward Hester, which showed Maxine's name. Angela answered and listened for a moment. "I'm sitting with her right now," Angela said, covering the phone. "She wants to talk to you."

"About what?" Hester asked.

"She won't say," Angela said, handing over the phone.

"We met last night," Maxine said. "At the gallery . . . and afterward."

Hester didn't need to be reminded. "What can I help you with?"

"I have a project for you. It's time sensitive, so I'll make it worth your while. I need your help finding some students. We lost track of them."

"Can I call you back?"

"I need this quickly," Maxine said. "If you can't do it, I'll need to find someone else."

"Got it," Hester said, hanging up.

"What does she want?" Angela asked.

"Nothing," Hester said,

She suspected that if she told Angela about Maxine's project, that she'd get a lecture on letting the police do their jobs, but when Angela folded her arms and waited, Hester relented. "Don't flip out. It's something about finding some missing students."

"I'm not flipping out," Angela said. "As long as you tell me all the details and don't go chasing serial killers."

"Even if you don't care, Morgan will," Hester said.

"Then tell us what you're doing and let us all flip out," Angela said. "Then make sure to stay away from trouble and keep your child out of danger. Girl, you're an adult. Do what you want to do." She stood. "And I think I'll get out of your hair and leave *Adam Bede* behind. It seems like a big waste of my time, unless you have other ideas."

"There's the really obvious."

"You left the really obvious to last? Spill."

"There's a dead baby in the novel," Hester said. "Killed by its own mother. The Matsons' youngest daughter died too. Rachel. Vanessa's sister. I'd start there."

BARRET

In the moment between sleep and awake, Barret forgot everything that had happened the night before. He hadn't been chased by a cop, twice; Gavin Dean hadn't paid him off; and he hadn't fought with Libby.

He dreamed that Vanessa Matson had discovered his mural. And he was happy.

But the morning forced itself on him. First, he heard thumping. Then came the light. The endless light, pouring through the car's windows. Then he took in the fist, and the construction worker attached to that fist, as it pounded on the glass of the rusted-out blue Nissan Sentra. Somehow, at 3 a.m., Barret had decided sleeping here was a good decision, a better idea than walking all the way to his dorm room.

"Poor judgment," his mother would have said. In the light of day, Barret had to agree.

"Move along," the construction worker shouted.

Barret sat up, bleary-eyed. He still wore the suit he'd rented for the gala the night before. The car smelled of twenty years' worth of cigarette smoke. Beer cans littered the back seat, and he swore he caught a glimpse of a used syringe poking out from under the driver's seat, not something he wanted an angry man in a hard hat to associate with him. He waved an acknowledgment at the man and shoved the seat in the coupe forward so that he could slip out the passenger's side door. On the sidewalk, he kept his gaze focused on the ground. Submissive. Apologetic. With angry men — whether they be Gavin Dean or this construction worker — it was best to avoid engagement.

"This is a tow zone."

Barret mumbled an apology.

The man took his hard hat off and ran a hand through his hair. "Are you going to do something about the car?"

Barret slung his bag over his shoulder and walked away.

"Come on, freak," the man shouted. "You gotta get this thing out of here."

Barret kept moving. If he had any luck left, the man would realize that dealing with him was more trouble than letting him go. Besides, what the guy needed was for that car to move so that he could start work on his project, and for that, he'd need a tow truck. Barret didn't own the car.

"This heap won't be here in five minutes," the man shouted.

Barret turned the corner. And he ran.

"Two strikes," Dreamessa said, when Barret rushed into the crowded café fifteen minutes later and stashed his bag in the break room.

"Two?" Barret said as he slipped an apron over his head and joined her at the counter.

He'd hoped that she'd overlook that he was five minutes late, even though the morning rush was in full swing, and a line stretched to the door. He took his place at the espresso machine, working through coffee orders and ending by adding a flourish of foam to a cappuccino. Behind him, the cook made breakfast sandwiches, and another worker moved through the café, clearing tables. Dreamscapes, right in downtown Jamaica Plain, with its interior decorated in ephemera and its simple food, was usually busy, especially at this time of day.

"You were late," Dreamessa said, when they'd worked through the line.

"I'm never late," Barret said.

"You were today so you can't claim never anymore."

The café door opened, and a woman with a baby carriage entered, followed by six more women, also with baby carriages. He and Dreamessa worked through this mini-rush again, so it wasn't till another half hour had gone by when Dreamessa said, "By the way, your second strike is that you're a mess. Did you sleep in those clothes? Go get cleaned up and then clear tables."

While the threat of job loss seemed to have passed, Barret knew that Dreamessa didn't suffer fools gladly. He'd have to weather her misgivings of him until she turned her attentions to someone else. He spent five minutes in the bathroom trying to wash away any residual smoke from the car. He also took off the black coat he'd rented, ran water through his hair, and dried it with the hand dryer. Out front, he maneuvered through the crowded café tables. At the counter, he slashed open a box with a kitchen knife, then slid pastries onto trays in the case.

Dreamessa hovered behind him.

"What's going on with you?" she asked, in either a managerly or a motherly way, he couldn't tell.

"It's nothing," Barret said, taking an order for a latte, glad that the noise from the steamer made conversation impossible.

With her mop of bright pink hair and tattoos, Dreamessa could have been thirty or fifty for all he knew, but she had the stern face and easy charm of someone used to working with the public. She knew more about him than most because of the tax forms he'd filled out when she'd hired him, and she'd taken everything in stride.

"I'm waiting," Dreamessa said when he'd finished with the customer.

"Girl trouble," Barret said. "It's nothing."

"Girl trouble?"

"Yes! Does that surprise you?"

"Not at all. And share away. Nothing much phases me."

"Then you've probably heard way more interesting stories."

"I bet it's less boring than mine. I used to be in a band. Heavy metal. I was a drummer, for Christ's sake. Now, I live in Readville with my husband and two kids. I live for other people's drama. If you want to spill, feel free."

Barret had built walls strong enough to withstand this line of questioning. He didn't know Dreamessa well enough to trust her with more than what she already knew. "I'll take out the trash," he said.

"Suit yourself."

He pulled the plastic bags from the bins

149

and carried them out to the alley behind the café. Cold, milky coffee sloshed onto his shirtsleeves. His head pounded from a lack of sleep, and more than anything he wanted to talk to Libby and find out what he'd done, even if he knew that she wouldn't tell him. No matter what she did say, even if she gave him a piece of the why, the answer would fracture into a thousand new questions, ones with even less satisfactory answers.

"Hey." Dreamessa stood in the doorway. "Get to work. You're not on break."

Kind Dreamessa had vanished.

Barret would have to find the answers to his questions for himself, and he suddenly had an idea of where to start.

MAXINE

The elevator doors opened on the sixth floor, and Maxine stepped out into Prescott University's brand-new administrative offices, a moment ten years in the making. She couldn't have been prouder.

"There's dirt on my desk," one of the instructional designers said.

So much for that moment.

Maxine ran a finger along the surface of the reception desk, through a layer of fine soot. Less than a minute in, and she'd discovered Building Kink Number One: Settling. Black tar was filtering through the roof. As concerns went, this one had OSHA written all over it. She dialed the building contractor and got voice mail. "Call me as soon as you get this."

"I wish there was a CVS in this neighborhood," the designer added. "Or a Starbucks."

That complaint, thankfully, was out of

Maxine's control. "I'll get right on it," she said, as she surveyed the sprawling, open-concept office where staff sat at long rows of workstations.

Maxine liked having a view of the entire staff. It kept people in line. At 9:30 in the morning, not enough of them had arrived for the day. She strolled through the floor, making a mental checklist of who'd shown up. Across the building in the marketing department, Jamie Williams had set up shop. "I'm surprised to see you," she said, "after your big night."

"Finishing for the semester," Jamie said.

"I hope you'll consider sticking around when your internship is over," Maxine said. "I could use you."

"Something to discuss."

It was exactly what Jamie should have said, and exactly why she'd pay good money to keep him. Maxine liked savvy, self-confident staff. She liked people who showed up with ideas and were willing to fight, but Jamie had the skills to go anywhere he wanted, so she suspected she'd be sending him off toward bigger horizons soon. "When you're ready, let's set up time to talk."

"I have designs to run by you," Jamie said, as the elevators pinged, and Gavin exited.

"I'll come take a look in a few minutes," Maxine said, and then hurried after Gavin to his office, where she paused outside the door.

Maxine had agreed to the open-concept plan to save space and money. Later, she discovered that Vanessa and Gavin had gone around her and asked the architect to build them both private offices.

With doors!

It made her want to strangle them.

Gavin was thirty-four years old, six years older than Vanessa, which didn't seem like much, now. But it had seemed like way too much when nineteen-year-old Vanessa had brought him home for the first time, and Maxine had had to remember her precarious — and often powerless — place in the Matson family hierarchy. Still, when she found out Gavin worked at Vanessa's school — her *high school* — as a business teacher, she went ballistic. Tucker dismissed the problem. And Jennifer, who'd been twenty-one when she married thirty-one-year-old Tucker, celebrated it. It was as though she saw herself in her daughter's decisions. All these years later, Maxine hadn't recovered from that first impression.

Vanessa eloped with Gavin two years later, the summer after graduating from college, and soon he joined the school as the CFO and began handling the Matsons' personal finances as well. "He has an MBA and he's a CPA," Tucker had said, when he told Maxine about the decision. "He's perfectly qualified."

"And four years of teaching at a private high school," Maxine said. "Don't you think he'd benefit from some real-world experience before taking on a job this big? We can find him a more suitable position for a while and see if he can handle more responsibility."

"You'll show him the ropes," Tucker had said.

And she'd tried. But Gavin didn't like to listen. Or to take direction. Maxine could have taken the situation to the board, but, as a privately held company, the board had little power or interest in change, and the people on it were friends of Tucker's who rubber-stamped any decision he put in front of them.

Now, Maxine supposed Vanessa was right. With the baby coming, she'd have to give in to having Gavin around.

She knocked.

He looked up. "Maxine!" he said. "Come in. The new office is awesome! I'm e-mailing Tucker right now to tell him what an amazing job he did!"

Gavin lived through exclamations. To Maxine, it was exhausting.

"I ran a 10k this morning to celebrate the little dude on the way!" he added.

"Or dudette," Maxine said. "But it's exciting, isn't it?"

"I'm stoked!"

Maxine smoothed the fabric on her skirt. "Listen," she said. "I went through the student data you gave me yesterday."

"Awesome!"

"Not quite awesome," Maxine said. "It's incomplete. The data on student job placement and satisfaction doesn't match enrollments. I need it for the alumni-outreach project I'm starting."

Gavin typed into his laptop, his fingers bouncing off the keys. He swung the screen toward her. "See," he said.

It was the same spreadsheet she'd spent the night reviewing.

"Exactly," she said, slowly. "It's not correct. There are students in our systems, students who paid tuition who have no data attached to their names. The data is incomplete."

Maxine had asked for contact information on alumni in three highly selective fields, architecture, graphic design, and UI/UX.

She'd also asked for any current students with 4.0 averages, but when she'd washed the data against her own spreadsheets, it hadn't matched. About a hundred students came back with incomplete information.

"I bet I screwed up the query," Gavin said. "Let me see what I can find."

"I asked you for this weeks ago," Maxine said. "What's taking so long?"

Gavin ran a finger across his desk. "There's dirt on everything."

"Try not to breathe," Maxine said. "You're in charge of student data. It's part of the CFO's job. Can you get me what I asked for? This morning?"

"I'll talk to Vanessa, see what she thinks."

"No, you'll talk to me," Maxine said, and she could kick herself for letting her voice rise. She paused, reining in her temper. "Forget it. I'll find what I need without you."

The smile fell from Gavin's face. "I don't appreciate the way you question my every move," he said, his voice low, the exclamations gone. "Lay off and let me do my job."

"Prove to me that you know what you're doing. I've covered your ass for years now."

Gavin stepped around the desk. She could smell the shampoo on his still-damp hair. "I'm the one who makes this place profitable," he said.

Maxine refused to back down or to let her gaze fall away.

"Now a good time?"

Jamie Williams stood in the hallway outside the office.

"Dude!" Gavin said.

He lifted a hand to high five like he probably had so many other *dudes* in his life, but Jamie, who towered over Gavin, ignored it.

"I'll meet you at your desk," Maxine said.

"You sure?" Jamie asked.

Maxine nodded and watched as he walked to the end of the hall and waited. Gavin returned to his desk and clacked at the keyboard, trying his best to dismiss her.

"Don't get in my face like that," she said.

Gavin mumbled, "Bitch," under his breath.

"Original," she said. "And don't forget, we have family night dinner tonight. I'll see you then. I can't wait."

"Everything okay?" Jamie asked.

"There's dirt falling from the ceiling," Maxine said. "It's probably a carcinogen. And the contractor won't return my calls."

Jamie nodded toward Gavin's office. "In there?"

Maxine knew Jamie was trying to be kind, chivalrous, even, but she didn't need an intern riding in to save her. She'd taken care of herself for years, and besides, this had hardly been the first time Gavin had reacted with anger when his manhood or competence had been threatened. He also wasn't the first man who'd tried to intimidate her with size or strength. Nor would he be the last. "It's nothing."

"See something, say something," Jamie said.

"Consider something said."

Jamie took the hint, and Maxine wondered what she'd have done in his place. She was glad that he let it drop. But as he walked her through his latest designs, she hardly retained a thing he showed her. A half hour later, when her phone rang, she still hadn't let go of the encounter with Gavin, as she had so many other times. "What?" she said.

"I'm calling you, like I promised," Hester Thursby said. "And I'm in. Tell me about the project."

Maxine dragged the spreadsheet she'd been working on into an e-mail and hit Send. "There's a list of a hundred or so student names on its way to you," she said. "Find contact information for each of them. You'll need to sign a nondisclosure agreement. And I need all of this yesterday."

"That's a quick turnaround."

"I'll pay you three thousand dollars."

"I'll have a preliminary report to you by tomorrow."

HESTER

At lunchtime, Hester found a stool at the Grafton Street Pub & Grill in Harvard Square, where she ordered a burger and extra fries, and opened her laptop. She put on her headphones and pulled up the video she'd found the night before. It was a *This Old House* snippet from nearly twenty-five years earlier when the show had descended on the Matsons' house in Jamaica Plain — Pinebank — the same house Hester had visited the night before. The host toured through the ground floor, which had suffered severe fire damage in the seventies. A temporary roof had sprung leaks in the ensuing years, and the host and his cohorts spent much time joking about mold spores.

The video showed its age, the colors muted, the hairstyles and clothing long out of date, but what Hester focused on were the few moments the host spent with Tucker and Jennifer, both of whom seemed impossibly young. Jennifer would have been twenty-seven when this taped, and Tucker thirty-seven. He had thick, dark hair, and even in the blousy shirts and loose jeans of the era, exuded sex appeal. He spoke with the bluster of someone who hadn't had a moment of self-doubt. Jennifer took the host on a quick, self-deprecating tour of the two rooms they lived in, complete with cots and a camping stove.

"Cozy," the host said.

"Oh, we get cozy every night," Jennifer said with a sly smile.

A huge black dog trotted in from another room. "I can't keep Shadow from terrorizing joggers," Jennifer said, crouching to let the dog lick her face. "They think she's a bear."

Jennifer had fine, classic features, long blond hair that cascaded around her shoulders, and a laugh that echoed through the enormous, empty house. She was nothing short of charming.

Four-year-old Vanessa ran into the room, and Jennifer pulled her close while the girl buried her face in her mother's leg.

"How do you like camping?" the host asked her.

Vanessa peeked at him, her brow furrowed. "Hate it," she said, sticking her lip out.

Then, in the last seconds of the video, another child toddled into the frame. Vanessa glared at the camera, while Jennifer scooped the second child up and kissed her about a dozen times. "There's my baby," she said. "Rachel the Rug Rat!"

The video cut off abruptly, leaving a sense of the incomplete.

Hester didn't have to read Rachel's short obituary again, the one she'd shown to Angela, the one that had run two months later that said Rachel had died in a tragic drowning. From this video, it was easy to see why Jennifer had retreated from the world. In her place, Hester might have done the same.

The bartender brought her plate. "Anything else?" he asked.

"Not right now," Hester said, dousing the fries in ketchup and taking a bite of the burger.

In her mind, she put Jennifer and Rachel away for now, and turned to Maxine's project, pulling up the spreadsheet and trying to orient herself to the student data. The list was short, about a hundred people overall, and included about twenty data points like date of matriculation, major, housing, and demographics. Maxine wanted Hester to find whatever she could about each person and pass it along so that someone at the school could reach out to the students. Maxine planned to interview them and use their testimonials in a marketing campaign about the school.

This was a basic data mining project, and the one danger it posed was killing Hester from boredom. Still, she couldn't wait to dig in. She'd walked away from finding missing people for many reasons, but mostly because she'd been sloppy and careless and had put Kate in danger. She had to trust herself to put Kate first — to make sure she'd never place Kate in danger again — and this boring project might be a path to finding that trust again.

Most of the students on the list had graduated in January, though a handful had graduated the prior May. She also noted that three of the students on the list didn't have graduation dates, meaning they either had dropped out or were still enrolled. She created a separate tab and pasted those names there, then focused on the alums.

There was an equal mix of men and women, a balance of majors, and the ages ranged from early twenties to the forties. Hester would do a first-pass search using social media, where she suspected she'd be able to find most of the students easily.

She sorted the list alphabetically by last name and added columns for each of the social media sites. The first name, Michelle Brown, was problematically common, so Hester wasn't surprised when she couldn't narrow in on a specific person. As she scanned through the list, she noticed that most of the names were common, even the non-European-centric ones. There were four Smiths, two Nguyens, and five Lees. A half hour in, and about fifteen minutes before her next meeting, she hadn't made any other progress. Of the dozen or so students she'd searched, she couldn't find any kind of confirmed digital trail. No social media. No websites. Nothing.

It didn't make sense. Young people, the ones that Hester worked with every day, the ones on this list, didn't know privacy existed. Even savvy and sophisticated students at a school like Harvard didn't know a world anymore where secrets stayed secret, or where their hearts didn't sit online for the world to find. She'd have believed that one or two of these students had chosen to disconnect, but not this many.

"Anything else?" the bartender asked.

Hester shook her head and checked the

time. She had ten minutes.

She read through the list again, moving across the data instead of down to see if she could spot any trends. Someone named Paul was marked as female, which could be true, and another student had a date of birth in the eighteenth century, but otherwise she didn't notice much else.

Instead, she moved to the second tab, where she'd pasted the anomalies, three women named Naomi Dwyer, Brittany Hardenne, and Libby Thomas. They majored in fashion, fine art, and architecture, respectively.

Hester started with Naomi. A few keystrokes later, she'd found an online profile featuring an athletic young woman standing next to an elaborately designed evening gown. Naomi had secured the profile with privacy settings, so Hester couldn't learn much more about her, but a search on Brittany Hardenne brought up a completely open profile filled with photos. Brittany had strawberry blond hair and a snarl, and most of the images had been taken alone, either at school or on a farm. The last post, a photo of farm animals, was a year old. Hester added the contact information to her spreadsheet, and then pulled up the messenger app and sent a note asking

Brittany to contact her.

This may take longer than I thought, she wrote to Maxine, who responded immediately.

Update me tomorrow no matter what you find.

Hester packed up and headed to campus, where she slipped into her 1:30 meeting right on time and forgot about the list as she went over requirements for the online catalog with the development team.

It wasn't till a few hours had passed and her mind had relaxed that she finally asked herself something that should have occurred to her immediately: Why were current students on a list like this one? Current students should be easy to find.

BARRET

Barret finished work at the café and went straight to his one o'clock class, art history, where he almost fell asleep as the instructor moved through slides from the Renaissance in a darkened auditorium. Afterward, he stopped by his room to change and shower. He'd memorized his roommates' schedules, Chris and Ash were both in the same drawing class, and Trace had a shift at the campus center security desk, so he knew he'd have the room to himself. He changed out of the suit, grabbed his shower caddy, and made his way to the bathroom, where one of the guys on the hall stepped out of a shower with a towel around his waist. A woman brushed her teeth. Even after a couple of months at the school, Barret hadn't gotten used to the coed bathrooms, though no one else seemed to notice them anymore. In truth, he hadn't gotten used to cohabitation at all, and spent as little time as he could here, which was another reason he wished he could patch things up with Libby. At least at her place it was the two of them — and the roommates. He slipped into the shower, and let the water wash away the last twenty-four hours. All of it.

When he returned to the room, he caught a whiff of the suit he'd been wearing and had the good sense to drop it in a plastic bag. He hoped he'd get his deposit back when he returned it. He changed into a bowling shirt and jeans, adding a key ring and chain. He spiked his black hair and headed out. At the elevator, one of his roommates, Chris, was getting off as Barret got on.

"Will you be around tonight?" Chris asked.

"I doubt it," Barret said.

Chris went to say something else, but the doors closed too soon.

Barret spent Gavin's hundred bucks at the art supply store on paints and brushes and returned to the Longwood T stop, to his mural, which had, indeed, been painted over in gray. He found a bench and sat as the cool air seeped in through his coat. Barret's first inspiration, the first time he'd discovered his creative side, had been when he'd read *The Plain Janes* in high school, a graphic novel about four teenagers who made guerrilla-style art, all with the purpose of getting the people around them to see their environment in a different way. Once, at home, he'd snuck out late at night and set up a series of scarecrows near the church, all wearing long prairie-style skirts like the ones Alice wore. The police investigated, and Father Todd condemned the scarecrows during the sermon on Sunday, but no one suspected Barret. He was too much of a non-entity to be seen. Nowadays, he still tried to emulate the Janes from the novel, even if he hadn't yet found his fellow misfits. Art, he believed, should say something true.

He thought of another mural he could paint, another canvas waiting to be filled, another statement to be made, one that Vanessa Matson would be sure to notice.

Which was how he wound up by the pond again, at the foot of that staircase, looking up toward Pinebank. It was four o'clock in the afternoon, so the path around the pond was crowded with people and dogs, and unlike the night before, Barret didn't have the cover of darkness to shield him. He took a few steps up, somehow imagining that he'd set off alarms for trespassing. When nothing happened, he completed the ascent, and stepped onto the hill.

Here, when he turned, he had views of the pond, and beyond it, all of Jamaica Plain and the southern parts of the city. With most of the trees still bare, the hill felt exposed, and Barret along with it. He edged across the gray lawn to the stone veranda, surveying the surfaces on the brick house for the best one to use. Here, he'd need to make it in and out in a single night, so his design should be simple but impactful, and whatever he painted would be the definition of ephemeral.

Right there was the perfect spot. On the corner, out of the line of sight from the driveway. Maybe it would even take them a day or two to notice.

He glanced toward the house and froze in place. One of the women he'd seen the night before, the one with the long, white hair, stood at the open French doors, a cocker spaniel on each side. The black dog barked, followed by the buff one. The woman reminded Barret of an older version of himself. She had his fair coloring and slight build. Now that he'd dyed his hair black, they were like opposites of the same coin, like yin and yang. As he turned to leave, she called out to him. "Are you cold?" she asked.

"Not really," he said. "And the rain stopped."

"For now," she said.

She reached into the cool air before yanking her hand inside.

"You're allowed, you know," the woman said. "It's public. The yard. It's part of the park system. We own the house, not the land, but sometimes people think they're not allowed, or sometimes they think the house is public too. It's the worst of both worlds. It drives Tucker crazy, even though he's the one who wanted it!"

Barret stepped forward, onto the veranda. The dogs barked again.

"That's not public," the woman said, quickly.

He stepped away.

"I'm supposed to cook," she continued. "It's family night. Maxine's usually here by now to help, but she's running late." She turned toward the interior of the house. "Do you want some tea?"

"Out here?" Barret asked.

"No," she said. "Inside."

Barret took a tentative step onto the veranda. When he was within an arm's length, the woman reached into the outside air and pulled him inside, surprising him with her strength. The dogs stood on their hind legs, pawing at his thighs.

"They're terrible," the woman said.

"I don't mind," Barret said, crouching to let the dogs lap his face. "I had a dog."

"I'm Jennifer," the woman said.

Barret introduced himself, and she poured vodka into two teacups, and then put the bottle away in a cabinet. "They don't like me to drink. I don't fool them, but the teacup helps them pretend."

Barret sipped the vodka, and the warmth of the alcohol spread through him. "What are you making for dinner?" he asked, walking through the room, taking in the art and décor. He stopped at a painting of a green sofa he recognized from a student show a month earlier. He wouldn't mind having something of his own hang in this house.

"Spaghetti and sausage," Jennifer said, taking a package wrapped in butcher paper from the refrigerator along with a head of lettuce. "And salad."

Barret unwrapped the sausage and took a pair of kitchen shears from a block, snipping the casings between each one. "What time do you eat?" he asked.

"Maybe seven."

"There's plenty of time for such a simple meal."

"I don't know where to start," Jennifer

said, sitting on one of the bar stools. "I'm hopeless in the kitchen."

"You'll want to broil these. And I'll mix the salad too. The rest, you can do later."

He washed the lettuce, spun it dry, and found a wooden salad bowl. In the refrigerator, he dug out carrots and cucumbers and added tomatoes from the counter. "Do you help your mother like this?" Jennifer asked.

Barret hadn't spoken to his mother, not since he'd left home. He tried his best not to think of her, or of how she'd see him now, even as an image of her, out in the fields, her skin covered in a film of grime while she worked the thresher, flashed through his mind. "I grew up on a farm," he said. "We all lent a hand."

"I grew up in the suburbs," Jennifer said. "In Michigan. A world away from here. What was it like, on the farm?"

"We de-tasseled a lot of corn. And shoveled manure." Barret added long peels of carrot to the salad. "Is Vanessa home?" he asked.

"You know Vanessa? She's having a baby."

"I was at the gala last night."

"I found out on Twitter. Or they think I did, but any mother knows these things, like your mother would know if you had a secret. I have two daughters. One of them is

173

like my drinking." Jennifer raised her teacup and took a sip. "We don't talk about her."

"Did she leave?" Barret asked.

"She did."

Outside, a car pulled into the driveway, then the front door opened. The dogs ran toward the noise, barking, and a moment later, Vanessa Matson walked into the kitchen. She stopped short when she saw Barret. He put the teacup aside and hoped he didn't reek of liquor.

"Can I help you?" she asked.

"This is my friend," Jennifer said, pausing a bit too long. "Bailey!"

Vanessa put her bag down. "You can't keep doing this," she said to Jennifer, and then smiled her most polished smile. "You weren't here last night, were you?"

Barret shook his head as Vanessa ushered him toward the French doors.

"Come back," Jennifer called after him.

"Don't even think about it," Vanessa said, shutting the door behind him.

Barret crossed the veranda to the grass, turning once he hit the public land. Vanessa stood in the doorway. He backed away till he reached the top of the stone staircase, where he paused, framed by the pond, the afternoon sun shining.

He wanted Vanessa to remember his face.

ANGELA

"Where did you go?" Zane asked as Angela tried to slink to her desk.

"Working a case," Angela said, regretting it when Zane's eyes lit up. "It's an old tax case," she added. "I pull it up whenever it's slow around here. This accountant was working with some local convenience stores and I swear he laundered cash, but I haven't been able to pin it on him. I have a box of statements to go through. Maybe a fresh set of eyes would help. . . ."

Zane's interest drained away visibly. "Not a problem," she said. "And not worth your time."

"Got it, Sarge," Zane said, heading across the room to bother someone else.

With him occupied, Angela took out the slim file she'd pulled from the archives on the Rachel Matson drowning. Everything she knew about the case so far came from the obituary Hester had shown her. Two-year-old Rachel Matson died in a tragic drowning in Ward's Pond, a smaller body of water near Jamaica Pond, located a few hundred yards from the Matsons' house. The obituary was brief, offering little of substance. Hester hadn't found photos of the child or additional news coverage, both of which troubled Angela.

Reading through the case, the first thing she noted was the sparsity of detail, which was explained by the lead detective's name. Bob O'Duggan.

Charming Bob.

Bob had been on the way out when Angela had been promoted to detective, but that hadn't kept him from asking her who she'd slept with to get the promotion — the first thing he ever said to her — or from calling her AA as a nickname. "Awesome Angela," he said when she called him on it, even though everyone knew he meant "Affirmative Action."

Bob cut corners. And rumors followed him, ones that claimed he was in the pocket of anyone who'd pay. He retired on the first day he was eligible, and no one fought him on the decision. Someone like Bob wouldn't have lasted a month on the force today, but that didn't keep him from living off his pension and remembering the glory days. Good riddance was all Angela had to say.

To his credit, Bob's brief notes on the case were clear. Rachel Matson had been home at Pinebank when her parents lost track of her. According to the report, Tucker and Jennifer thought Rachel had wandered somewhere in the house, and spent time looking for her before expanding the search outside to Jamaica Pond and the area surrounding the house. Tucker found Rachel in Ward's Pond and called the paramedics, who tried to revive her. Jennifer Matson was sedated and taken to the hospital. Tucker Matson left four-year-old Vanessa Matson with a friend and went to the station to answer questions. Angela searched through the file for additional interviews, but there weren't any. The detective hadn't spoken to Jennifer, nor had he spoken with Vanessa or the nameless family friend. Angela bet she could name that friend in one guess: Maxine Pawlikowski. When the coroner ruled the case an accidental drowning, Detective O'Duggan had signed off and filed the report.

Case closed.

The problem was that Angela had questions, even from reading these skimpy details. A lot of them. And any good detective should have had the same questions.

Did the Matsons have childproof door-knobs, and if so, how had Rachel gotten out of the house on her own? How had Tucker Matson thought to look in Ward's Pond with so many other closer places to search? And had the Matsons seen anyone around the house, anyone lurking or watching the children? A child had died, and the investigation reeked of convenience, of easy answers, and of lazy, lazy detective work.

But it wasn't till Angela got to the last page on the report that her heart sank.

She closed the folder and put it in her drawer. There'd be a record that she'd retrieved it, but she didn't care. If anyone asked why — if Stan asked why — she'd tell him she wanted to investigate the Matsons' backgrounds. In a way, he'd brought this on himself when he'd asked her to stay close to Maxine.

Angela went to his office, where he sat hunched over a report. She thought about the years they'd worked together, how well she believed she knew him. She'd joined the police force right out of college, in 2002, and had moved up the ranks quickly. She remembered meeting Stan for the first time, with his fierce loyalty and adherence to the law. Stan didn't bend the rules. Not the Stan she knew.

"Everything okay?" he asked.

"Heading out," Angela said.

"Any big plans?"

"Picking Isaiah up at swim practice, if you can call that exciting," Angela said. "You?"

"A date with the TV."

"Don't do anything I wouldn't do." She turned to leave. "Remember Bob?" she asked. "Bob O'Duggan."

"Charming Bob. How could I forget?"

"What happened to him?"

"Still lives in West Roxbury, last I heard," Stan said. "He used to split his time between the Corrib and Doyle's till Doyle's closed."

"You're not in touch."

"No more than I have to be. Why do you ask?"

"No reason," Angela said. "Catch you to-morrow."

Out in her car, it killed her to do it, but she called Cary's ex-wife, Brenda, who answered with a chipper hello.

"I'm stuck at work," Angela said. "Would you mind picking Isaiah up at swim practice?"

"Not a problem," Brenda said, which is what she usually said when Angela asked her for a favor, which made Angela resent her more.

"Would you give George dinner too? Cary

won't be home till seven-thirty or eight."

"We'll take him for a walk on the beach," Brenda said. "And I'll get dinner started too. Who knows how long you'll be!"

Angela hung up and lectured herself about being nicer.

Then she sat in the car for a moment, working through her next steps. There *had* been a reason she'd asked Stan about Bob, because what bothered Angela the most about Rachel Matson's drowning wasn't Bob's sloppy work. That was a given. What nagged at her was that Stan was listed as the second detective on the case. He'd even signed off on the final report. Detectives shouldn't work cases when family members were involved, and Maxine Pawlikowski had said last night that she was an associate member of the family. Cops didn't forget dead children. Ever. These were the cases that seared onto your memory and ripped you out of a deep sleep, the ones you returned to whenever you had a free moment. These were the cases you wondered if you got wrong. Stan should have told Angela about Rachel Matson's drowning the moment she mentioned going to that house. It should have been the first thing he'd said. That death demanded justice, and

Angela promised herself, she wouldn't rest till she knew what had happened.

HESTER

At the end of the day, Hester walked the few blocks from Harvard Square to Somerville to pick Kate up at kindergarten. Outside the brick building, a phalanx of teachers stood guard as parents arrived to take their children home. As Hester waited, Mrs. Brough, Kate's teacher, waved.

"I'll miss her next year," Mrs. Brough said. "Kate's a student who'll stay with me. She's special."

These words, these kind words, filled Hester's heart with pride and love, especially in light of what she'd learned about Rachel Matson that day. Lately, Hester had given herself permission to hope and to dream and to believe in a future that would always include Kate. She liked that hope more than she wanted to admit, more than she sometimes dared to admit.

Kate was Morgan's niece, his twin sister Daphne's daughter. The girl had lived with

Hester and Morgan in their Somerville apartment for more than two years now, ever since Daphne had skipped town. Hester had seen Daphne once, briefly, since then. The meeting had come close to ending Hester's relationship with Morgan, but somehow, they'd managed to heal stronger than they'd been before. Now, Hester and Morgan still did their best to keep Daphne real and present in Kate's life, talking about her in big and small ways when it made sense, though recently, Hester had noticed that Daphne came up in conversation less frequently, and when she did, it was Kate who often steered them to a new topic.

Now, Kate dashed out of the building, her curls bouncing beneath the spring sun, and when Hester offered her a hand, she took it without reservation. How much longer would that last? They walked the few blocks toward the house while Kate yammered about her day and her friends and everything she'd learned. A few weeks earlier, she'd started writing out numbers on copier paper, going higher and higher each day. Yesterday, she'd reached the nine hundreds.

"What comes after nine hundred ninety-nine?" Hester asked.

"Dunno," Kate said.

"But you'll figure it out?"

"Duh."

Kate released Hester's hand and skipped forward. Hester jogged after her.

"Mommy came to school today," Kate said.

A part of Hester shattered at the mention of Daphne. What could she possibly want, here, today? And how would Hester and Morgan mobilize to take this on, together, as a team? Hester's mouth felt dry as she managed to say, "Where is she now?"

"April Fool's Day," Kate said, skipping ahead another few steps.

Hester grabbed the girl and yanked her from the street, rougher than she'd planned. "Careful," she said.

Kate seemed to consider a tantrum. Hester crouched and hugged the girl. Kate submitted to the hug for all of two seconds before squirming away.

"I forgot it was April first," Hester said. "What would you have said if your mother had shown up?"

"I don't want to talk about it," Kate said, the tantrum, and hopefully any other mention of Daphne, averted.

The threat, though, remained. Hester decided that the best course of action right now might be to ignore the whole conversation.

"How about ravioli for dinner?" she asked as they arrived home.

Kate ran up the front steps. "What kind?" she asked.

"Spinach and walnut."

"Yuck!" Kate said.

"April Fool's Day," Hester said. "It's plain. But don't think you'll get out of eating salad."

"Double yuck," Kate said.

Once inside, Hester lifted Ian the iguana from his enclosure and rested him on the counter.

"You set up your Legos while I start dinner," she said, to Kate, as she sautéed an onion, dug out a can of tomatoes, and took a box of Dave's Fresh Pasta from the freezer.

A moment later, Morgan's truck turned into the driveway, followed by the patter of paws on the stairs. The front door opened. O'Keefe galloped in and did a lap around the house, followed by Waffles, who lumbered and sniffed for any new scents, and then Morgan, who greeted Kate by holding her upside down and swinging her back and forth while she shrieked. When he finally got to saying hello to Hester, she nodded at the iguana. "Ian's hungry," she said.

"I'll get him some greens," Morgan said, hanging his coat in the closet.

Hester glared at him.

"No one takes stray iguanas," he said. "Not full-grown ones. He's six feet long!"

The leathery creature flicked his tongue. If the worst thing Morgan Maguire did was take in animals in need, then Hester supposed she'd found the right person for her. Besides, she could use Ian as leverage.

"Go watch TV," she said to Kate.

In Kate's world, TV was forbidden before dinner, so she tripped over her own feet running for the remote. Soon, she'd set herself up at the coffee table, Legos spread across the surface and one dog on each side of her, while a cartoon flashed across the screen.

"She told me Daphne showed up at school today," Hester whispered. "She was joking."

"If it happens, we'll figure out what to do."

Hester resisted a retort, knowing it might blow up into an argument. She and Morgan disagreed on what to do about his sister. Hester wanted Daphne's parental rights severed — a decision she'd made after the last time she'd seen Daphne — but Morgan wouldn't hear of it, and Hester didn't think the case would move forward without his support. Hester, after all, wasn't even Kate's actual aunt. "One of these days, this'll turn into a problem," she said.

"When it does, we'll face it," Morgan said. If Morgan didn't want to deal with that reality, then he could deal with another one. "Someone hired me to do a job today," Hester said. "Maxine. She wants me to find some students."

Morgan took down two dog bowls from over the refrigerator. At the sound of kibble hitting steel, both dogs ran to the kitchen, where Morgan made them sit.

"Did you take the job?" he asked.

"I thought we could talk about it," Hester said, even though, technically, she'd already begun the work.

"Very mature."

"Shut up."

Morgan cordoned off part of the kitchen for Waffles, who inhaled her food, and another part for O'Keefe, who nibbled. He released the dogs from their "sits." They each descended on their bowls, while Hester filled Morgan in on the project.

"Any serial killers involved?" he asked.

"Angela asked the same questions. But you can't know, right? And if so, I'll hand it off to the cops."

"Again, very mature."

"And again, shut up," Hester said, as her phone pinged with an incoming call from Maine. "You want to say hello to Ethan?"

Kate jumped from the sofa and ran to join them as the face of five-year-old Ethan popped onto the screen.

"Ethan, my man!" Morgan said.

"It snowed today!" Ethan said.

"So much for spring in Maine," Ethan's guardian, Lydia, called out from somewhere behind him.

Hester had met Ethan a year and a half ago when his mother had died. Hester had pushed to have the boy come live with her here in Somerville, but in the end, he stayed in Maine with Lydia and his half brother, Oliver, where he seemed to be thriving. Most nights, he called at about this time to say hello and talk about his day. Tonight, he played his recorder for a few minutes while Kate showed him her pages of numbers.

After they hung up, Morgan said, "He'll outgrow calling us one of these days."

"Maybe," Hester said. "Eventually. But not yet."

Morgan filled a pot with water and put it on the stove. "Tell me more about the project."

Hester diced a cucumber for the salad. "You might die of boredom," she said. "Unless . . . there's something more to it."

"You already started, didn't you?" Morgan said. Before Hester could deny it, he added, "What did you find?"

Hester put the knife down and faced him. "The students don't exist," she said, and she could hear the excitement in her own voice. "At least most of them don't."

"If they don't exist then they can't be dangerous. That's a plus. Maybe Maxine pulled the data from the wrong field."

"Maybe," Hester said. "I'll run that by her tomorrow. But I did find three students. I'll talk to them too and see what I can learn."

Waffles finished her dinner and tried to break through the barrier to get to O'Keefe's bowl. Morgan cut her off, heaving the fifty-pound dog onto his shoulder. She sneezed and sprayed them both with doggy drool. Hester tossed Morgan a roll of paper towels.

"Remember our game?" he asked.

How could she have forgotten? "Are we still playing that?" she asked.

"Ready?"

"Do I have a choice?"

"How did it feel to tell me about this project? To let me help?"

Hester considered the question, and how little she wanted to answer. "It scared me," she said, finally. "I thought you'd be pissed off. What did it feel like to have me ask for help?"

Morgan leaned in and kissed her. "It was okay," he said. "Nothing special."

"Don't be a sap," Hester said, even though, in her heart she knew his real answer, and she felt the same.

The front door opened. Butch ran into the apartment, paws barely finding purchase on the wooden floor, followed by Jamie.

"Just in time," Hester said.

"Soup's on," Morgan called to Kate.

"We're not having soup," Kate said.

"Technically, that is one hundred percent correct."

As they sat down to dinner, a text beeped onto Hester's phone from Angela. I need your help, she wrote. Tonight.

"Intriguing," Morgan said.

"Now, am I supposed to tell you what she wants?" Hester asked.

Morgan piled salad onto his plate. "I'm pretty sure that's how this works."

"I'll let you know when she tells me."

MAXINE

When Maxine let herself into Pinebank, the
only greeting came from Adele, followed by
Fred, both of whom stood halfway up the
staircase and yapped. "You two have a vet
appointment tomorrow," Maxine said, offering each of them a treat. "You'll get about
ten shots each."

They followed her as she wandered
through the first floor, into the front parlor,
and around to the kitchen, where a pot of
water sat on the stove, boiling away. Maxine
took the lid off and turned the gas to low.
Outside, gray clouds hovered over the pond
as the sun finished setting. The flowers in
the vases around the house had begun to
wilt. Maxine sent a quick e-mail to the
florist reminding them to deliver fresh ones
to Jennifer in the morning. From Tucker, of
course.

Then she checked that off her mental
to-do list.

"Anyone home?" she shouted to a silent house.

Upstairs, she found Vanessa, in her sitting room, tapping at her phone. "The coverage from the gala last night is good," Vanessa said as she flipped through online photos. "Here's one of you," she added.

"I look prehistoric," Maxine said.

Why on earth had she worn that eggplant-colored suit? It made her hair look purple, and not in a hip way. Between dirt falling from the ceiling and everything else that went into moving into a new building, not to mention the conversation with Gavin, the gala seemed as if it had happened weeks ago.

"Haven't you heard?" Vanessa asked. "Fifty is the new twenty-five. That makes you younger than me. I have to get these to the PR department. Which one?"

To Maxine, the two photos looked the same, and in both, Vanessa seemed impossibly young, impossibly carefree and hip, something Maxine hadn't managed to experience once in her lifetime. She collapsed onto a gray, overstuffed armchair and let her shoes fall to the floor. "The second one."

Vanessa clacked something into a message, hit Send, and fell into the chair beside her. "What a day!" she said.

Maxine couldn't have said it better. "What a day," she said.

"I've been talking to the press since we finished the video shoot. Did you hear me on Radio Boston?"

"You were great," Maxine said, making a mental note to listen to the broadcast later tonight.

"I wish I could have a drink," Vanessa said, and Maxine allowed herself a touch of excitement. It would be nice to have a child around again.

"Is Gavin home?" she asked.

"He's here somewhere. Did something happen between the two of you? You have that look. The pissed-off one."

For a moment, Maxine considered telling Vanessa about the morning's blowup, but she didn't want to test loyalties. It wasn't fair. To any of them.

"It's those pipes in the dorm," Maxine said. "The ones that burst. And the dirt falling from the ceiling. I wish things could go smoothly for once."

"It'll all settle itself out," Vanessa said, flipping through more photos.

The only way anything settled itself out was if Maxine made sure it did.

"My mother had a guest when I got home

this afternoon," Vanessa said. "A Goth with those stretched-out earlobes. Anyway, be careful with the sausage tonight. She asked for help cooking."

"Where is she?"

"She went to lie down."

"Your father?"

"He went with her."

Jennifer and Tucker slept at the front of the house, two doors away. Maxine closed her eyes. Was it her imagination, or could she hear them now, together, *tucking.*

She stood to leave.

"Where are you going?" Vanessa asked.

"Someone has to cook dinner," Maxine said. "And I'm starving."

"Gavin's team has done a kick-ass job with recruiting," Vanessa said. "The numbers are up . . ."

"Two percent," Maxine filled in.

"Two percent!" Gavin said.

As CFO, Gavin managed the recruiting department, so Maxine supposed he could take credit for the success. They hadn't spoken, not since this morning, and he sat across from her at the dinner table, refusing to make eye contact.

"That's not us!" Tucker said, from where he sat at the head of the table and wrestled

with a bottle of pinot noir.

"The ads help," Vanessa said. "But that's only part of it. There's a whole, integrated outreach plan that Gavin and his team put in place last year."

Maxine had developed every aspect of that recruitment plan.

"The cork's broken," Tucker said.

Maxine pushed the cork through with a butter knife.

"Do you know what that bottle goes for?" Tucker snapped, and for a moment she forgot their game: they hated each other in public.

"Desperate times," she said, pouring herself a glass and fishing out the broken bits of cork with a spoon. "And it tastes as good as Gallo to me."

Jennifer swept in from the kitchen. She wore a string of pearls and a loose-fitting garment that would have been called a hostess dress in another time. "No more business. No more bickering," she said. "And if we don't eat soon, I might waste away."

Maxine stood as if on command and followed her into the kitchen. A moment later they returned to the dining room with a platter piled high with spaghetti and sausage, the salad bowl, and two loaves of garlic bread. "I made enough for an army," Jennifer said. "Eat up."

Maxine piled spaghetti and sausage on her plate, and bit into a chunk of bread. Like usual, Jennifer took a quarter of a sausage and a few strands of spaghetti, and then barely touched either as the conversation rolled along. Occasionally, she slipped bites to Fred and Adele, who waited anxiously at her feet.

"Tell us more about the baby," Jennifer said, a few moments later. "Last night, it was a surprise."

"We don't know much," Vanessa said, putting a hand over Gavin's. "I'm a week or so past the first trimester, so six months to go!"

"Six months to go," Jennifer said, drinking down her wine and topping it off again. "Boy or a girl?"

"We don't know," Gavin said.

"If you find out," Jennifer said, "you'll have to tell me. I'll want to know who I can look forward to babysitting."

The words hovered among them, sucking the oxygen from the room.

"We're already interviewing nannies," Vanessa said. "The whole process, it's daunting." She paused. "We'll be moving too. We're looking at a house in Chestnut Hill."

"Moving?" Jennifer said. "Why?"

"Don't you think it's time?" Gavin asked.

"I don't think so at all," Jennifer said. "I don't want you by yourself. Not with the baby. It's not a good idea. You'll need help."

Tucker topped off Maxine's wine. Again. She had no idea how much she'd had to drink, but her tongue felt loose as this conversation headed toward disaster. "There's plenty of time for plans," she said, hoping to steer toward a new topic. "And plenty of time to think about the future. You'll be out for a few months," she said to Vanessa. "We'll need some initiatives to work on while you're gone. Now that you've saved our recruiting, what's your next big idea, Gavin?"

Gavin glanced at Vanessa.

"Go for it," she said.

"A shift in focus," Gavin said. "Away from traditional students. Those enrollments are on the decline anyway, nationally and here in Massachusetts. We need to bring in more adults. More continuing education students. More corporate education."

"And we'll use the gallery, like last night," Vanessa piped in.

"I hope so," Tucker said. "It cost enough to build."

Gavin sat up. "Last night, we focused in on the career side of creative by bringing in graphic designers. Students aren't interested in the arts anymore, liberal or any kind. They don't want to be sold a dream, which is what the old Prescott University did. They want to leave college and find a job. If we connect the school to those types of careers, and show that we can help students get there, we'll reach a new market segment."

This was the exact idea Maxine had been selling for the past year — almost her exact words — and like the new campus center or these family night dinners, it would come true now that one of the Matsons had claimed it as their own. "Sounds like something worth looking at," she said. "Good idea."

"I have them every now and then," Gavin said. "Don't sound so glum."

Dinner was over.

"Sit, everyone," Maxine said, standing to clear the table.

"Who wants coffee?" Tucker said. "It's monkey-shit coffee. Costs me forty bucks a pound."

"Oh, Tucker," Jennifer said. She laughed in a way that made Maxine hope she'd had enough to drink to forget the earlier conversation.

"You are vulgar," Maxine said, hoping to

sound prudish and angry, but even she caught the note of flirtation in her voice, one that she hoped would be absorbed by the wine they'd all been drinking. Everyone but Vanessa.

"It's a delicacy!" Tucker said. "The monkey gobbles it up and shits it out and somehow the shit leeches away the bitterness."

"It's civet-shit coffee, to be precise," Gavin said. "Civets aren't related to monkeys."

"I'll stick with Sanka," Maxine said, as she left with plates piled high.

In the kitchen, she slid the dishes onto the counter for later and searched the fridge for the box of cannoli she'd ordered from Modern Pastry. Tucker shimmied behind her, his hand brushing her backside. "You can uncork me anytime," he whispered.

Maxine shoved past him. "Stop," she said, taking the box out to the table.

After dinner, in the kitchen, Maxine and Jennifer cleaned up while the others watched a Celtics game. Maxine put on yellow rubber gloves and got to work on the pots and pans. Jennifer made a show of rinsing a few dishes, but eventually poured herself a mug of vodka. Maxine didn't bother to say anything. Not tonight. Tonight, she'd lost herself in dinner and family. She'd even forgotten to be angry at Gavin.

"The flowers are faded," Jennifer said, to herself, maybe, or to no one.

"There'll be new ones soon, I'm sure," Maxine said.

The dogs scampered into the kitchen and stood at the back door. Jennifer joined them, peering into the night air, at the dark surface of the pond. "They need to go out," she said.

"I'll take them in a minute," Maxine said. "Who came by today? Vanessa told me there was someone here when she came home."

"Bailey, I think," Jennifer said.

"He didn't come by last night, did he?" Maxine asked.

Jennifer shook her head. Fred barked at something in the yard. Maxine pulled off the rubber gloves and went to look for their leashes. She took them outside onto the grass and waited for them to finish their business, while she listened to the night and held her arms to her sides for warmth. It was quiet here with the pond lapping at the shore. So much more peaceful than her apartment.

Inside, she let the dogs off their leashes. "They have a check-up in the morning," she said. "Why don't I bring them home tonight, and I can take them from there?"

"It's not out of your way?" Jennifer asked.

Roslindale and Dr. Maguire's office in Cambridge were on opposite ends of the city, but who else would take the dogs to the vet? "Not at all," Maxine said.

Her phone beeped, right as Gavin walked in to grab a beer from the fridge.

"Damn it," Maxine said, reading through the message from campus security.

Gavin pointed to himself.

"Not you," Maxine said. "There's a party at Warhol that's out of control."

She'd have to go over there now, make a show of being present.

"I can go," Gavin said.

"I'll take care of it," Maxine said.

"You do everything," Gavin said. "Stay. Enjoy the game. I'll head over and see what can be done."

"Let him," Jennifer said.

Maxine almost dug in her heels, but she was tired. Exhausted. "Have at it."

After Gavin left, Jennifer gazed out the French doors for a moment. "Do you ever wonder how our lives could have been different?" she asked.

Maxine asked herself that all the time. If things had been different, she wondered what Rachel would be doing right now, whether she'd have stayed in Boston, or gone away and escaped. But then, if Rachel had lived, if she'd turned twenty-six in June the way she should have, maybe there wouldn't have been anything to escape. Maybe Vanessa would have moved out long ago. Maybe she'd have seen Gavin as a creepy old man when he'd hit on her in high school. Maybe Maxine would have moved on to another job, to another boyfriend, to another life, and maybe she'd have trouble remembering who the Matsons even were. "It's not worth dwelling on hypotheticals," she said, returning to the dishes.

BARRET

For Barret, there was a thrill in working so close to his subjects. He could hear them, through the windows — the laughter, the occasional eruption in conversation — as he painted his way across the wall. He kept the design simple, the colors bold, since the only light came from the moon whenever the clouds cleared long enough for him to see. Later, the rain would start again, and he hoped enough time would pass for the paint to dry solid.

He lost himself in his brushwork so that he barely heard the dogs barking, or the French doors swing open. He was adding in the last detail on a twenty-dollar bill when Maxine came to the edge of the veranda, not ten feet away from him, and stood looking out at the evening. Barret froze in place, not daring to move. He held his breath, hoping that the dogs would remember him from earlier, but Adele barked. Fred did too. Barret willed himself to disappear into the shadows.

"Do it or don't do it," Maxine said, her words slurred. "But I'm not staying out here for the entire night."

She yanked at the leashes, pulling the dogs away from him and across the grass. Thankfully, she went back inside a few moments later.

He returned to the design, working in a few more details, but alert now, wary. When the front door opened and the floodlights came on, he retreated again. Gavin Dean crossed the driveway to a Tesla and sped away.

"This is for you," Barret whispered.

He dared to flip on his phone's flashlight. There was the slick suit, the five o'clock shadow, the hand on a knee, and the five twenty-dollar bills. A speech bubble over that strong jaw read, "You look like someone who can keep secrets."

An exposé in acrylic.

This one Barret signed with a flourish.

It was on the south side of the house, facing the pond, but not large enough to see from the path. He wondered how long it would be here before someone found it, and he hoped it would be enough to ignite a whisper. He hoped that other students who'd found themselves in Gavin's office would see it and come forward, and that their voices could all merge into one.

For the first time in months, Barret stood tall. He took a photo of the mural, and then left, running till sweat poured down his forehead and his breathing stabilized. He ran without knowing where he was headed, and yet he still wound up there, on Libby's block, looking up at her window. Tonight, he could make anything happen. He believed that. And yet he stood there till he worked up the courage to climb the trellis and sit outside her window. And to hope.

The bedroom was empty. Inside, someone passed by the doorway, lingering in the hall. One of the roommates stepped across the threshold as she pulled a sweater on over her bra. She paused before coming farther into the room and running a hand over Libby's pillow. Was this Emma or Sasha? It was the one with dark hair that stuck up all over the place. The one who worked as an editorial assistant and corrected people's grammar. And the one who'd hovered outside Libby's door last night, listening.

She opened a tube of hand cream and dabbed some on her palm, replacing the tube on its side even though it had rested on its cap before. Libby would know someone had been in her room. Anyone would know. She'd probably believe it was Barret.

The roommate turned with a start. "Coming," she said, her words muffled through the glass. A moment later, both roommates left through the overgrown garden, their heads together.

Barret tried the window.

ANGELA

The sun had set over the surface of Jamaica Pond. Across the water, lights in Pinebank blazed.

"I thought we'd be going there," Hester said from the passenger's seat in Angela's car.

"We'll see where the night takes us," Angela said. "What did you tell Morgan?"

"As much as you told me. He and I are playing this annoying game. His idea. Questions. Telling each other our secrets. It's like nonstop therapy."

Since Angela had known Hester, the woman had been tight-lipped about anything that had happened to her as a child or, to be honest, the week before. Hester seemed to live for the present and future. "It'll do you good," Angela said. "You're like San Quentin with the private life. And don't bother arguing. You know I'm right."

Angela dared to look at her friend, who

glared back.

"Take my side," Hester said.

"You know I take your side when it matters," Angela said. "Even over that handsome husband of yours."

"Non-husband."

"Whatever. When are you giving that one up, anyway? Everyone is sick of waiting, including Morgan."

Angela's phone rang. It was her sister Amelia. She put the call on speaker before Hester could get in another word. "I'm with my friend," Angela said.

"I'll keep it clean," Amelia said.

They talked about Amelia's upcoming trip to Vancouver for the few moments it took to reach a credit union parking lot in West Roxbury. "Gotta go," Angela said, cutting Amelia off mid-sentence.

"Bye," Amelia said, and the call disconnected.

"That must be nice," Hester said. "Having a sister to talk to."

Angela's sisters were numbers one through three on her speed dial. She even reprogrammed her phone every few months to change up the order so that none of them could get jealous of the others. Her parents were number four and five. And Cary was number six. If Hester used speed dial,

Angela suspected she might be number two, right after Morgan. "It's not all it's cracked up to be," she said. "She thinks I'm bossy. All my sisters do."

"Could have fooled me," Hester said. "Now tell me what I'm doing here. I assume we didn't drive all the way over here for a Black and Tan."

Across the street, the Corrib Pub sat on the corner, a single-story building built of red brick, its gold-lettered sign lit up with green bulbs. Angela stared out the windshield, engine still running, both hands gripping the steering wheel. She considered how to start. She didn't want to reveal too much about her earlier conversation with Stan, at least not yet. "That obituary you showed me today," she said. "It bothered me. For a lot of reasons. But mostly because dead children make headlines, especially rich blond ones. This barely registered a blip."

"You think there was a cover-up?" Hester asked.

"I don't know what to think."

Angela took out her phone and brought up the photo of Bob O'Duggan she'd found online. "My bet is this guy'll be in the bar, probably drinking his dinner."

Hester took the phone. "He's handsome, in an old-guy way."

"This photo's from ten years ago, so who knows what's changed, but Bob has these eyes you can't miss. Bluer than the sky."

Hester looked across the parking lot toward the restaurant, and Angela could almost see her friend pulling the pieces together on her own. "He worked the Rachel Matson case," Hester said.

Angela nodded.

"And you're not talking to Stan about this because Bob and Stan are tight." A statement, not a question.

"Not exactly," Angela said. "They're not tight. I wouldn't even say they're friends, but they're more than friends too. They're both in the boys' club."

Hester chuckled. "Boys' clubs are everywhere. We even have a boys' club at the library of all places. Kevin's the captain, and he doesn't even know it."

"That's the problem with Stan. Take any boys' club you have ever experienced in your entire life, multiply it by a million, and you'll get what the Boston police force looked like when I joined it. Parts of it are still like that, but more covert. I almost miss the days when it was out in the open."

"And Stan plays along without knowing he's doing it," Hester said.

It had taken Angela a long time to figure

that out for herself, because most men showed you who they were without being asked, but Stan knew how to play both sides. He knew how to be one of the boys and her friend and confidant at the same time. "I'm good at my job," she said. "So Stan keeps me close. And he knows I despise the status quo, and that I fight it when I can. When we're alone, he hates all that as much as I do. But out in the world, he has the privilege. He uses it even without knowing it. But when you're on the inside like that — when you're part of the conversation without having to ask — you can't really understand the power, or know what it's like to be on the outside looking in."

Hester tapped a finger on the console. "Stan was on the inside on the Rachel Matson case," she said after a moment. "He watched out for someone he shouldn't have."

"I'm not sure," Angela said, "But he worked the case with Bob." She nodded across the street to the pub. "I need you to go in there and get Bob to talk and make sure he doesn't connect you to me. Can you handle it?"

"What do you think?"

"Have a text ready," Angela said. She then added, more for her sake than Hester's, "It's a public place, and I'll be sitting across the street if anything happens. Hit Send the second you smell a whiff of trouble."

Hester saluted, reminding Angela of Zane, who'd be giving *her* orders if Stan found out about this little escapade and put her back in uniform. "Whatever you learn in there," she said, "whatever he tells you, you have to promise me you'll keep it to yourself."

"I'm good with secrets," Hester said.

"It's one of your best qualities."

HESTER

Hester jaywalked across the street and glanced over her shoulder. Angela gave a thumbs-up, and Hester pulled open the heavy oak door and stepped into the warmth of the pub, which was still packed with the Thursday night dinner crowd. The smell of grills and fryers and beer taps wafted over her as she scanned the bar area for "Charming Bob" O'Duggan, whom it took a moment to locate. In the last decade, Bob's midriff had expanded, and his hairline had receded, but his eyes still sparkled blue. Hester took a seat two stools down from him. "Whisky, neat," she said to the bartender. "Make it a double. French fries too."

The bartender left the tab in a glass. Hester drank down half the whisky, in part for show, and in part for liquid courage. She was used to questioning people, to getting into their heads, but the thought of interrogating an interrogator thrilled her, even as it filled her with dread. Bob would see right through her if she wasn't careful. She waited for the fries to arrive, before saying, "Keeps me from getting blotto," right into her glass.

Bob took her in at once. He had the skills to know she wanted to start a conversation, and she hoped he was self-aware enough to know it wouldn't be about sex.

He smiled. A rosy splash covered his nose and cheeks, but shadows of his legendary charm still showed. "I can help you get blotto," he said. "What're you drinking?"

"Johnnie Walker."

"Red or black?"

"Blue, if you're buying."

"We'll stick with red." He nodded at the bartender, who poured another shot.

"You a cop?" Hester asked.

"That obvious?"

"I can spot 'em. My father was a cop." Before she even knew the words had formed, they spilled out of her mouth. "Maguire. About your age. Did you know him?"

"You couldn't swing a cat without hitting a Maguire at the station," Bob said. "What's his first name?"

Hester was shocked to suddenly realize she didn't know Morgan's father's name. "He lived in Southie," she said.

Bob had had a few already, and he was out of practice, but his eyes cleared with her evasion.

"That don't help," he said.

"He was shot on the job. When I was eleven." Hester did the math in her head. "In 1993."

Bob finished his beer and signaled for another. "I knew him," he said. "Good guy. Lots of kids. He had jet black hair, like you, but his wife was a redhead. All those kids were carrottops, not a black Irish in the lot."

Hester laid her phone on the bar, ready to text Angela.

"You don't look like you grew up in Southie," Bob continued. "Not the old Southie. And besides, Steve died in ninety-four, not ninety-three. Get your facts straight."

Steve. Steve Maguire. Hester saved that one for later. "I'm being nosy," she said. The truth could be a tool in the most surprising times. "My husband, he's the Maguire. He doesn't like to talk about where he grew up. I look for tidbits whenever I meet a cop who may have worked with his father. You can give me more of the story than an obituary."

Bob studied his glass, and Hester wondered if she'd lost him.

215

"I didn't know the guy that well," he said. "He was one of those cops who wanted to make detective, but, you know, the force changed. . . ."

He paused, letting Hester fill in the gaps herself. Women, people of color. Cops, like Angela, who were on the outside.

"I made detective right before the door closed," Bob said. "I think Steve kept hoping his turn would come."

"What happened to him?"

"Now you're testing my memory. I don't think they caught the guy who did it. It happened in Roxbury."

Another pause to allow Hester to fill in her own details. To some people Roxbury meant home. To certain people, to the Bob O'Duggans of this world, it was shorthand for dangerous.

"Neighborhoods change," she said. "I mean, look at Southie."

"Yuppies."

"I work in Jamaica Plain. Over on Amory."

"You wouldn't have seen me there after dark, not till recently," Bob said, in a way that made Hester think of her conversation with Angela in the car, about Stan being on the inside.

Hester was on the inside too — something she often forgot — and she used that status

216

here in a way Angela couldn't have. "It's nice now," she said. "The school has a new campus there."

Bob seemed to pick up on her lead. "What're you doing over there?" he asked. "What school?"

"I'm a librarian. At Prescott University. They opened a new building there."

"That's not us!" Bob said.

"The place is lame," Hester said. "The library is a shelf of books, and some days I don't talk to a student. I've been looking for a new job since the day I started."

"That school always stunk," Bob said.

Hester let the comment hang between them for a moment. She swirled a wad of fries through ketchup. "You ever met the people who own the place? The Matsons? They're a piece of work. And I hear things. That they pay off the mayor and have deals with the zoning board. How else could they buy up half the city?"

"It's more than that," Bob said.

Hester drank down the last of her whisky. "I should hit the road," she said.

She went to put on her coat.

"I worked a case with that family," Bob said. "Saw them up close."

"The college president is all over the place," Hester said. "I wish my dad had owned a college. And I hear her mother doesn't leave the house."

"Jennifer Matson," Bob said. "Used to be in the papers all the time, when there were society pages. She was pretty. She and her husband went to all that swanky shit. But that was before. It wouldn't surprise me if she went off the deep end after everything that happened."

"With Rachel?"

Bob sobered up.

Instantly.

"Who the fuck *are* you?" he asked, swinging off his stool with surprising dexterity and blocking Hester's exit.

"Back off," she said.

She'd dealt with enough drunks in her life to handle Charming Bob, and she wasn't ready, yet, to call in the cavalry. "Tell me about Rachel," she said. "What happened?"

"You should keep your nose out of things that don't concern you."

"Bobby," the bartender said, "pick on someone your own size."

"You worked the case," Hester said. "Cleared it too."

"Sure, I worked it. And there was nothing to find."

"If there was something to find, what would you have looked at?"

Bob pulled a few twenties from his wallet and tossed them on the bar. "Take your best guess," he said, and then sauntered out the door and into the night air like a man trying his best to appear sober.

Hester followed a few moments later.

"Well?" Angela asked.

"Bob's an angry old man," Hester said. "Racist. Sexist. All of it. But it went well."

"Good. When I saw him stumbling off, I thought it had gone another way."

"Well, April Fool's," Hester said. "It went pretty shitty. I think I blew our cover."

MAXINE

As Maxine drove home, she swam in the
warm afterglow from dinner, from sitting
on the sofa beside Vanessa as the Celtics
won in overtime, from allowing herself to
let Gavin take the lead with tonight's dorm
crisis. Maybe, she thought, she'd judged
him too harshly. Maybe keeping him on this
tight leash had been a mistake. Maybe she
would trust him after all.

Beside her, the dogs curled against each
other on the passenger seat. They were getting on in years, Fred and Adele, though
Maxine couldn't help but remember seeing
them for the first time as puppies, each the
size of a teacup, curled against each other at
the bottom of a wooden crate. They'd been
the last two puppies from a litter of five,
and Maxine had driven all the way to
western Connecticut to choose one. "If you
take both, they'll only have eyes for each
other," the breeder cautioned, as Maxine

rested a hand against each of their translucent bellies, and their hearts pounded away.

The black one — Fred — opened a sleepy eye and curled in closer to Adele, and ten minutes later Maxine held them both, cradled against a shoulder. "They'll need each other," she told the breeder, but in truth, she wasn't able to choose. She hadn't been able to make one the last to go.

Before Fred and Adele, there'd been Daisy, a Boston terrier. And before Daisy, Shadow, the huge, loping Newfoundland that Vanessa and Rachel had tried to ride like a horse. When Tucker and Jennifer first moved to Pinebank, Shadow would plunge into Jamaica Pond in a way that made joggers believe a bear had crashed out of the trees. She paddled away from shore, toward flocks of ducks and geese, refusing to return no matter how much Jennifer cried after her.

That was before, of course, when Jennifer would laugh while she wrestled with the enormous dog and tried to towel off her sodden coat, when Shadow would stand on her hind legs and greet Maxine with a huge, slobbery kiss. And when children played on the grass.

Shadow was the dog Maxine missed most.

Maxine wedged her car into a space farther from her apartment than she liked. She armed herself with her keys, balanced a sleeping cocker spaniel on each shoulder, and walked the block and a half toward home.

Stan sat on the front steps, waiting.

He reached out to pet Adele, who nipped at his fingers. "Do they live with you now?" he asked.

"They have a vet appointment in the morning," Maxine said. "It was easier than driving over to pick them up."

"You'll do anything for those people."

Maxine didn't want to listen to Stan criticize her. Not tonight. She wanted the warmth of the evening to last, somehow.

"How's your dating life?" she asked. "What's her name these days, RCA or Samsung?"

Stan ignored her. "Let me pour you a drink."

"I've had enough. And it's late. What are you doing here anyway?"

"Bob called me. Bob O'Duggan. Someone was asking questions."

Any good feeling Maxine had left from

the night dissipated. "Who could possibly care?" she asked.

"I'd ask you the same thing."

Stan waited for Maxine to make the next move, like, she suspected, he would with any criminal. She turned and took step number one. Eighty-six to go. But Stan grabbed her arm.

"You disappeared for two days," he said. "And took that child with you. Where did you go?"

"Why does it matter? After all this time?"

"There's no statute of limitations on murder."

Maxine looked to the buildings around them. Sound traveled up on this street. Anyone could hear them. "I didn't murder anyone," she whispered.

"Did someone else?"

"You're the detective," Maxine said.

Stan was a good detective. Maxine knew that. He'd faced down murderers, rapists, the worst of the worst. And he didn't let emotions cloud his decisions, not usually. But he gave in to Maxine tonight, and she knew he did it for the same reason he told her to carry Mace or to park under the streetlamp. He did it to protect her.

She left him to fill in the blanks himself. Like she had for over twenty years.

In the apartment, she caught a glimpse of her face in the mirror. The bruise from this morning's fall had spread under her eye and across her cheek. She barely made it into the front hall before she collapsed to the floor, her legs splayed around her, her face in her hands. She let the dogs go, and to their credit, they pawed at her till she let them crawl onto her lap, her fingers buried in their fur.

She remembered that night, her first night in this apartment, her first of freedom. The night Rachel died. She remembered the way she'd danced through each of her rooms, a slice of pizza in one hand, a beer bottle in the other, "Mo Money Mo Problems" blasting from her radio.

It wasn't till the song ended that she heard the pounding. It came up through the floor, from the apartment below. She turned off the music and stopped dancing. By then it was late.

She kicked off her shoes and padded outside onto the front porch. She took in the Boston skyline. She even said a little prayer of happiness to the moon. She set up a single deck chair and stretched out in the cool, late-summer air.

She must have closed her eyes because later, she woke with a start when a fat raindrop splashed her nose. A summer deluge followed. She even loved the rain. She gathered what she could, dragging the chairs and piles of cardboard boxes in. Then someone knocked at the apartment door.

Pounded, really.

That neighbor had nothing to complain about. Maxine walked down her hallway, still smiling as she yanked open the door.

Tucker stood on the landing, water pooling at his feet, Vanessa balanced against his shoulder.

"You okay?" The second-floor neighbor's disembodied voice floated up the stairwell.

"It's fine," Maxine shouted. "What are you doing here?" she added in a whisper.

Tucker thrust the girl at Maxine. "Watch her," he said. "Don't let her out of your sight."

Maxine took Vanessa. Her blond hair was damp, her skin cold. "What happened?" she asked, the panic already rising in her voice.

Tucker reached toward his daughter, stopping short of stroking her hair. For someone who took up all the space in a room, he seemed to have shrunk. "She can't talk to the police," he said.

"What the . . ." the neighbor began, coming halfway up the stairwell and taking in the scene in front of her. "This is a quiet building," she said. "We respect each other. You're not off to a good start."

"I'll take care of it," Maxine said to Tucker.

He turned and headed down the stairs, right past the neighbor.

Vanessa stirred and mumbled something in her sleep.

"It won't happen again," Maxine said.

"God willing," the neighbor said, turning to head downstairs. "Princess Diana died," she added. "It was on the news."

Maxine shut the apartment door, remembering Jennifer's phone calls from earlier, the ones she'd ignored. She dialed in to voice mail and listened to Jennifer's sobs. "I don't know . . ." Jennifer had said. "I don't know what to do."

Maxine's phone vibrated. She read the text through. No one had shown up at the dorm to take care of the party.

Wherever the fuck you went, she wrote to Gavin, you better get over to that dorm like you said you would. It's gotten worse, and it's yours to solve.

He was a prick, after all.

Maxine let the phone fall to her side.

That night, Vanessa had clung to her, and Maxine had held her close while the tiny child sucked her thumb. Her arms were covered with bruises. As Maxine loaded them both into her car and drove out of the city, she vowed to protect Vanessa. And ever since, Maxine had held Vanessa as close as she dared. She'd watched her and protected her and kept her safe. Every day. She'd continue to protect her from Gavin. Or anything else that came her way. Whatever the cost.

■ ■ ■ ■

FRIDAY, APRIL 2

■ ■ ■ ■

HESTER

Somewhere between sleep and awake, Hester's face grew wet, and then wetter. Paws dug into her stomach and chest, and the sound of rain pattering on the roof filled the bedroom. "Stop," she mumbled into her pillow while trying to bat Waffles away.

The dog stood on her chest, tail wagging, her snout an inch from Hester's nose. Beside her, Morgan snored away.

"You should be more like O'Keefe," she whispered.

The greyhound was probably curled in a ball in the next room, right next to Kate, where she'd stay till the girl woke her.

Waffles lapped Hester's face. The battle had been lost.

"Let's go," Hester said.

The dog leapt to the floor and waited at the top of the stairs. Hester checked Kate's room, where, indeed, O'Keefe and the girl slept soundly beside each other. Downstairs, she led the way into a rainy April morning.

The night before when she'd come in from her jaunt with Angela, Morgan had been working on the puzzle while the dogs dozed on the sofa. She was still on an adrenaline high and had told him about going undercover to meet with Charming Bob. At first, she didn't mention that she'd asked Bob about Morgan's father, about the shooting, but keeping that secret without offering something in return felt wrong. "My mother's name is Josephine," she said. "Most people call her Jo."

Morgan fit a piece of the puzzle into place. "I didn't ask," he said.

"Well, I did," Hester said, studying the parts of the puzzle they'd managed to put together so far. "This is a map of the world. See, that's Africa, the part you're working on."

Morgan nodded.

"I got nosy and asked Bob about your father," she added, filling him in on what she'd learned.

"I figured you already knew that," Morgan said. "It wouldn't have taken much more than an online search to learn it on your own."

Hester filtered through the box of pieces till she'd sorted out a new set of yellow ones. "This makes me uncomfortable," she said.

"Being with me?"

"No. Your game."

"Why?"

"Because I think you won't like everything you find out about me."

"That's true of me too."

Morgan gave her a squeeze, and let the conversation dwindle away. He usually knew when he'd pushed too far, even if she'd done most of the pushing this time.

Hester returned to the apartment and let Waffles off her leash. The dog ran to the center of the living room and shook the last of the rain from her coat while Hester kicked off her wet shoes. By now, the day had officially begun. Kate sat at the counter gobbling cereal, while O'Keefe lay on the sofa. For a dog that spent her youth at a racetrack, the greyhound seemed more than content as a couch potato. Morgan handed Hester a bowl of oatmeal, and she chose not to mention the bacon and maple dough- nut she'd stopped for at Union Square Do- nuts.

There'd been enough honesty lately.

"Where did you grow up?" Morgan asked.

"Already?" Hester said. "I haven't even

had coffee!" Which wasn't true. She'd had a cup with the doughnut.

Morgan filled a mug and added seven sugars for her. "Your adventures last night have me curious. They gave me lots to think about while I was sleeping. What town?"

"Is that one question or two?"

"It's one, with a clarification."

"Fine," Hester said. "I grew up on the South Shore. Near the beach. In Marshfield."

Her heart pounded at the revelation, however meager. It was more than Morgan had ever pried out of her, and certainly enough for him to use to dig further, if he wanted.

"The Irish Riviera!" Morgan said. "Fancy people from South Boston went there in the summer. Maybe they knew you."

"I doubt it," Hester said, remembering the tiny apartment over the restaurant that she'd shared with her mother.

"Near the beach too. I appreciate the extra detail," Morgan said. "Your turn."

"I know your father's name is Steve. What about your mother? Is she still alive?"

"That feels like two questions in one," Morgan said. "You're trying to find out if my mother is alive, but also slide in finding out her name."

"I gave you a lot!"

"Are you fighting?" Kate asked, finishing her cereal and shoving the bowl into the sink. " 'Cause it sounds like you are."

"We're not," Hester said.

"Aunt Hester doesn't like it when I'm right," Morgan said. "But here you go. My mother's name *was* Maureen. How's that?"

"Generous," Hester said, adding, to Kate. "Your uncle is generous, so ask him when you need to borrow money. Maureen Maguire. Morgan Maguire. I like the alliteration. Were there other *M* children?"

"We're late," Morgan said, ending the interrogation.

For the next ten minutes, they went through the typical mad dash while Hester got Kate dressed and ready, and Morgan gathered the dogs for a day at the office. Soon all twelve of their legs had tramped down the stairs to the truck, leaving Hester alone in the apartment with Ian and her thoughts. She wondered what Morgan might do with this newfound information. Would he show up in Marshfield for a sit-down with her mother?

In her memory, her mother seemed old, though Hester was thirty-nine now, two years older than her mother had been when Hester had left for college. Her mother had grown up in that town, gone to high school there, had a baby at age nineteen. Her mother's world probably ended at the town line.

Hester remembered one night, when she'd been alone in their apartment. A steady rumble of music and voices floated through the floor from the restaurant below where she and her mother both worked in the summer. Hester held a frozen Coke can to her forehead, her arms and legs splayed against thick air, the kind of humid even an ocean breeze couldn't remedy. She watched an old VHS tape of *Shogun.* When it got to be nine o'clock, she flipped the TV off and left. By then, dinner had gotten cold.

Downstairs, the restaurant was filled, music blared from the jukebox, and a line of customers in T-shirts and sandals waited for tables. Hester searched the bar area where her mother sometimes wound up. She wasn't there. Outside, people packed the streets, couples, entire families. It was Labor Day weekend, and they were celebrating the end of summer. Brant Rock was a tiny village set high above a rocky shore and protected by a seawall that stretched in both directions.

Hester walked along narrow Ocean Drive, away from the bustle, till she found herself standing in front of the Connors' house, with its beach roses and tiny lawn. She touched the picket fence. Here, away from the streetlights, it was dark, and, at first she thought she was alone. Then she saw the red glow of a cigarette. A cloud of smoke wafted through the heavy air. "I'm not supposed to smoke." It was Mrs. Connor's voice. "She's down on the beach, if you're looking for her."

Hester pulled her hand from the fence, embarrassed to be caught here, to be outside, looking in. She hadn't spoken to Mrs. Connor, not for years, nothing beyond a polite hello in the supermarket. She took a step away.

"You're off to Wellesley," Mrs. Connor said. "When do you head out?"

"Tomorrow," Hester said, shocked that Mrs. Connor would know anything about her, let alone that she was going to college. "In the morning."

"You'll have a great time." The cigarette fell to the porch. Mrs. Connor ground it out with her heel. "And you can be anyone you want to be. Don't let anything hold you back."

She went inside and closed the door.

Hester stood on the sidewalk for a few moments. The next morning, she'd lug her suitcase downstairs and through the restaurant, and then she'd take a commuter bus into Boston, to an unknown future. For the first time, she realized that she had a say in what that future might be.

She skirted the house to a path that led to the seawall. Below, on the rocky beach, a line of bonfires stretched as far as the eye could see. Hester took a set of stairs down and kicked off her flip-flops. The sand felt cool between her toes as she walked to where four- and five-foot waves crashed on the shore. She waded into the frigid water till it threatened the hem of her shorts. Eventually, she headed down the beach, to the spot where her mother went to get away, the spot she went when she wanted to be found. A group of kids Hester had graduated with sat around one fire. Kelly Pratt called her name, but Hester waved and kept going, while Mrs. Connor's words echoed. Yes, she could be anyone she wanted to be.

At the end of the beach, a stone jetty jutted into the ocean. High tide was an hour off, but soon water would cover much of the jetty's granite surface. Hester leapt from one rock to the next till she came to the end and sat beside her mother. "It's cooler out here," she said.

Her mother had Hester's coloring, fair

skin and black hair, though hers had begun to go gray. The moon lit up her face as she stared out to sea, her eyes glazed and unfocused. She lifted a bottle of Jack Daniel's to her lips.

"If the tide comes in much farther, we'll be stuck out here," Hester said.

"You ruined it," her mother said, her words slurring together. "Everything. My whole life. You ruined it."

Hester didn't say anything. It was late and her mother was drunk, and besides, she'd heard it before. She felt herself lifting away. She'd begun her escape. She thought of the next day, of the suitcase and the bus and of arriving on campus. She thought about the future. She *could* be anyone she wanted to be.

In the kitchen, Hester tried to shake the memory away. She distracted herself with the iguana, lifting Ian onto the counter and enticing him toward a pile of greens. "Good boy," she said, as he chewed on some spinach.

It felt like talking to a shoe, but she'd learn to love this creature, eventually. She listened to the silence of the apartment. She'd taken a Sunday shift this week for the sole purpose of having a comp day, and there'd been a time not long ago when Hester had yearned for nothing more than a day to herself. Now, when she had one, she hadn't a clue what to do with it. For a moment, she even considered vacuuming.

Instead, she made a plan for the day. She wanted to talk to Jennifer Matson, alone. She also wanted to delve further into Maxine's list. She pulled the list up on her laptop and narrowed it on Brittany Hardenne, whose Facebook page provided plenty of open content. A quick search brought Hester to an online yearbook with a photo of Brittany, a pretty young woman. The small, regional high school near DeKalb had fewer than a hundred graduating seniors, but the only other photo of Brittany was from the class play, where she seemed to be part of the tech crew and stood at the back of the group, scowling.

Hester focuseded her search on the name Hardenne within DeKalb and then on a cluster of family-owned farms on the outskirts of town. She searched on images, followed a blurry one of Brittany, and found an out-of-date family-run blog with content about a reunion two years earlier. It also included a phone number for Elaine Hardenne, which Hester punched into her phone. When a woman with a smoky voice answered, Hester fumbled for her words. She'd expected to leave a message.

"Who is this?" the woman finally asked.

"I'm looking for Brittany," Hester said. "Is this Elaine?"

"Oh." The woman paused for a moment. "Yeah, this is Elaine. Join the club. And let me know if you have any luck."

Hester imagined the woman in her living room, a cigarette burning in an ashtray, a drink in hand. Even if it wasn't yet noon.

"She left in January," Elaine said. "Haven't heard from her since."

"She enrolled in college," Hester said. "In Boston. At an art school."

"Yeah, she was always drawing and painting," Elaine said. "And I knew that anyway."

"If you know where she is, why haven't you reached out to her?"

"I don't think that's your business, stranger on the phone. And I need to get to work. The farm doesn't run itself."

"Please," Hester said, before Elaine could hang up. "It sounds like you want to know what's going on with her. If I learn anything, I'll pass it along. How's that? It'll be like we're working together. My name is Hester Thursby. Look me up online. You'll see. I find missing people."

"That name sounds fake," Elaine said, but

Hester could hear the clack of a keyboard in the background, and a moment later the woman said, "Looks like you do more than find missing people. What's this about a serial killer?"

"Ignore the rest of it."

"It's already been seen. But Brittany wanted to leave. What was I going to do to stop her? She was here one day, working at the Dairy Queen, smoking dope in her room, telling me she'd apply to the community college next semester, and screaming her head off at me like any normal teenager. Next day, she's gone. She leaves a note that says I don't get her and not to worry. Guess what I've done ever since?"

"I have a daughter," Hester said.

"Then you know what a pain in the ass they can be," Elaine said.

"She's five. Sweet but bossy."

"Appreciate it while it lasts."

"Brittany graduated from high school?" Hester asked. "Who were her friends?"

Elaine didn't respond, and for a moment Hester thought she might have lost the woman. "Didn't have any," Elaine finally said. "She used to. They'd make TikTok videos and giggle, that kind of crap, but something happened with a friend of hers at the church. Kids think you don't see things, even when they're obvious. I should have stepped in, but my hands were full since my husband died, and for a while I thought I might actually lose this place, so shame on me." Elaine's voice broke. "She was so unhappy, and I thought it would pass. But it didn't. Now look where we are."

Hester clicked on one of the photos on the family blog. In it, Elaine, who was probably close to the same age as Hester, had bleach-blond hair and the suntanned face of someone who worked outside. She stood with an arm wrapped around Brittany as the two of them tumbled over the finish line in a three-legged race. Unlike the photos from the yearbook, in this one Brittany grinned from ear to ear, the kind of happy that any parent hoped would last a lifetime. "I'll find her," Hester heard herself say. "I promise."

After hanging up, she clicked through a few more of the family photos and committed to keeping her promise to Elaine Hardenne. If Brittany was enrolled at the school, it wouldn't be hard to keep the promise anyway.

Hester took out a photo of Kate, and thought about that moment on the beach, with her mother. She'd escaped that town, and she *had* become who she wanted to be, at least mostly. When the bus had driven away from Marshfield, Hester hadn't known that it would be the last time she'd see Brant Rock, or the people who lived there, or that, after a single, strained call from the dorm phone, that the days would turn into years, that she wouldn't speak to her mother again. She couldn't have imagined any of it, because if she had, it would have hurt too much.

Looking at the photo of Kate made Hester realize, again, how lucky she was to have landed in this family, to be part of the life she'd built, here. She wanted to stop holding back, to stop protecting herself from hurt. In the end, that's what Morgan's game was all about. And it's what they both deserved.

Her fingers began typing, and before she could stop herself, she'd read an obituary for Maureen Maguire, Morgan's mother. It was a few lines long, but it gave away plenty. Maureen had taught kindergarten in the Boston public schools, and had raised ten children, including Daphne and Morgan. The other eight children's names were all listed, along with fifteen grandchildren — Kate's too. Maureen Maguire had passed away, surrounded by family and friends.

But what caught Hester by surprise, the

part that made her truly see how much she'd missed in her strange relationship with Morgan, was the date of his mother's death. She'd died last year.

She'd passed away surrounded by family and friends.

Had Morgan been there too? Alone? Had he brought Kate?

Hester closed the obituary and erased her browser history. What she didn't know about her non-husband could have filled an entire search engine, and what she did know was that she'd betrayed Morgan with this search into his life, as she'd betrayed him the day his mother died and forced him to face it on his own. For the first time, she admitted that his game wasn't such a bad idea, and she promised to make up for those betrayals.

ANGELA

Angela parked by the Stony Brook Reservation, where three cruisers and an ambulance sat with their lights flashing. She strode past a few bystanders, met Zane, and they began the hike into the wooded area while water dripped off the hood of her raincoat.

"This is more like it!" Zane said.

"Zip it," Angela said. "And respect the victims. How far from the road?"

"About a half mile."

The dam had broken on Boston homicides this morning when a woman walking her Labrador retriever in this enormous park had followed the dog into a thicket to where he'd nosed at a body. Now, most of the area had been cordoned off with police tape, and, as Angela and Zane arrived on the crime scene, the medical examiner was releasing the body.

"Male, early twenties, Caucasian," he said. "A single gunshot wound to the chest, and plenty of track marks. This'll be pretty straightforward."

"As straightforward as they get," Angela said. "We'll be done here within the hour."

One of the cops who'd responded to the call had found another male in his early twenties, passed out and holding a recently fired handgun. Paramedics had already wheeled him out of the park, cuffed to the gurney.

"We'll work the scene," she said to Zane. "The way to mess up a case like this one is to screw with the evidence."

"Got it, ma'am," he said, before dashing off with one of the evidence techs.

Angela conferred with the two officers who'd responded, and then squinted down the path through the trees as two men in dark raincoats approached. It wasn't till they came closer that she recognized Stan's familiar gait. He was with Roy, the other detective in Angela's unit.

"Not worth your time," she said to Stan, walking toward him. "Not worth mine either, to be honest."

"Roy's going to work with the kid on this one," Stan said. "Let Zane take the lead. He can get his feet wet."

"We'll all get wet today," Angela said. As Zane's supervisor, she didn't have enough faith in him to leave. "Let's make sure we get the DA what she needs."

"Trust him," Stan said, "like I've trusted you."

Something in his voice told Angela to listen. She caught up with Zane. "Roy's going to work with you on this today but call me if anything out of the ordinary happens. Got it?"

Zane nodded, and then Angela walked to the street with Stan. "I'm starving," he said. "Leave your car. I'll bring you back here."

"What's going on?" Angela asked.

"We haven't talked for a while," Stan said, getting into the driver's seat and flipping the locks open. Angela hesitated before getting in beside him.

"We talk all the time," she said. "Sometimes too much. I see you every day."

"Do we?" Stan asked, heading into West Roxbury, where he parked illegally and led her into the Rox Diner. The small restaurant was packed. Stan chose a table toward the back, where a server brought them coffee and menus.

He knew.

About Bob. About bringing Hester out the night before. About the questions Angela wanted answered. She knew it. And Stan was letting her sit with the feeling, the way he would with any suspect.

But she wasn't above delaying the inevitable or holding her cards close, even if Stan had interrogated better criminals than she and knew how to draw out her punishment. He put on his glasses and read the menu. "I should get a poached egg," he said. "Or the granola, but there's a lot of hidden sugar in granola." He patted his flat stomach. "Maybe I'll stick to coffee. Have you heard about that diet, the one where you eat between one and seven o'clock every day?"

"The starve yourself diet?" Angela asked.

"Something more scientific. Based on facts. We like facts, don't we? Evidence."

"Sometimes you have to go with your gut."

"Maybe I'll get French toast. That'd be good for my gut."

Angela relented. "What do you want?" she asked.

"How's the family life?"

"Fine," she said. "We have the dinner tonight. You know, the one where Brenda comes over and annoys me."

"You still hating on Brenda?" Stan asked. "She seems nice to me. Generous."

"Don't take Brenda's side."

"Maybe I'll get waffles."

"What can I get you?"

A server hovered at Angela's shoulder. She

was young, pretty, and Angela caught Stan taking her in. "Bagel with lox and cream cheese," Angela said.

"Two eggs, over easy, bacon, and hash browns," Stan said.

He'd ordered the same thing every time they'd gone to breakfast for the last fifteen years. His eyes hovered on the waitress's legs as she walked away. Sometimes Angela forgot that he was more than her lieutenant, more than her friend.

Much as Cary had brought the baggage of middle age into their relationship, Angela had brought her own baggage. Her list of conquests could have filled a phone book. It was a rare night that Angela and Cary went out without bumping into one ex or another, mostly men and a few women, which, at this point, made Cary laugh. Angela had been married once before — to Rick — for about six months, long before she'd discovered her gay side, or her lesbian side, or her queer side, or whatever people wanted to call it. She didn't care.

But one bit of baggage that Cary didn't know about was that Angela had had a fling with Stan. Years ago. When they both had been married. It had lasted three days while they hunted a serial rapist, and had ended without discussion — deferred maintenance

— as soon as they nabbed the perp. The fling could easily have driven a wedge between them. Instead, it bound them closer. They both got divorced that year — Stan after a decade of marriage — but neither mentioned rekindling the affair, and they'd managed to keep it to themselves. It would have ruined both of their careers, especially Angela's. Was there anything more clichéd than sleeping with a superior? Angela hated being a cliché.

"How's the single life?" she asked Stan now.

"I do what I want. Whatever I want. The only girlfriend I have is Alexa."

"Would Alexa lie for you?"

"I think she'd do anything I wanted," Stan said.

"I won't."

Stan sat forward. "Bob O'Duggan called me last night. Told me that a tiny woman with black hair and glasses was asking him questions about the Matsons at the Corrib. Sound like anyone you know?"

Angela didn't answer. She wanted to see how much of his hand Stan would play.

"And," he continued, "I checked the archives. Turns out you pulled the file on Rachel Matson's death yesterday after-noon."

"You're the one who told me to stick close to this case," Angela said.

"But why dig into something that closed so long ago?"

"Because it stinks, and you know it does."

"You weren't there," Stan said. "It was open and shut, an accident. That's it."

The server brought their breakfasts and asked if they needed anything else while topping off their coffees. "Not now," Stan said. "Thanks."

"Do you trust me?" Angela asked.

"Mostly," Stan said.

"Then you'll have to trust me on this."

"Do you still trust me?" Stan asked.

After working with Stan this long, Angela trusted him more than anyone else she knew. More than Hester. More, even, than Cary. But, truthfully, she didn't trust anyone that much. "Of course," she said.

HESTER

Hester had the driver drop her on the southern shore of Jamaica Pond, where the boathouse and bandstand sat by the water. She jogged through raw, wet air around the perimeter of the pond. It was right after nine, not too early for a social call, even a spontaneous one, and if she was lucky, Jennifer Matson would be home alone.

In the light of day, Pinebank was still grand, with its red and yellow brickwork, ornate veranda, soaring gables and multiple chimneys, all framed by the bare cottonwoods. Whereas at night the structure had seemed remote, at the center of a vast wilderness, the daylight revealed how exposed it actually was. An open field sat not fifty yards away, and a walking path led right along the south side. Hester also noted that someone had painted graffiti on the brick. The rain had streaked away some of the paint, blurring part of the image and lettering, but, to Hester, the design reminded her of Roy Lichtenstein, with bold colors, the sharp angles of a man's face, the dark silhouettes of two women, and a speech bubble in the style of a comic strip. She traced what was left of the lettering and came up with *keep secrets.* She snapped a photo of the whole thing and took a second of the smeared signature.

At the front door, she rang the bell. A moment later, Jennifer Matson answered. Today, she wore capri pants and a pink sweater set, her white hair tied in a low ponytail, ready to take on the day. "I thought you might be someone else under all that gear," she said.

"Were you waiting for someone?" Hester asked.

"I met a new friend yesterday. I thought they might come for another visit."

Hester swiped at the rain dripping from her hood. "Someone painted a mural on the side of the house."

Jennifer hovered in the doorway. "Is it nice?"

"I took a photo."

"Then you'll have to come inside and show me!"

Jennifer faded into the dimly lit house. Hester followed, through the foyer, and around to the kitchen where Jennifer perched at the island, a tablet in front of her. "Reading the paper before I get going," she said. "I have a yoga class this afternoon. Have you done yoga?"

"Not with the kiddo and work. I don't have time, not anymore."

"If you make time for yoga, yoga makes time for you."

"Very centering."

"You can take your shoes off," Jennifer said.

Hester kicked off her sneakers and hung the coat on a hook.

"Coffee?" Jennifer asked. And when Hester hesitated, Jennifer added, "It's coffee, nothing else. I don't get going till after noon."

"Restrained. Sure, but sit. I'll get it myself." Hester took a mug from an open shelf by the sink and filled it from an urn.

"There's cream in the fridge, and sugar over there," Jennifer said. "How many kids do you have?"

"A girl," Hester said, taking the stool opposite and sipping the coffee. "Rich," she added.

"It's monkey-shit coffee." Jennifer laughed and covered her mouth. "That's what Tucker calls it. He'd kill me if he knew I'd added cream. He says it spoils the finish."

"Do what you like, right?" Hester said, spooning more sugar into her own mug.

"Show me a photo of your daughter."

Hester scrolled till she came to her favorite image of Kate, from the school's nonsectarian holiday production in December where Kate had played a walrus. "She's five going on thirteen."

"Vanessa was like that too, taking charge." Jennifer touched the screen, her fingers brushing Kate's curly hair, the walrus tusks, her grin. "You're lucky."

Hester scrolled to the image of the mural.

"That'll have to go," Jennifer said. "It's happened before, with the house out in the open like this and people constantly wandering by. Comes with the territory, I guess, but it's annoying."

"I bet," Hester said. "Where are the dogs?"

"Maxine took them last night. It's quiet here without them. They have a vet appointment."

"With Morgan!" Hester said.

"That's right! You're married to Dr. Maguire!" Jennifer's eyes creased into a grin. "Maxine has such a crush on him. She'll talk and talk about the appointment later."

Hester suspected many of Morgan's clients had a crush on him. Who wouldn't? "You can't get much sexier than a handsome veterinarian. I'm lucky he's mine."

"That's how I feel about Tucker."

Hester took out her laptop. "Do you have Wi-Fi?" she asked.

Jennifer gave her the code, and Hester logged on. "I was thinking about our conversation the other night and remembering a paper a student wrote last semester on lesbian tropes in television. She referenced an episode of *Police Woman.* I thought it would be fun to watch it together."

An image of Angie Dickinson flashed across the screen, and Hester hit Pause.

"You remembered," Jennifer said. "I've never seen the show! I'd listen at my mother's door but most of the time, I couldn't even make out the dialogue."

"These shows don't age that well."

"It doesn't matter," Jennifer said, taking Hester's hand and leading her out of the kitchen, through the house and into a media room with a giant flat-screen television. Hester connected the laptop while Jennifer curled up on the overstuffed sofa.

"Do you always let strangers into the house?" Hester asked.

"You're hardly a stranger. You're Maxine's friend!"

"More like acquaintance."

"You're *my* friend, then," Jennifer said, as credits rolled, and the episode began with Angie Dickinson's Pepper Anderson running out of a rainstorm and into police headquarters, shaking out her coat as she strode along a hallway.

"The same weather as today," Jennifer said.

"This episode is called 'Flowers of Evil'," Hester said. "It's about three lesbians who rob and murder the residents of a nursing home. Apparently, it caused quite a stir when it aired. There's a butch, a femme, and a bitch who conspire together, hence the paper on lesbian tropes. I bet you can guess who takes the fall in the end."

"The femme?"

"We'll see."

"We should have popcorn."

They settled in as Pepper went undercover at the nursing home, fending off awkward sexual innuendos from all three murderers. In the end, the femme took the fall for the others, as Jennifer had predicted. "I knew it!" Jennifer said, her eyes glowing. "You weren't even born when this show ran. How do you even know about it?"

That was a question Morgan could have asked as part of their game, but Hester found it easier to answer Jennifer, someone she barely knew. "When I was growing up, my mother would sometimes disappear for a few days. I'd fend for myself. One thing I did was watch videos, anything I could take out at the library, so I know seventies miniseries and movies really well. TV shows too."

"Where would she go?"

"She'd drive," Hester said.

"Did she ever take you with her?"

"Sometimes. We went to Lubeck in Maine, once. It's as far as you can drive before getting to Canada. You didn't need a passport to cross the border then. We could have kept going."

"What stopped you?"

The police had stopped them. They'd taken the Connors' car, after Hester had snuck into their house in the middle of the night to steal the keys, the real reason, if Hester was being honest, why Mrs. Connor had stopped asking her to babysit. "It was time to go home," Hester said.

"I'd love to drive to Lubeck," Jennifer said. "And I wouldn't stop there. Where's your mother now?"

Hester closed the laptop. "You guessed the ending. It was the femme who took the fall."

"I'm good at guessing the end. And it was worth waiting forty-seven years to see it!"

"I'm good at endings too," Hester said. "Tell me something. Why did you leave that copy of *Adam Bede* for yourself the other night?"

Jennifer began answering and then stopped herself. She brushed at an imaginary stain on her capri pants. "Sometimes I think people will forget," she said. "And I don't want them to. I want them to remember what happened, and how it happened."

"What do you need to remind them of?"

"That she was," Jennifer said. "That she was ours. That she shouldn't be forgotten even if it hurts too much to talk about her. About Rachel. Even when other good news pushes her aside."

"Rachel the Rug Rat."

Jennifer looked up.

"I saw a video," Hester said. "She was adorable. You loved her a lot."

"More than you can imagine." Jennifer crossed to a window that looked out through the trees. "You can't see it from here, but the pond where it happened isn't far. Ward's Pond. Across that field and through those trees. In the summer, the field is overrun with families. Dogs. Children playing. I hear them. All day long."

Outside, a car pulled into the driveway.

Jennifer swiped at her eyes with a fist. "You'll have to go," she said, her voice flat. "That's Vanessa. She doesn't like when I have friends over."

Hester paused.

"I'm fine," Jennifer said. "You should go."

Hester gathered her bag and followed Jennifer to the kitchen. "Maybe I can come back. We can watch something else another time."

Jennifer took out the vodka and topped off her cold coffee. "You seem like a friend," she said. "That mural on the house. It looks like Gavin. Don't you think."

Hester could see it. "You're different when you're sober," she said.

"And you should call your mother," Jennifer said, drinking the coffee down in one gulp, and ushering Hester through the French doors. "I told you I was good at predicting endings. I can tell you haven't talked to her, not in years. Give her a break. You'll be happier in the end. And it's not like she killed you."

Those final words lingered in the damp air as Jennifer closed the door and melted into the dimly-lit house. Hester imagined her standing at the window on a gorgeous summer day, hearing children crying, seeing the world at play. She hurried across the veranda and then skirted the house and headed down the driveway, away from the pond. She checked a map of the park, and then took a path that ran through the field. It took a moment to orient herself, but a hundred yards later, she found herself at a busy intersection, waiting for traffic to subside till she could cross the street and head down a set of stairs. Here, she found Ward's Pond, a small body of water surrounded by trees and a narrow walking path. Unlike Jamaica Pond, which was broad and sunny and public, this felt like a hidden oasis deep in the forest, even as traffic on the Jamaicaway roared on the road above.

Hester stopped at the edge of the pond, where reeds and grasses poked up through the water. Across, on the opposite bank, a sandy shoreline marked where the Muddy River ran.

She climbed the stairs to the sidewalk and looked back, across the field, to where Pinebank rose through the trees. It hadn't taken more than five minutes to walk from the house to the pond, but it hadn't been an easy trip, either, and had involved crossing an open field and a busy road. How could a two-year-old have possibly wandered here on her own?

Hester dialed Maxine's number. It was time for them to talk.

on her own?

Hester dialed Maxine's number. It was ... for... ... ...

MAXINE

All around the waiting room, dogs lifted their heads in unison when Maxine's phone rang and Hester Thursby's name flashed across the screen. Maxine hit Ignore. It was her own fault for choosing the barking dog as her ringtone, though Fred and Adele were used to the sound by now. They barely woke from where they curled against each other on Maxine's lap.

"Will Dr. Maguire be ready soon?" she asked the receptionist.

"A few more minutes," the receptionist said. "Sorry for the wait. There was an emergency surgery."

Maxine leaned her head against the wall and closed her eyes, trying to escape her own thoughts. Since Stan's visit the night before, she'd been assaulted by *what ifs.* What if she'd answered that call from Jennifer all those years ago? What if she'd driven the ten minutes from her house to Pinebank instead of dancing around her apartment with a slice of pizza? What could have been different? How could all their lives have changed?

"Mrs. Pawlikowski?" a vet tech said from an open doorway.

"Ms.," Maxine said automatically.

The vet tech tried, and failed, to look at anything but the bruise on Maxine's face, which had managed to get worse overnight. In the exam room, both dogs shuddered with anxiety when the tech offered treats as she asked about their health. "Up," Maxine said, scooping under their bellies and lifting them onto the table.

The door to the exam room opened. Dr. Maguire came in wearing his blue scrubs, followed by his own slobbering basset and a greyhound. "I have the whole menagerie with me today," he said, pausing. "First things first." He lifted Maxine's chin. "That's a nasty cut."

"I'm a klutz," Maxine said.

Dr. Maguire dipped a swab in something. "I'm not supposed to do this, but that looks like it might be infected, or on the way there."

He was fit, but not too fit, and probably not worth seeing shirtless, but with a kind face and a disarming grin. And the attention felt nice.

"How's that wife of yours?" Maxine asked.

"Having fun with the project you gave her," Dr. Maguire said. "And remember, she's my non-wife, and will be till she changes her mind. I'm not one for ultimatums. I ask her to marry me every few months. She says no. Maybe I'll ask again soon. But you can only take so much rejection, right?"

Dr. Maguire prodded the dogs' abdomens. He ran a hand along their hind legs. He distracted them with treats as he gave them each a series of vaccinations. "They both look great," he said. "Healthy. Keep doing whatever you're doing."

The flowers would arrive at the house by eleven, like every Friday. From the car, Maxine dialed and drove despite the hands-free laws — the Trans Am certainly didn't have Bluetooth — and listened as the phone rang. "Tell me exactly what's in the bouquets," she said when a timid-sounding woman answered.

"Daffodils, tulips, baby's breath, lilies . . ."

"No lilies!" Maxine said.

She'd told the florist a hundred times not to include lilies because lilies made Jennifer think about drowned babies and funerals and gravesites. She hung up and careened through town till she turned into the trees toward Pinebank. She parked and headed inside.

"Hello, darling," Jennifer called from the kitchen.

Maxine dropped the dogs to the floor. They barked in tandem and ran across the carpets.

Maxine had a to-do list a mile long. She had to review the designs for the summer courses. She had to go over that new diversity and inclusion proposal. She had to call Hester back and find out what she'd learned. And now, she had to wait here to check the flowers.

Maxine followed Jennifer's voice, to where the woman sat in a salmon-colored chaise, looking out over the veranda. "It'll be nice once the weather is warmer," Jennifer said. "We can sit outside."

Maxine poured herself coffee and noticed an empty mug in the sink. "Was someone here?"

Jennifer shook her head in a way that told Maxine she was lying. "Anyone else home?" Maxine asked.

"Vanessa's around here somewhere," Jennifer said. "And Tucker's at the chiropractor. He is very stressed out."

What, exactly, did Tucker find stressful about playing golf and squash all day? Still, Maxine was relieved to hear he wasn't home. Even after decades of subterfuge, she found not speaking to him in public exhausting. "I'd like an hour to de-stress one of these days," she said, her words purposefully clipped.

"Honestly, Maxine. You can be so unpleasant sometimes. I'd have thought you'd have softened toward him, after all these years."

"I should try harder."

She and Jennifer spent the next half hour going through Jennifer's plans. Today, Jen wanted to head to the Museum of Fine Arts for a new exhibit then take a yoga class in Brookline, one she'd already registered for online. Maxine made a mental note to cancel the registration before they got charged.

"Did you hear me?" Jennifer asked.

"Sorry?" Maxine said.

"I could tell you were off somewhere. But I was saying that it was silly. I was silly. I realize that now. The other night. The book." Jennifer's lips quivered. "I overreacted. To the news. About the baby."

This was as close to a confession that Maxine would get, and, if she was being truthful, it was as close as she wanted. It was so much easier to leave all they had to talk about unsaid. "We'll forget it happened," she said.

"I know you worry."

"I worry about everything," Maxine said, touching her friend's hand. It was as cold as ice. "You'll have to be more specific."

Jennifer lowered her voice. "About the new baby. About what will happen when it comes. What Vanessa might remember."

"Watch her," Tucker had said. *"Don't let her out of your sight."*

Maxine would keep watching, to make sure the new baby was safe. She'd pay attention and wouldn't make the same mistakes, not this time around. And Jennifer wouldn't ever be alone with that baby, not while Maxine had breath in her body. "Everything will be fine," she said.

"You take care of us," Jennifer said. "You always do. You always have."

"Even when I can be unpleasant?" Maxine asked.

Jennifer poured herself a cup of coffee. "Especially then," she said.

The doorbell rang.

Finally, the flowers. "Let me deal with the delivery," Maxine said.

In the foyer, the deliveryman carried the bouquets in and lined them up on a table.

Fourteen in total. While he retrieved the old arrangements, Maxine ran her hands through the flowers, breathing in the sweet smell of roses till she found a single, over-looked lily hiding among tulips. She crushed it in her hand.

"Aren't those lovely," Jennifer said. "After thirty years, Tucker still thinks to send me flowers each week!"

"He's a dear. And I have to run."

"The list calls?"

"Always."

"If you see Tucker," Jennifer said, "tell him I'm busy, but that he should telephone if he needs anything."

Maxine cupped her friend's cheek and kissed her gently. "I will," she said.

Outside, as she went to get in the car, she noticed Vanessa standing by the south side of the house, studying something Maxine couldn't see. Vanessa left the yard and joined her. "I'll see you tonight for dinner?" she asked.

They met for dinner on Fridays — just the two of them — and had for years. "Of course," Maxine said.

"You headed to school? If you see Gavin, would you tell him I need to talk to him?"

"What were you looking at over there?"

"Nothing important," Vanessa said. "I

forget how beautiful the house is. It's good to be reminded sometimes. I'll see you to-night!"

In the car, Maxine checked her phone. Hester Thursby had tried calling twice and had also sent a text. Maxine punched in her number.

"I'm almost done," Hester said, walking Maxine through what she'd found — nothing, basically — about most of the students on the list. They'd been registered at the school, they'd taken courses, had grades, and graduated, but they didn't exist, not online at least. "Do you want me to keep trying?" Hester asked.

"Not at all," Maxine said. "That's everything I need."

There was a pause on the other end of the line.

"What?" Maxine asked.

"I went to see Jennifer this morning," Hester said.

That explained the extra coffee mug.

"And I talked to her about Rachel," Hester added.

Hearing the girl's name, every time, hurt like the first time.

"I have questions," Hester added.

Maxine cut her off. "I'll send you the check for your time. And don't forget that you signed an NDA on this," she added, before clicking off and calling Gavin.

He didn't answer. Not a surprise. He rarely took calls from Maxine. She sent him a text before speeding toward the school.

I know what you did.

HESTER

Hester slid the phone into her pocket as the Red Line train hurtled through a tunnel. Maxine had something to hide — that was clear — but Hester wasn't sure if it was about Rachel or the missing students or both. She planned to find out, whether Maxine liked it or not.

After leaving Jennifer at Pinebank, Hester had found an up-to-date LinkedIn profile for Libby Thomas, including a current photo and a listing for a spring internship at a small architectural firm. The profile trumpeted her 4.0 grade-point average at Prescott University, but not much else. Libby seemed to have materialized out of nowhere. She didn't list jobs or an educational background prior to the fall semester, a red flag Hester would have noted herself if she'd been the hiring manager for a position.

The train stopped at South Station. Hester

headed upstairs, into the rain, and crossed Fort Point Channel into the Seaport District. Until ten years ago, the Seaport District had been a mostly abandoned stretch of land consisting of industrial buildings and parking lots. Now, it was transformed into one of the most sought-after business locations in the city, with new buildings going up seemingly every month. Hester hadn't been down here in a year or two, and she was shocked by how much had changed in that short time. It took her a few moments to locate the building where Libby worked, but inside the lobby, a security guard sat at a desk checking IDs, and when Hester tried to talk her way to the elevator, the guard told her she wasn't on the guest list.

Outside, Hester called the firm, but the phone went right to a directory of employees, and when she entered Libby's name, she got voice mail. At least Hester knew the woman still worked there, even if it felt as though she'd wasted her time coming here. She could try going to the school to find information on any of the students, but that risked alerting Maxine.

She pulled up Libby's LinkedIn profile again. Libby had thick hair that framed a pale face in tightly wound curls. Even in a thumbnail photo, her eyes hinted at someone who took life seriously. Hester waved to the security guard, yearning for the days of open access.

Then Libby left the building.

Sometimes, all this job took was patience. And a little luck.

Libby wore a raincoat with a green hood pulled over those distinctive curls. She walked with determination, across the street, and around a corner, where she ducked into a deli. Hester followed, squeezing into the crowded store and taking a place in line behind Libby, where the woman bent over her phone till she ordered a chicken parm sandwich.

"I'll have a Reuben," Hester said.

She stayed beside Libby, who seemed to sense the intrusion, and slowly turned away. When their orders were called one after the other, Hester carried her tray to where Libby sat. "Do you mind?" she asked, sliding into the chair before Libby could put the phone down or answer.

"Weren't you outside my building?" Libby asked. "What do you want?"

"To talk to you."

"My mother told me not to talk to strangers."

"Maybe we'll be friends," Hester said.

Libby fumbled with her bag. Her phone dropped and skidded across the floor. "Fuck, fuck, fuck," she said, loud enough so that the man at the next table turned. Libby matched his stare, her eyes as intense in real life as they were in her profile photo.

Hester softened her voice to a whisper. "It's nothing. I want to ask you a few questions. It'll take two minutes."

"Why not e-mail?"

"Do you answer e-mails from strangers?"

Hester retrieved Libby's phone from where it had fallen and laid it on the table between them. "You don't want people to stare."

"Put your own phone on the table," Libby said. "And don't even think about recording a word I say."

Hester lay her phone next to Libby's, making a show of powering it down.

"Who are you telling?" Libby asked.

Telling?

"I'm not telling anyone anything."

"Yeah, right."

"I have a list of names," Hester said. "Nothing else. Let me know if you recognize any of them. You may have gone to college with some of these people."

"Even if I knew them, they don't want anything to do with me. Leave me alone."

"This is for Prescott University," Hester added.

"Prescott?" Libby said, relaxing noticeably. "Whatever. That place is a joke."

"They're looking for data, on graduation rates, that sort of thing," Hester said, laying the list on the table.

"What does a list of names have to do with graduation rates?"

"They want to talk to alums."

"I'm not an alum. Not yet."

"Okay, they want to talk to good students. Like you. You have an internship in your field."

"If you can call it that. Who knew working could be so boring? All I do is respond to e-mails all day. And who knew being an architect could make you such an asshole?"

"There are assholes everywhere," Hester said. "Even at nice people conventions."

That earned the tiniest of smiles.

"That was a lame joke," Hester said, pushing the list toward Libby. "The lamest. But would you look?"

"Fine," Libby said, reading through the list quickly. "Don't know any of them," she said. "But I don't know many people. Not these days."

Hester flipped the page to the shorter list. "How about Naomi Dwyer? Or Brittany

Hardenne?"

Libby's eyes shot up. "Why would you want to talk to Brittany and me? What could we possibly have in common?"

That was the exact question Hester wanted answered.

"And besides, if you're looking for Brittany, you won't find her," Libby said. "She doesn't exist, not anymore. But then again, neither do I. And I have a lot bigger problems to deal with right now than Brittany and her drama. Go to Dreamscapes in Jamaica Plain. You seem smart. You'll figure it out."

Libby stood and threw most of her uneaten sandwich into the trash, the momentary trust Hester had established having evaporated. "Is this for Gavin?" she asked. "He's coming for me, isn't he? You can tell him I'm tired of this. Tell him I don't care anymore. I survived it once, and I can survive it again. He has a lot more to lose than I do."

The mural painted on the side of the Matsons' house, of that hand on a woman's knee, flashed through Hester's mind. "What will he lose?" she asked.

"Fuck you," Libby said, stalking out of the restaurant, which had grown quiet at the outburst.

Hester ignored the people staring at her, slowly working her way through the Reuben and fries, and soon the noise around her returned to a dull roar. She'd been in the news herself a few years earlier when she'd helped capture a serial killer, and the attention hadn't been all positive. She remembered being watched, and the random calls late at night from reporters looking for a scoop. Most of all, she remembered wondering what would surprise her next, and when she'd read something else new and untrue about herself.

She wouldn't get any more information out of Libby Thomas, not now, because Hester knew one thing: Libby had a secret, one that made her feel like prey. And today, Hester had unwittingly played the hunter. Now she needed to know why and what it had to do with Gavin Dean.

Maxine

Like most colleges, Prescott University relied on federally funded grants and loans that came through student tuition. Their very survival was dependent on this money flowing frequently, and often, but there was also a federal regulation called the 90-10 rule that applied to all for-profit colleges, schools like Prescott University, and it was simple and easy to follow. It capped the percentage of revenue that the school could receive from federal financial aid at ninety percent. The remaining ten percent had to come from other sources, whatever they might be. The whole goal of the rule was to single out poor performing institutions, ones that treated students like figures in a ledger, the same institutions Maxine had spent two decades fighting from getting lumped in with. Breaking this rule could shut a school down in a matter of weeks, especially if the press got wind of it. Maxine had seen it happen plenty of times. She sped into the campus parking lot, almost forgetting to take her keys as she parked across two spaces and headed into the building.

That's not us?

That's exactly who they were.

She should have seen what was going on. She should have seen it last night, at dinner, when Gavin had bragged about increased enrollments. And she should have seen it months ago. She should have dug into the data as soon as enrollment numbers rose, but she'd been too relieved. Too ready to accept good news.

College enrollments were down nationally and had been falling for a decade. Small liberal arts colleges were closing. Students wanted to major in STEM, not the arts, so why, of all schools, would Prescott University be the one to buck the trend? She knew where she worked. She knew that the school's declines should have been steeper than traditional colleges not beating them. But she'd opted for blinders.

She punched at the elevator button, and when the doors didn't open, she took the stairs instead, running up three flights, two steps at a time, and met Gavin on his way down.

"Trying to make your escape?" she said.

He stopped, looming over her.

Coward.

"You made up those students," Maxine said. "The ones on the list, and probably others as well. You made it look like they paid a full ride. And you doctored admissions data so that we could take in more student loan money. Have I missed anything? We'll lose the school over this as soon as it hits the news."

Gavin puffed his cheeks out. "You live in la-la land," he said. "How do you think we paid for all of this? For this building, for your vision? Or Vanessa's gallery? We should have been looking for ways to economize. This whole thing has been your pipe dream."

"You stole money from the government," Maxine said. She spoke slowly, hoping he might understand the gravity of the situation. "That's fraud. It's a felony, and don't think for a second I'm taking the fall."

Gavin stepped toward her, his fists clenched, and Maxine finally paused to take in where they were. The stairwell, a fire escape, was lined with concrete thick enough to absorb any sound. She'd overseen the designs herself. Gavin could do anything he wanted, and no one would hear. But she didn't back down. She wouldn't give him that satisfaction, not here. Not anywhere. "Don't try to intimidate me," she said. "I bet you've leveraged the properties too. How else would you have come up with all this money?"

He lunged at her, fist raised.

And in that second, Maxine noticed the razor-sharp part in his hair, the way his polished shoes glistened in the fluorescent light, the way his eyes shone with unadulterated hatred. She imagined a fist to the face, the sharp jab of pain, cracked bones and teeth, the explosion of tinny blood in her mouth. She also imagined falling backward, into oblivion. When the fist stopped an inch before contact, she wanted to slap herself for flinching.

"Don't worry," Gavin said. "I don't plan to expose myself to assault charges, or worse. But do you want to know what I know?"

"You don't know anything," Maxine said.

"Try me," Gavin said. "I know that you're meeting Vanessa for dinner tonight, like you do every Friday night. Man, do I hate that. All these years we've been married, and I can't take my wife out on a Friday night because she's meeting some old hag. And I know that she means more to you than anyone else in the world. I also know you'd do anything for her. Anything at all."

"I already called Vanessa," Maxine said. "Tucker too." She hadn't, but Gavin didn't need to know that. "They're on their way here so that I can tell them about this mess in person. We'll figure a way out of this, but it won't be with you. Consider yourself relieved of all duties, effective immediately. You can leave on your own, or I'll call Security and have you escorted out. Your choice."

Gavin snapped his fingers. "We *should* call a meeting," he said. "We can have it in the conference room upstairs, the new one, the one with all that audiovisual equipment. That cost a lot of money too. You can lay out your case for them. Show what you've found."

Maxine stepped away from him.

"Or maybe," Gavin said, "we should talk about *your* secrets, and we can meet at your dumpy apartment instead."

"I don't have secrets," Maxine said, even as a feeling of dread blossomed. Gavin was too stupid to bluff when he didn't have cards to play.

He leaned in and whispered, "Tuck the Tucker."

Maxine's mouth went dry.

"I have you on tape," Gavin said. "I hired

284

a private investigator, just in case I needed something in my back pocket. What do you think Vanessa would do if she found out about you and her father? Would she want you coming to the house? Playing with the baby? Do you think she'd let you interfere in every single aspect of our lives like you do with my mother-in-law? You thought you'd take over and make our child yours to fill that sad empty life. There's no way in hell I'll let that happen. Come to think of it," Gavin added, "maybe I'll tell her everything anyway, because, man, am I sick of seeing your ugly face."

Maxine met his stare. It was all she could do till she got away and could think through her next steps.

Gavin sauntered by, his shoulder brushing hers. "I wonder if *you'll* need to resign," he said, as his phone rang. He flashed Vanessa's photo at Maxine. "Look who's calling," he said. "She and I, we have a lot to catch up on." He clicked into the call. "Hey, babe. I'm here. With Maxine. She said she wanted to talk to you about something."

He held the phone out, and Maxine took it. "We're on for dinner, right?" she asked, her voice shaking

"I told you that already," Vanessa said. "What's wrong?"

"Nothing."

"Let me talk to Gavin."

"Give me till tomorrow," Maxine whispered, as she handed the phone to him.

"We'll see," Gavin said.

He descended to the ground floor and left the building.

BARRET

Barret barely had fifteen minutes to get from campus to work, but that didn't stop him from allowing a flash of hope when he checked his phone for texts. No one had sent one — certainly not Libby. He ran through the rain toward Centre Street, wondering if anyone had found the mural he'd painted, wondering if it had even survived the weather. He remembered painting another mural on the side of his high school. It had been hot and dry, not a chance of being washed away, and the mural had shown a line of people, at attention, shoulders squared, facing in the same direction toward an unseen beacon, while another person danced behind them, leaving the crowd behind. Below, he'd painted "See What You Want" in block letters, and he'd waited for the message to cause a stir. But in the morning, the cleaning crew had already arrived to begin removing the mural, and by the afternoon, it was gone. Not a single teacher or student talked about the mural that day, but when Barret got home, his mother called him into the barn where she was tending to a pregnant sow.

"Anything you want to talk about?" she asked.

For a long time, Barret's mother had called him her best friend. But lately, they barely spoke.

When he didn't answer, she said, "Come find me if you do."

And he knew she knew. What other secrets did she know?

He'd decided right then; it was time to leave.

Someone grabbed Barret from behind. He swung around, shrugging off the hand. But it was Libby who faced him.

"Were you in my room last night?" she asked.

Barret kicked at the wet ground. He'd tried to get into her room, but the window had been locked. Now, he didn't want to admit to even being there.

"Someone was," Libby said. "And there were fingerprints on the outside of the glass."

"Everything seemed fine," Barret said. "I

liked being with you. What went wrong?"

Libby looked down the street. "I can't give you the answer you're looking for, and it doesn't matter how you ask. I'm sorry."

"You can tell me *something.*"

"It's not what you think, that's all I can say."

She turned to leave but stopped herself. "You might hear some things about me. Some things I didn't want anyone to know. If you do, well, I hope you'll understand."

"I'll always understand."

"Maybe you will. Maybe you won't. Also, a woman came by my office today. She had a list and was asking nosy questions I didn't want to answer. She asked about Brittany."

"Why would anyone care about her?" he asked.

"No idea. But this woman is coming your way."

Libby left, leaving Barret standing in the rain. He wondered if they'd ever speak again. But the last person in the world he wanted to think about right now was Brittany Hardenne.

"Better," Dreamessa said, looking Barret up and down as he arrived for the shift with seconds to spare. She handed him an envelope. "Payday," she added.

Barret tucked the envelope into his bag. The money couldn't have come soon enough. He got to work and spent the next half hour restocking grab-and-go items and trying to push Brittany and Libby from his mind. But when he finished the task, he caught Dreamessa watching him.

"Your face doesn't say *Can I help you?*" she said. "It's more like *Get away from me.* What's going on with you?"

"I'm nineteen," he said. "Drama."

Dreamessa wiped down the counter and brewed a carafe of dark roast.

"Where are you from, anyway?" she asked.

"You saw my ID when you hired me."

Dreamessa raised an eyebrow. "I did," she said. "DeKalb. What's it like there?"

"I'm from the outskirts of DeKalb. There were lots of farms. We raised pigs and grew corn."

"How'd you wind up here?"

"You know, luck."

Dreamessa tossed a rag beneath the counter. "Look," she said, "you're pissing me off. It doesn't have to be this hard. The world's a big place, with all sorts of people. But you have to be open to it. Stop being scared. Or be scared. Do whatever you need to, but you're here now, not there. You can find your place in this world."

Barret knew she wanted to help, but it didn't keep him from shutting down. He wished he was bolder, one of those people who took on the world, who declared who they were without regard to anyone but themselves, but that wasn't him. Except with Libby. And Alice, before.

"Here, I'll tell you something about myself. My name's not Dreamessa."

"I'd never have guessed."

"Want to know my real name?"

"Not if you want something in exchange."

"It's Lisa Simpson. Try going through life with that name. It'll scar you."

Barret fought back a smile. "You are the sensitive and thoughtful one," he said.

"Zip it."

A pack of teenagers stormed into the shop right then, lining up and cutting off the conversation. They were the type of high school students Barret used to dread seeing on the street, the type he imagined might single him out, but now he barely noticed them. That, he supposed was a kind of progress. Still, as he moved through their orders, Dreamessa's question stuck with him. How had he gotten here, to Boston of all places? He hadn't said goodbye when he'd left the farm, only a note, one that told his mother she didn't understand him. He suspected that she was glad he was gone. When he thought about why he'd run away, he realized now that it was easier in the end than facing his truth or allowing anyone he loved to face it with him.

"What can I get you?" Barret asked.

Dreamessa had gone into the kitchen, and a tiny woman with a black ponytail stepped up to the counter. She took in his name tag and his face in a way he'd gotten used to. And he remembered her, from the gala, and from seeing her through the Matsons' window the other night. "Looking for your kids again?"

"Barret?" she asked. "Do you go to Prescott University?"

He nodded.

"Could I ask you a few questions? I have a list. Would you take a look at it?"

This was the woman Libby mentioned, the one looking for Brittany. Thankfully, his phone beeped, and a text popped onto the screen. "I'll have to catch you later," he said.

He took off his apron. He had an hour to go before the end of his shift, but he left the café without telling Dreamessa where he was going. The text was from Libby. She wanted to see him. And nothing else mattered.

HESTER

Barret ran right past Hester, the café door slamming behind him as he took off into the rain.

A woman in her thirties walked out of the kitchen with a tray of clean mugs. She had a shock of pink hair and the look of a manager who'd seen it all. "Where did he go?" she asked.

"He got a text," Hester said.

"Strike three," the woman mumbled to herself, and then gave Hester a practiced smile. "Sometimes it's for the best. What can I get you?"

"Has he always gone by Barret?"

The woman's smile faded.

"He looks like someone I used to know," Hester said. "How long's he worked here?"

"Yeah, I'm not going to tell you that, or anything else about him. Do you want something? Otherwise, I have plenty to do, especially now that I'm shorthanded."

"I'll take a coffee," Hester said.

"That, I can help you with."

Hester carried the cup to a table, and then booted up her laptop. One of the big pieces of the puzzle had fallen into place with one look at Barret. She returned to the Hardenne family blog and found the photo of Elaine and Brittany running the three-legged race. Despite the tattoos, the earlobe plugs, the cropped hair, and dye job, Hester could still see Brittany Hardenne in Barret's features. They were the same person. Somewhere along the line, Brittany had transformed herself into Barret. If one good thing came out of this, maybe Hester would convince Barret to call his mother.

She returned to her conversation from earlier with Libby Thomas, who'd said that Brittany didn't exist. Unless there was more to that story, Hester had what she needed, but Libby had said that *she* didn't exist either. A simple search on Libby's name, filtering for news, returned too many results. Hester thought through the conversation for other information. When Hester first told Libby about the project, Libby said that the people on the list wouldn't want anything to do with her. It was when Hester told her that the project was for Prescott University that she seemed to relax a bit.

What if she'd enrolled at another school before moving to Boston? But why keep that a secret, why leave it off her résumé? She texted the question to Morgan, and he responded a moment later

Because she flunked out, got kicked out, or was forced to leave?

With Prescott University's open-enrollment policy, the admissions department wouldn't care about any records or past transgressions. I should have thought of that, Hester replied.

Distance helps. You should see how many scans I've studied for hours before one of the other doctors points out the problem in about two seconds. We're a good team!

They were, Hester thought.

She returned to the spreadsheet and read through the columns. Libby was from California, but narrowing the search to that state didn't help either. None of the results was about a woman in her early twenties. She tried adding the word "college" to the query, but most of the results that returned were about sporting events.

According to Libby's online profile, she'd enrolled here in Boston in the fall. Hester narrowed the search to cover the spring semester, a year earlier. She removed "Libby" from the equation and added the word "scandal."

Bingo.

A YouTube video came to the top of the query with a headline that read "Stanford Student Rips into Pharmacy Employee," and linked to a Bay Area news story from the year before. Hester plugged headphones into the laptop and began the video, which she had a vague memory of having seen. It took her a moment to recognize Libby, aka Mary-Elizabeth Thomas, in the grainy footage. This woman had the same dark curls and intense eyes, but she also seemed open and carefree, like someone who hadn't yet learned how much life could hurt. She stood in line at a pharmacy, the video starting up mid-sentence as Libby asked a salesclerk if there was something wrong.

"It's hard," the clerk said. "Ah . . . I can't . . ."

"You can't what?" Libby said. "It's a fucking pair of sunglasses. Ring them up."

"The scanner. It doesn't . . ."

" 'It doesn't,' " Libby said, imitating the way the cashier tripped over his words.

"Take a chill pill, Mare," one of her friends said.

"All I want is a fucking pair of sunglasses," Libby said. "And this fucking god-damned retard can't work the register. How hard

296

can it be? Are you a fucking retard?"

Hester had seen enough. She remembered now; this video had spread across the Internet, playing in Twitter and Facebook feeds for a few days till it had been replaced by some other scandal. She remembered that feeling of schadenfreude that it wasn't her own worst moment caught on camera for the world to see. Even now, she couldn't quite look away.

Libby snatched the sunglasses from the cashier, put them on, and attempted to leave the store without paying. A security guard tackled her and hauled her to the ground. "I'll sue you," she shouted. "Do you have any idea who the fuck I am? You're retards. All of you!"

The video stopped abruptly. The first of thousands of comments read, *Bitch is CANCELLED.*

Hester thought of the terrible things she'd said in her life, of her worst moments, and imagined seeing them play out on video. And she judged too. She could understand how the video had gone viral. She imagined the hate mail Libby had received, the death threats on her social media.

Hester searched again, this time using Mary-Elizabeth Thomas in the query, and the search returned thousands of results.

Libby had been in her junior year when the video went viral. The public shaming began at once, with follow-up videos of Libby being chased into her dorm by a group of students chanting, "Do you know who we are?" Within a few days Libby disappeared from campus, and soon she disappeared from the news cycle.

Hester took a sip of her coffee. It was stone-cold.

Libby had a secret. Like other people who'd been publicly shamed, she'd tried to leave her past behind and reinvent herself. In a way, Barret also had a secret, but an open one, at least to anyone who met him in person. Maybe the third student on that list, Naomi Dwyer, had a secret too.

BARRET

Brittany was Barret's deadname, a name he hadn't used since his hair had been blond, when his mother still called him her daughter. He hadn't used it since that last day in Illinois, one he could still remember like it happened yesterday.

The day had been frigid, with an unrelenting wind screaming across the bare fields and snow in the forecast. He'd packed a bag, mostly art supplies, but also a few changes of clothes, jeans and flannel T-shirts. He left the skirts behind. He didn't take photos either, nothing to weigh him down. His room, with its toys and posters of boy bands seemed like it belonged to someone else.

Downstairs, he scribbled the note to his mother and left, and outside he tried his best not to turn around, to take in the farmhouse, with its peeling paint and patchy front lawn and unpaved driveway, or the sadness that had infused everything, every moment, since his father died three years earlier.

As Barret headed toward the old highway, Rusty emerged from the warmth of the barn, collapsing with a sigh on the frozen ground. Rusty was fifteen, going on sixteen, and now, Barret wondered if he'd lasted these months. That day he'd stopped to let the dog lap his face in exchange for a belly rub, but even Rusty couldn't keep Barret from leaving the farm. "Take care, boy," he said, as he dragged his suitcase down the long driveway and the sound of Rusty's thumping tail faded away.

Barret sensed a new life opening in front of him. When he hit the road, he turned left, toward DeKalb, ten miles away. Eighteen-wheelers sped by, leaving sonic blasts in their wake. A mile in, he stopped at the 7-Eleven for a hot chocolate and a bag of Doritos, paying with one of the twenties lining his backpack, forty-one of them in total, saved from months of working at the Dairy Queen, months of skimming off what he handed his mother, months of imagining this day. The guy working the register barely looked up as he handed him the change. Barret finished the hot chocolate and plunged into the cold to continue his journey.

The church rose from a sea of fresh asphalt. Barret knew every inch of this building, every member of its community. Inside, at this very moment, Father Todd might be preaching about destiny. Maybe Alice was there too, her skirt falling below her knees, her hair curled around her shoulders. Alice had mastered a smile, one that masked her secrets. Their secrets. Her touch, like Libby's, had surprised him, mostly because he'd thought he was alone in the world, and for a while, a few days, really, he hadn't been. Losing Alice had made him lonelier than he'd ever felt in his life. But that loneliness had given him the resolve to leave.

Brake lights shone. Tires squealed across the blacktop. A pickup truck reversed. The passenger-side window slid down and a blessed cloud of warm air enveloped Barret before dissipating into the cold.

"Want a ride?" the driver asked.

He wore a checked dress shirt and tie and a heavy overcoat, and he probably had a clown suit in the rear cab. Barret kept walking. The truck inched along beside him. "Come on, babe," the driver said. "Hop in. I got nowhere to be. You'll freeze your ass off out here."

Not in a million years.

"Suit yourself, freak," the man said, driving off fast enough to kick gravel in Barret's face.

Barret was a freak. And every step he took, every advance he rejected, every potential serial killer he spurned, took him closer to embracing his difference. And this guy, with his pickup and checked shirt, was a surprise blessing. He distracted Barret long enough to forget the church and the minister and his mother and Alice and Rusty till they were all far, far behind him. Good riddance to them all.

Except Rusty. And his mother.

Eight miles to go.

"Chicago," Barret said that afternoon at the bus depot.

"Sixty-five dollars."

Barret handed over three twenties and the change from his stop at the 7-Eleven.

"ID?"

He slid his ID beneath the bulletproof glass.

"Don't look much like you."

"Glasses," Barret said. "And I cut my hair."

"It looked better before, missy."

The man wore a name tag that read TOM. Maybe Tom sat here all day saying things to piss people off, but what did it matter what Tom thought of Barret's hair? He wouldn't see him again.

On the bus, Barret took a window seat. Other passengers filtered on, each stopping at his seat and staring too long. There was power in being a freak. His phone beeped with a message from his mother. Can you pick up your brother at Bible camp?

The bus driver eased onto the interstate, and a few hours later, when they stopped at Popeye's for a break, Barret bought a small order of French fries, loaded them with ketchup, and tossed his phone in the trash.

He couldn't wait to see the world.

A day later, his train pulled into Boston and his new life began. Three months had gone by now, and he could barely remember Brittany. Brittany had giggled at boys and baked cookies and lived most of her existence outside her body, looking in. Barret was still getting to know himself, but he didn't live his life like an endless dress rehearsal anymore. He was small and slight, shorter than most women, let alone men. He usually wore jeans and bowling shirts and a sports bra tight enough to keep his breasts in place. He hadn't yet considered

any kind of surgery — it was beyond anything he could afford — but Libby had
taken that all in stride, and that had been
enough. He wondered whether it ever still
could be.

The heavy rain seeped into Barret's worn
sneakers, but he hardly cared. His feet felt
light, like he might lift into the air and fly
away.

Meet me, Libby had written. By the boathouse.

Their special place.

He came to the traffic light and waited,
squinting through the rain to where the
boathouse rose out of thick fog. Early-
evening traffic passed by him, wipers fighting against the deluge. He stepped into the
road before the light changed. A truck sped
by, horn blaring. He remembered that night
with Libby all over again, the touch of a
gloved hand, the burn of the cold. He'd
begun calling himself Barret as soon as he
arrived in Boston, but the new name had
sounded strange, translated, like speaking a
foreign language.

That night on this pond, he'd put his hand
to Libby's hair. He pulled her toward him.
He pressed his lips to hers. With that kiss,
he left Brittany behind and became Barret.

He became someone he wouldn't ignore again. That's what Libby meant to Barret.

She meant everything.

The walk sign flashed. Barret dashed across the street. The city seemed miles away. "Libby?" he said. "Where are you?"

No one answered.

"Is someone there?"

He took a step forward, into the dark.

ANGELA

Angela pulled in front of the UMass Boston campus. She was late to pick up Jamie, who stood outside waiting while rain poured off an awning. He managed to slide his enormous frame into the front seat of the car by jamming his knees beneath the glove box. "Could have taken the bus," he said.

"You probably could have walked at this point," Angela said. "Sorry to be late."

For most of the day, she'd avoided having to talk to Stan again, but as the afternoon wound down, Zane returned from the crime scene at Stony Brook Reservation. Or to be precise, from the hospital, where the suspect they'd picked up had woken and confessed without being asked so much as a single question. "A win is a win," Stan said, insisting that they go for drinks to celebrate Zane's first close. At the bar, Zane sucked down a cosmo and told every detail of the confession, while Stan watched Angela from across the room. She'd finished her wine and gotten out of there as quickly as she could.

Now, she kissed Jamie's cheek, her hand brushing the scar, which, like his stammer, had faded but not yet disappeared.

The reminder.

Two years ago, someone under Angela's command had shot Jamie during a raid on his apartment, during a raid that shouldn't have happened. As a black man in this world, he'd suffered the exact fate that Angela feared every day for Isaiah. She hadn't pulled the trigger, but she still blamed herself for being part of the problem.

Good had come from the whole situation. Jamie, who didn't have much family, had moved from a lonely apartment in Everett, to the one in Hester and Morgan's house. He'd brought Butch with him, and he'd become a part of their lives. Now, he came to Angela's house every Friday night for dinner, and she'd committed to making sure he could become the best he could be. It wasn't that hard of a job. He came with the goods.

"How's the internship going?" she asked.

"Keeps me busy. Especially Maxine. Wants

me to stay on after I graduate, work full-time."

"What do you think?"

"Won't graduate till next year. But something to consider. I'll want to see if there are other offers."

"Sounds about right," Angela said. "What do you think of that organization?"

Jamie gave the question some thought. "They try," he said. "They're trying, but there's a stigma with a for-profit. It may not be possible to overcome. I learn from Maxine, though. Tough but fair. She got in a fight with Gavin Dean yesterday. Not sure what it was about, but I was glad I was there."

"Did something happen?"

"Nothing I could point to, but, you know, there was something. Asked Maxine if she needed anything, and she said no."

Maxine Pawlikowski hadn't given Angela the impression of someone who couldn't take care of herself. Still, like any good cop, Angela took even a hint of workplace violence seriously. She made a mental note to follow up as she drove into Savin Hill, the quiet Dorchester neighborhood on the southern edge of Boston where she lived with Cary, and parked in front of their small bungalow. Before she could get out of the car, the front door opened. Isaiah dashed out with George at his heels. He passed right by Angela without so much as an acknowledgment and headed right to Jamie. George chose her first. "Damn dog," she said, as he leaped up to greet her.

Despite the rain, Isaiah dribbled a basketball, pivoting to keep it from Jamie. The trio ran to where the basketball hoop hung over the garage. Cary stood in the doorway, while her ex-wife, Brenda, hovered at her shoulder with a contented look on her face that made Angela feel like a stepparent. Angela locked her firearm in the vault in her trunk and called to George.

"Let him play," Cary said. "He's been cooped up all day."

"He'll smell like a wet dog," Angela said.

"He is a wet dog," Cary said.

"They'll stink like wet boys."

Cary took Angela's hand and pulled her into the house. "Let them have some fun. We can have five minutes of adult time."

"ABC!" Brenda said, handing Angela a glass of red wine.

Brenda was short, with practical salt and pepper hair. She was from an old WASP family on the North Shore, the kind of family that spent summers at the country club. Like Cary, Brenda was a therapist, and between the two of them there was way too much processing for Angela's comfort. In their defense, they'd remained close after their breakup and committed to raising Isaiah together. Happily single, Brenda usually came to these dinners with tales of weekend getaways, or spinning class, or binge-watching an entire season of some new TV show, which made Angela resent her more. "What's ABC?" Angela asked. "The wine?"

"Angela, Brenda, and Cary," Brenda said. "The Awesome Threesome!"

She raised a hand to high five, and Angela knew that she, herself, was the jerk who waited a split second too long before succumbing. "ABC!" she said.

"Brenda brought Thai," Cary said.

"I know it's your favorite," Brenda said, as the door opened and the boys piled in.

All three of them.

George shook water from his coat, while Isaiah led Jamie to the TV, and soon the sounds of a video game filled the house. Angela took a moment to appreciate the scene unfolding around her. In truth, it wasn't so bad, even with awful Brenda. "I'm starving," she said, as the stresses of the day began to dissipate.

She finished her wine and refilled her glass.

"That's more like it," Brenda said.

"Did you get Drunken Noodles?" Angela asked.

"You know I did," Brenda said.

Why? Angela asked herself. *Why am I such a terrible, ungenerous person?*

Angela's phone rang. "Damn it," she said. "It's Stan. We're in a fight."

"You better answer then," Cary said.

"Don't let that stuff fester," Brenda added.

"The two of you are like the dynamic duo," Angela said.

"That's what I used to say," Brenda said. "Before we broke up."

"What?" Angela said into her cell phone.

"I know you have the dinner tonight," Stan said.

"Is this about our conversation?"

"No, I need you. In JP."

"Jamaica Plain? What happened? Is it the Matsons?"

"It's a murder," Stan said. "And it'll be all over the news in about two minutes flat. I'll tell you the rest when you get here."

"What about today?"

"We'll talk about that tomorrow."

Angela clicked off. "Sorry," she said.

Brenda filled a plastic container with din-

311

ner to go, adding a brownie wrapped in plastic.

"Duty calls," Cary said. "We'll make sure to get Jamie home."

MAXINE

Maxine was out of breath. And she was tired of the rain, and the cold, but she jogged the last half block to the intersection, trying to keep the wind from turning her umbrella inside out. When she reached Ten Tables, she paused to collect herself, swiping water from her face, and putting a hand to her hopelessly windswept hair. She'd need calm and assurance tonight with Vanessa, no matter what secrets had to come out. She had to face this problem in the same way she'd faced everything else that had ever come her way in life. She had to be strong. In the end, Vanessa would understand the choices she'd made, even if she couldn't find a way to forgive them. Maxine had to believe that.

She ducked into the restaurant, a tiny bistro in Jamaica Plain with a warm interior and a hearty menu. The hostess greeted her by name and let her take her usual seat, where the bartender handed her a towel and slid a Manhattan onto a coaster without asking. "I must look a fright," Maxine said.

"It's that time of year when we all give up," the bartender said.

"If we're all giving up, I look worse than bad."

Maxine kept herself from gulping the cocktail, letting the sip of rye sit on her tongue and warm her mouth. And she thought about the afternoon, about Gavin, about everything that had been said and done. After Gavin had left her in the stairwell, Maxine had taken advantage of the soundproof walls to scream till she went hoarse. After she'd finished that little show of emotion, after she'd crumpled to the stairs and stared numbly at the concrete walls for God knows how long, she'd taken a pragmatic view of the situation. Secrets didn't stay secret, not once they'd made their way out. She'd given her life to the Matsons, to this school, to Vanessa, and she could lose it all so easily, but a calm had settled over her as she realized what she needed to do.

"She coming tonight?" the bartender asked, nodding toward the second, empty stool.

Vanessa was late.

"She'll be here soon."

Maxine checked her phone for messages, but no one had written. I need to talk to you, she wrote to Tucker, and then deleted it. Tucker was useless in a crisis and had been since the day she'd met him. Anytime the school had faced any scrutiny, Maxine had taken the hit. And anytime the family had faced a crisis, Maxine had dealt with that too.

But the longer she waited, the more her imagination shoved any calm aside. Maybe Vanessa wasn't coming. Maybe Gavin had already gotten to her. What if she never came? Maxine shifted in her seat. Pinebank was a half mile from here. She could make it there in less than fifteen minutes. She could plead her case. She could make them understand.

And then the door opened, and Vanessa walked in.

Maxine hadn't realized she'd been holding her breath, waiting. She released it now in a gasp.

Vanessa was drenched, her face ashen. She closed her eyes, her hand on the hostess station. Then she shook her head and seemed to release whatever she'd brought with her. In one fluid movement, she took her coat off, stepped across the bar, and kissed Maxine's cheek. Everything Maxine had held close, all the dread and fear, all the images of endless nights alone, released. She clutched at Vanessa, pulling her in close. "What's wrong?" Vanessa asked, her voice shaking.

"Nothing," Maxine said. "I had a day."

"Sorry I'm late. I went to see my mother. She's upset that I didn't tell her about the baby. She's upset that we're moving out of the house. She was drinking." Vanessa's face broke as she slid onto the stool. Her hands flew to her face as she rubbed tears away with fists. "Sorry," she said.

Maxine couldn't help it. Big, fat tears of relief spilled from her own eyes. "Don't apologize."

"It's only hormones," Vanessa said, squeezing her eyes shut as though trying to will away the tears. "It feels like I have no control over my body, like it's been hijacked."

She pushed the stool away and leaned forward, putting her head between her knees. Maxine lay a hand on her back. Vanessa sat up and embraced her. "I thought I could do this," she said, gasping, sobbing like she hadn't sobbed since she was a child. "I thought I was strong."

Everything would be fine. Maxine knew that now. "People have babies all the time," she said. "And most of them survive us."

"Not all of them," Vanessa whispered.

No, Maxine thought to herself. Not all of them.

A moment later, Vanessa pushed herself away and dug a tissue from her bag, glancing around the restaurant. She blew her nose and swallowed. "That was embarrassing," she said. "Like I mentioned, hormones."

"Everything okay?" the bartender asked.

"You didn't see any of that, did you?" Vanessa asked.

"Not a thing," the bartender said, as she went to pour Vanessa a glass of cabernet.

"I'm into club soda these days," Vanessa said quickly. "With a lime."

"Good news, I hope," the bartender said.

"The best," Vanessa said, taking a quick sip of Maxine's cocktail as soon as the bartender turned away. "Don't tell. The pregnancy police might arrest me. And I need it, as you can see."

"Is everything else okay?" Maxine asked. "You're awfully upset."

"A little morning sickness. Actually, a lot of all-day sickness."

"You should take it easy."

"Not with the gallery open for less than two days," Vanessa said. "Besides . . . Gavin

317

told me you had it out with him today. He's pissed off. Worse than normal. He told me to ask you about it."

Thankfully the bartender returned. They both ordered hamburgers, like they did most weeks. "You should get yours well done," Maxine said.

"I'll have it medium rare," Vanessa said. "Everyone's full of advice now, especially people who haven't had children."

Maxine let that one pass, even if it left a small bruise. It was the least of her worries today.

"What happened?" Vanessa said. "Tell me. It couldn't have been that bad."

This was Maxine's chance to confess, to take the power from Gavin. But she couldn't find the right words. "Oh, you know," she said. "The two of us fight. But in the end, we love each other because we love you."

"Could have fooled me," Vanessa said.

Outside, on the street, a police cruiser flew by, sirens blazing.

"Refill?" the bartender asked.

Maxine nodded as another police cruiser flew by, followed by a third. "What happened?" she asked.

"Haven't a clue," the bartender said.

Maxine swiveled away from the window. The blood had drained from Vanessa's face.

Running late, Hester texted to Morgan. Can you get dinner started?

It was heading toward seven o'clock, and with the way the subways worked, it would take an hour for Hester to make it from Jamaica Plain to Somerville, which was on the other side of the city.

Her phone rang.

"What are you doing?" Morgan asked.

Hester huddled under a bus shelter across the street from Naomi Dwyer's house. She filled Morgan in on her day, and what she'd learned. After she'd found the video of Libby on YouTube, she'd searched more closely on Naomi Dwyer's name. Naomi also came from California, and it took a few queries to connect her name to that of her mother's, a well-known actress who'd gone to jail for paying someone to take Naomi's SAT test. Naomi had been a minor at the time, so the press had mostly left her out of the coverage. She also had a different last name than her mother, but once Hester made the connection, she was able to piece together more of the story.

"She'd been admitted to some pretty prestigious schools," she told Morgan. "The offers were rescinded once the case hit the news."

"Did she know what her mother had done?"

"From the interviews, I'd say no," Hester said. "But who knows? It's another scandal. Like Mary-Elizabeth Thomas. Another secret to hide."

"Call if you need to bounce any more ideas off of me," he said.

"There's some chili in the fridge."

"It's Friday," Morgan said. "We're ordering pizza."

"That'll get me home faster. See you in a bit."

She clicked off and ran across the street, through a chain-link gate, and into a small garden, where a door was propped open with a cardboard box. One of two mail slots was labeled clearly with Naomi's name. Hester rang the buzzer, and a voice came through an intercom system. "Naomi moved," a man said.

"Do you have her phone number?" Hester asked.

"Not for strange people who show up ringing my bell."

The intercom cut off, and Hester dialed again. When no one answered, she walked in, leaving the box where it was.

On the second floor, two more boxes propped open the apartment door. Beyond it, was a utilitarian one-bedroom with slanted ceilings and furniture from IKEA. Footsteps approached as a man emerged from the bedroom with a third box. He was more like a man-boy, lanky, with curly hair that needed a trim.

"Naomi went to stay with a friend," he said. "We broke up. This is her stuff, if you want any of it. Here, you can help me. Grab something."

Hester lifted one of the boxes and followed the man as he lumbered down the stairway and onto the sidewalk, where he dropped the boxes on the curb.

"It's raining," Hester said.

"She was fucking someone else," the man said. "I don't give a shit. Good thing my name's on the lease."

He stopped at the front door and peeled Naomi's name off the mail slot, flicking the label into the mud. "There's some hand cream in that box that costs like twenty dollars a tube," he said. "Take it. Or someone else will. And if you find Naomi, tell her to go to hell."

He went inside and made sure the door latched behind him.

So much for that lead. Hester's stomach rumbled. A few slices of pizza and a beer suddenly held more appeal than a rainy night. Finding Naomi Dwyer could wait till morning.

Cary's car sat in the driveway when Hester trudged from the bus stop. Jamie rolled down the passenger's side window as she approached.

"How was dinner?" Hester asked, leaning into the car.

"Awesome," Isaiah said, from where he sat in the back seat beside George. The dog snaked his snout around Jamie's shoulder and lapped Hester's face while she ran her fingers through his rough fur. "Good boy," she said.

"I won Horse," Isaiah continued. "Twice! And I got three new levels on Captain Toad!"

"Amazing! I'm still on level one."

"Angela got called in to work," Cary said. "So now you know, I check for messages."

"I bet she's already home," Hester said. She wondered how often Cary found herself lying in bed staring at the ceiling and hoping. "But why don't you come in for a bit? We can have a drink. Morgan would love to see George."

"We'll be up forever as it is," Cary said. "We should get going."

Jamie unfolded himself from the front seat and thanked Cary for dinner.

"We'll see you next week," she said.

Upstairs, barks and scurrying paws greeted Hester and Jamie when they opened Morgan's door. Jamie scooped up Butch, whose white tail swatted back and forth, while Waffles and O'Keefe greeted Hester. "She in bed?" Hester asked, before running upstairs to check on Kate.

The girl slept with a notebook lying beside her where she'd continued with her numbers. Hester slid onto the mattress, and Kate stirred.

"What comes after nine hundred and ninety-nine?" Hester whispered.

"Tousand," Kate mumbled.

"Good girl," Hester said.

Downstairs, she grabbed cold pizza from the fridge then told Morgan and Jamie about her conversation with Libby Thomas, as well as what she'd learned about Naomi and Barret.

"I think I may have gotten Barret fired," she said. "He ran out of work as soon as I showed up, but tomorrow's Saturday. I'll try finding Naomi and Barret again. Maybe I'll run by the school and see who knows them."

"Or," Morgan said, "you could tell Maxine you're done. Who knows what the truth is here, and whether you even want to find it?"

"We'll see," Hester said.

They chatted for another half hour, till Jamie stood and stretched. "I'll take the dogs out," he said.

Hester untangled leashes and harnesses and got the dogs suited up for their walks. Once Jamie left, she settled into the sofa.

"I talked to Barret's mother today," she said. "Or Brittany's mother. He left in January, and she hasn't heard from him since."

The conversation with Elaine Hardenne had hit close to home, and one thing in particular had stuck with her. Elaine knew that Barret had enrolled in school, that he lived in Boston, but she hadn't tried to contact him. "Do you think my mother knows where we live?" she asked.

"Probably," Morgan said. "My guess is that she knows anything she can learn about you, which is a lot. You have the profile on the Widener website and social media. I bet she follows it all. I bet she has a Google alert on your name too."

When Hester had left her mother's house, she'd thought she'd cut all ties, but that's not the way the world worked. Not these days. Her life was subject to the same scrutiny as anyone else's. "When your mother died," she said, "did you go to the funeral?"

Morgan stood. He crossed to the kitchen, where he rinsed the beer bottles and put them in the recycling. "You asked your question this morning," he said.

"It's tomorrow somewhere. I'm jumping ahead."

"Would you go to your own mother's funeral?"

"Not in a million years," Hester said, but as the words spilled from her lips, she thought about Elaine Hardenne, sitting in that Illinois farmhouse, worrying.

In Hester's own narrative, she was brave. She'd left her mother's home and headed to Wellesley. She'd taken charge of her life and her future in the way she'd known how. But she thought of herself now, today, and what she'd do if Kate disappeared, how she'd manage to make it through the hours and days. In the twenty-one years since she'd climbed onto that bus to leave for Boston, she hadn't questioned her actions or her selfishness. Not once. "Maybe I would go," she said.

"There's your answer," Morgan said.

"What was it like? The funeral?"

"Strange," Morgan said. "And full of regret. You can't make up for things after the end. You can't make it better."

He leaned across the sofa and kissed her on the cheek. "That's enough for tonight," he said.

She nodded. It was enough for her too.

ANGELA

Triple-deckers in various states of repair lined the narrow street. Squad cars, their lights flashing, had blocked access. Angela pulled onto the curb and showed her badge as she ducked under the yellow crime scene tape running around the perimeter of one of the houses. "Where?" she asked Roy when she saw him.

"Second floor," he said, nodding toward a house covered in weathered shingles. "In the kitchen."

Across the street, the first of what Angela assumed would be many news trucks had pulled onto the sidewalk, and a bevy of neighbors had gathered. Heading up the walkway, she noted that the front light was out, and the shrubs surrounding the entrance were overgrown. Upstairs, she found Stan talking to the medical examiner, while Zane hovered. The apartment was a typical railroad design, a long hallway with rooms off it at intervals, and a kitchen in the caboose.

"Blunt force trauma to the head," the medical examiner said. "But no defensive wounds that I can see. My guess is she hit her head on the marble counter, but I'll confirm when I get the body on the table."

"Yowzers!" Zane said.

"Shut. Up," Angela said, grabbing his arm and dragging him to the front room, where she pointed outside. "Do you want something like that to wind up on TV? If it did, you'd be done. Finished. In uniform for the rest of your career. Understood?"

"Sorry."

Paramedics carried the body down the narrow stairs.

"Don't move," Angela said to Zane, and then pulled Stan aside. "Is he a moron?" she asked, jerking her head toward Zane, who offered a high five to one of the uniforms.

"He's batting a thousand right now," Stan said. "Besides, he's part of the team whether you like it or not."

"Is this punishment?"

"It could be," Stan said. "But it's not. I need you on this."

Angela often took the high-profile cases, especially ones involving women. She knew how to handle herself on camera, and she knew how to answer tough questions without giving away too much. She understood the role, even if she didn't always like it. "Resident black lesbian reporting for duty. What can you tell me?" When Stan began to answer, she nodded toward Zane. "Not you, him."

"Hot dog!" Zane said.

"Perez!" Stan said. "Don't make me regret this. Give the report."

That wiped the grin from Zane's face, and it pissed Angela off that it had taken a rebuke from Stan for this kid to start listening.

"Vic is female, late teens or early twenties. Her roommate found the body on the kitchen floor. She tried to administer CPR and called nine-one-one."

"She touched the body?"

"She's covered with blood," Zane said. "Head to toe."

"What's the vic's name?"

"Thomas," Zane said. "Mary-Elizabeth Thomas. Goes by Libby."

"And where's the roommate?"

"Neighbor's house."

"Great," Angela said. "You stay here. Work with the techs and let us know if they find anything important. We'll be talking to . . ."

"Sasha," Zane said. "Sasha Howell."

Stan led them across the street to a house from a different socioeconomic class. This one had been painted recently and had a well-maintained garden and ample lighting. The door to the third-floor apartment was propped open, and a woman sat at a dining room table with a uniformed cop, who nodded and left when Angela walked in. Two men hovered in the kitchen. Stan went to speak with the owners, leaving Angela to take the lead on the interview. "Mind if I sit?" she asked.

Sasha Howell had mousy hair held in a barrette. Her eyes were bloodshot, and Angela suspected that whatever Sasha had taken that night — alcohol or something else — still coursed through her bloodstream. Angela hoped it softened what she'd seen, because, as Zane had indicated, her jeans and blouse were covered in drying blood. So were her face and hands. It took a moment for her to nod, and even then, Angela waited to ask her first question.

"Is she dead?" Sasha asked.

"I'm afraid so," Angela said, softly. Witnesses often grasped at hope, even when there was none. "Tell me about tonight," she added.

"When I got home?"

"Even before that," Angela said, trying to ease Sasha into the story.

"Emma and I went out. We went to Tres Gatos. It's a tapas bar."

"Good food there. Great drinks. Who's Emma?"

"My roommate." She paused. "My other roommate."

"Emma lives with you and Libby."

Sasha nodded. "We're best friends, Emma and me, but if I'd stayed much longer, I'd have been sitting by myself anyway. She was flirting with a guy at the bar. I got bored and left."

"Have you texted Emma?"

"She hasn't answered."

One roommate dead, the other unaccounted for.

"Send me a photo, would you," Angela said, jotting down her number.

Sasha sat up. "Oh, God. You don't think . . ."

"I don't think anything. Not yet."

When the photo beeped into Angela's phone, she forwarded it to Roy and told him to canvas the restaurant and the surrounding area. Take as much help as you need. This is a priority.

"You walked home by yourself," Angela said to Sasha. "Did you see anything?

Anyone leaving the house."

Sasha stared at the table. "I found her. Sprawled on the kitchen floor. There was blood everywhere." Sasha touched the dried blood on her own face. "Can I take a shower?" she asked.

"Not yet," Angela said, as Stan stepped into the room behind her.

"Your friends are making up a bed for you," he said. "One of the police officers can get some things for you to wear from your apartment, and you can shower after we process what we can. But tell us what happened, and don't hold back on details. You don't know what'll wind up being important. Start with walking into the house. Was anything out of the ordinary?"

Now that Angela had established a level of trust, Stan could play bad cop when necessary. The two of them had played this game countless times over the years.

"The front light was out," Sasha said. "But it's been out for months. I called the landlord. He didn't do anything. We tried changing the bulb ourselves, but it didn't work."

"What about the front door?" Angela asked. "Was it locked?"

"The door to the apartment too," Sasha said. "If they'd been open or unlocked, I'd have noticed."

"Once you were in the apartment," Angela said, "was anything out of place? Did you see or hear or smell anything unusual?"

"You mean besides blood?" Sasha asked, softly. She paused, and her head snapped up. "She knew him, didn't she?" she said. "How else would he have gotten into the apartment? Does he have keys? A murderer has keys to my house!"

Angela leaned forward. "You'll stay here tonight, and hopefully by morning this will all be sorted out. Most murderers are idiots and easy to catch. Tell me about Libby. How did you meet her?"

Sasha slumped in her chair, the momentary burst replaced by exhaustion.

"We put an ad on Craigslist. Maybe six months ago. Emma and I already lived here. We went to Simmons together, and another friend lived here too, but she moved in with her boyfriend."

"Does that friend have keys?" Stan asked.

"They moved to Seattle," Sasha said.

"What was Libby like to live with?" Angela asked.

"She kept to herself, mostly, which was strange because we did everything together, and we even said that in the interview, and she said she was excited to move into a place with friends, but when she did move in, it was like she didn't want to do anything. I even asked her to come with us tonight, and she said no."

Again, Sasha caught her own words. "Oh, God. Do you think . . . I mean, would she be okay if she'd come with us?"

"Hypotheticals don't help," Stan said.

"He means that you can't plan for these things," Angela said. "Ever."

"Sounds like you didn't like Libby that much," Stan said.

That woke something in the woman. Her eyes darted from Stan to Angela. "I liked her fine. I didn't *know* her. I probably said ten words to her last week."

"What did you know?" Angela said. "That can be a good place to start."

"She was from California," Sasha said, quickly, eager to show her cooperation. "And she was always working. She told me she was an architect when she moved in, and I sort of wondered why she even needed roommates because don't architects make a lot of money? But then I found out she had an internship. And she was still a student."

"That bothered you," Stan said. "That she lied."

"She didn't lie," Sasha said. "It was me. I assumed."

"But she let you assume," he said. "I bet

you said something like *Libby is an architect,* and she didn't correct you."

"What else did she lie about?" Angela asked.

"I didn't know anything about her," Sasha said. "She was *so* intense. If you asked her how her day was, you could get caught listening for an hour to every single detail. We used to imagine what she'd do on a date."

"You and Emma?" Stan asked.

Sasha shrugged.

"And what did you imagine?" Angela asked.

"A lot of direction."

"Not very nice," Stan said.

Angela swiveled toward him, a fraction of an inch to tell him to lay off. He nodded, barely.

"It happens," Angela said. "But it sounds as though you knew more about her than you thought. You imagined her having sex. That's intimate. Was she planning to have sex last night?"

"Was she raped?" Sasha asked.

"I don't know. The ME will tell us."

"What if I'd been the one here alone?"

The horror of what had happened had begun to hit Sasha. Any useful time with her would be short now. "Did she have a boyfriend? Or a girlfriend?" Angela asked.

"Sort of. His name's Barret. But I think they broke up."

"Last name?" Stan asked.

"I barely knew him."

"Describe him, then," Angela said.

"Black hair, those plug things in his ears. He goes to school with her."

Stan took notes and went into the other room, where Angela could hear him relaying the description. Angela flipped through her notes, and when Stan returned, she said, "Tell me about your conversation from earlier. You said that you asked Libby to come out, and she said no. What else did you talk about?"

Sasha sighed. "A lot."

Angela waited.

"Her day," Sasha said. "That it was long. That someone followed her during lunch."

"Stop," Stan said. "Someone followed her. You might have mentioned that ten minutes ago. Did she say who?"

"Some woman," Sasha said. "Libby kept rambling on about a list and the school. This was Libby's last semester at Prescott. She said the school wanted information on her."

"Prescott University?" Stan asked. When

Sasha nodded, he added, "Just what we need."

Angela waved Stan into the kitchen. Something about Sasha's story was sounding too familiar.

"Tell Zane I need him to run an errand," she said, taking out her phone and hitting speed dial number 7.

"Cary told me you were on a case," Hester said when she answered.

"I'm sending a car over," Angela said. "I need you in JP."

"I was there a few hours ago."

"I'm not surprised," Angela said. "You can tell me about your day when you get here."

BARRET

Barret huddled in the corner of the bandstand, shielding himself as best he could from the wind and rain. Libby hadn't texted again, even after over an hour of waiting. He read her last message. Meet me. By the boathouse.

He was here. Waiting. And he didn't know why she'd written or had a change of heart, but no matter what, he didn't want anything to jeopardize it. He couldn't appear needy. He stood and walked down the stairs, into the rain. A man with a dog hurried by. Barret squinted after him as he turned the corner of the jogging path. He approached the wrought-iron gate that led to the docks. The boats had been pulled up for the winter and were covered with tarps. He tested the locked gate, before heaving himself up and over it. He maneuvered around the boat hulls till he reached the end of the dock and sat, his feet dangling over the rough surface of the pond.

He imagined Libby, in her room, working. The drawing of Rusty still hung on her wall — at least it had till last night — and he wondered whether she'd stared ahead, pondering a design, and had found herself focusing in on Rusty's wagging tail, and remembering the night Barret had given her the drawing, the night on this pond. He wondered if she'd found herself smiling without knowing why, and if she'd rolled onto her side and glanced at a photo of him before tapping in the text. Did she regret the text the moment she hit Send, or had she found room for him in her heart again? He could go home, to the dorm, and wait. Or he could go to Libby's house, like he had last night. He could shimmy up that trellis and sit in her window and hope she wanted him there.

Across the pond, Pinebank hovered over the foggy darkness.

Barret's feet moved, almost on their own. He found himself skirting the pond, and then on that staircase, creeping through the dark. In the Matsons' yard, he pressed his back to one of the cottonwood trunks and surveyed the house. Inside, the lights on the first floor were ablaze. He slunk across the lawn, his shoes sinking into the mud, and turned the light on his phone toward the wall. The mural was gone. Erased. Had the paint washed away in the storm? Or had Gavin found the mural this morning and scrubbed most of it away?

Barret kicked at the foundation and rested his head against the brick. He tried to tamp down the growing sense of hopelessness that he'd kept at bay since Libby had thrown him out. When he'd come to Boston in January, he'd seen the future. He'd dreamed of becoming someone new, and he'd accomplished that, but now he created art to see it destroyed. He loved women — first Alice, then Libby — who couldn't love him for who he was, and he wondered if any of this had been worth it. He thought about the farm, about Rusty lying in the driveway, about the relentless wind in the winter and sun in the summer. He remembered his mother, her arm around his waist, holding him up as they stumbled across the finish line in that stupid three-legged race that he'd sulked about till he'd loved every minute of it.

He could talk to his mother. He knew her number by heart.

He punched it into his phone, his thumb hovering over Send. He wondered what he'd tell her, what he'd say when she called him

Brittany.

Inside the house, the dogs barked.

Barret hit Cancel. Across the veranda, Jennifer Matson came to the French doors and peered into the darkness, clutching a fireplace poker in one hand while the dogs flanked her on each side. She took a step back, and then launched forward, as though willing herself to cross that threshold into the night.

"Who's there?" she said, her voice barely a whisper.

Barret could leave. He *should* leave.

But he stepped away from the house and into the light. "Is Gavin home?" he asked.

"No one's home," Jennifer said. "Only me. Me and the dogs. It's lonely."

"It's cold," Barret said.

"Would you come inside?" Jennifer asked. "You can help me."

Barret looked at the poker in her hand. Jennifer leaned it against the wall. "There's nothing to worry about," she said.

Behind her, a kettle whistled.

HESTER

The unmarked cruiser sped along Storrow Drive. "Can't you tell me what this is about?" Hester asked, one more time.

The detective driving made a zipping motion over his lips. "Sarge would kill me," he said.

"I can feign innocence," Hester said.

"But I couldn't. That's part of the job."

Hester rested her forehead on the passenger's side window as the lights of MIT shone across the Charles River. A few moments later, the detective pulled onto a residential street, where Angela met the car. "She give you any trouble?" she asked.

"A barrage of questions," the detective said.

"Great," Angela said. "Help Roy with the canvas on the other roommate. There's still no word on her."

The detective gave her a mini-salute and jogged off, while Hester stepped out of the car to where lights flashed, and cameras rolled, and police tape surrounded a run-down house.

"You met with Libby Thomas today at lunch, correct?" Angela asked.

Hester was dealing with Sergeant White again. And Sergeant White's question hit her in the pit of the stomach. Homicide detectives didn't ask anything without a purpose. "She was on that list from Max-ine," she said. "The one we talked about at the library. I found out what I could about her and then met her for lunch, but she wasn't interested in sharing. And you wouldn't be involved if she'd simply made a harassment claim. Would you say it?"

"Libby was murdered," Angela said.

Hester closed her eyes and leaned into the car. Angela took Hester's arm.

"Was anyone else hurt?" Hester said, her words sounding as though someone else had spoken them.

Angela flashed a photo of a woman with short dark hair. "One roommate's across the street at a neighbor's house. This one, Emma, is still unaccounted for. And I don't need to say this, but I will anyway. You need to tell me everything you can about your conversation. Anything you've learned."

"Did I do something?" Hester asked. "Is

this my fault?"

"That's why you need to tell us everything," Angela said. "And hopefully we rule that out."

Hester followed her friend to a police van, where Stan met them a few moments later. "Been a while," he said. "I guess it could be under better circumstances."

Hester couldn't even muster a smile. She slid into the van's rear seat, while Stan and Angela swiveled around to talk. "Sorry about the accommodations," Stan said. "It's better than the rain. And we wanted to talk to you now, not later."

"Do I need a lawyer?" Hester asked.

"Do you want one?" Stan asked.

"You don't need one," Angela said, glaring at him.

"Fine," Stan said.

"You met with Libby Thomas today for lunch," Angela said. "We know that much. Tell us about the meeting. Why were you there?"

Hester told them what Maxine had hired her to do. "It was a list of students," she said. "That's it."

Angela turned to Stan. "Any idea where your sister was this afternoon?"

"Don't drag her into this," Stan said.

"She dragged herself into it," Angela said.

Stan left, slamming the van's door behind him. He lit a cigarette and took a heavy drag. "Back in a minute," Angela said, as she followed him.

Even through the thick glass of the police van, Hester sensed tension between them. She didn't know Stan well, but in the years since she'd met Angela, her friend had had nothing but praise — reverence, almost — for her boss. Tonight, though, Hester could see the murky labyrinth of conflict that this case presented. Both detectives were too close, and she wondered if either of them would be working the case come morning? Stan ground the cigarette out with his heel and jabbed a finger at Angela as he spoke. Angela shoved his hand away. But when the pair returned, they were back to business. "Tell us everything," Angela said. "We may need to hand this case off, but we'll decide later."

"I found Libby's profile on LinkedIn," Hester said. "That made it easy enough to figure out where she worked. I waited outside her office till she went to lunch and followed her to a restaurant. I tried to talk to her, but she was paranoid."

"About what?" Angela asked.

"That I was stalking her."

"You *were* stalking her."

"That's exactly what you were doing," Stan said.

"And last I heard," Angela said, "this project was supposed to be you find information and send it to Maxine. Not, you troll people on the Internet, dig up their personal information, and harass them. And the project certainly had nothing to do with finding people who wind up dead less than twelve hours later."

"Maybe I do need a lawyer," Hester said.

"You don't," Stan said.

"Do I?" Hester asked.

Angela shook her head.

"Remember what you said about flipping out and me being an adult," Hester said. "You're flipping out."

"You better believe I'm flipping out," Angela said, her voice low and steady.

"All right." Hester held up her hands in surrender. "I did what I did. Do you want to know what I found out or not?"

"My blood pressure can't go any higher than it already has," Angela said. "Spill. Everything."

Hester continued, telling them about the students she couldn't find, and the three that she could.

"You talked to all three of them today?" Angela asked.

"Two. Libby and Brittany."

"And the third? Naomi, right?"

"I talked to her boyfriend." Hester tried to remember the second name on the mail slot. "David something," she said. "Or ex-boyfriend. He claimed she moved out of the apartment because she'd been sleeping around. He'd packed up some boxes and put them out on the sidewalk."

"Text me the address," Angela said. "And remember. We're the detectives here. Thanks for your help on this, but now it's time to let us do our jobs."

"Is that what you told her at the bar last night?" Stan asked.

Angela turned on him. "Are we doing this again? Find out where your sister is. We need to talk to her too."

Stan ignored her. "What else?" he said to Hester.

Hester pulled up the YouTube video of Libby and showed it to them, but right as it finished, one of the evidence techs tapped on the van's window. "Don't move," Angela said.

She and Stan followed the tech to the apartment, where he showed them the contents of a trash can, and a moment later Stan went into the second house, across the street, while Angela waved Hester toward her.

"I need to get you home," Angela said. "We have a lot to follow up on tonight. Libby's ex-boyfriend is our number one suspect. We found a home pregnancy test. It was positive. Stan's making sure it doesn't belong to one of the other roommates."

"Who's her ex?" Hester asked, testing a theory. "Gavin Dean?"

Angela let that one sit for a moment. "Remember when I told you to spill everything?" she said. "Why would you think Gavin is involved in this?"

"There's the connection to the school to start. And she mentioned him today when we were talking. She wanted to know if I was working for him. She said something like he was coming for her."

"Sounds like a threat to me," Angela said.

"And this, too," Hester said, pulling up the photo of the mural from the Matsons' house. "I found it this morning. It's wrecked from the rain, but it looks like Gavin. At least his mother-in-law thinks so."

Angela forwarded the image to her own phone. "We'll look into it. As in, me and my police colleagues, not you. Gavin isn't the boyfriend, though. The boyfriend's name is Barret. Any chance you've run into him?"

Hester almost didn't answer. She wondered if this last connection might finally break Sergeant White. "I know Barret," she said. "But if Libby was pregnant, you have another suspect on your hands. It's not Barret."

"And how the hell would you know that?"

"I was trying to tell you before we got interrupted. Brittany Hardenne is a trans man. He was born a woman. He goes by Barret. They're the same person."

"That complicates things," Angela said, jogging across the street to Stan.

Hester watched the two of them talking to each other for a moment, and then called Morgan to tell him she'd be gone for a while.

"Jamie's still here," Morgan said, as the scream of NASCAR blared behind him. "You were right about the puzzle. It's a map of the world."

"You'll probably finish it without me now."

"If I know you," Morgan said, "you'll swoop in and add the last piece. What's happening there?"

"I don't know how much I can tell you."

"How about all of it so that I don't imagine much worse?"

"It's Libby Thomas, in the kitchen, with the candlestick," Hester said. "That woman

I saw during lunch today, someone bludgeoned her to death."

Despite the attempt at levity, the truth hit Hester in the gut. "I'm ready for this night to end."

"Should I come get you?"

"No, I might call an Uber. Now that Sergeant White knows everything I do, she wants me out of her hair. And by the way, don't get on her bad side. She's not someone I'd want to face during an interrogation."

"I've seen it," Morgan said.

Hester ended the call as Angela returned.

"Zane'll take you home in a few minutes," she said. "Don't wander off. And it kills me to say this, but thanks for your help."

"Anytime," Hester said.

"Make this the last time."

Angela left Hester to wait in the cool, rainy night. Across the street, the eleven o'clock broadcasts had begun, and reporters decked out in rain gear stood in a line speaking into cameras. Hester joined the growing crowd of onlookers. She spotted Zane and tried to wave him down, but he went into the crime scene house. Up the street, a woman walked toward them wearing a thick wool coat over a short dress, her gold sneakers flashing in the streetlights.

Hester left the gawkers and met her. The woman had short, dark hair that cowlicked from the back. The dreamy look in her eyes faded as she took in the crime scene.

"You're Emma," Hester said, recognizing her from the photo on Angela's phone. "They've been looking for you."

Emma fumbled in her purse, the contents spilling across the sidewalk. "My phone died," she said.

"You have about a million texts and voice mails. I bet someone called your parents too. Sorry."

"Is Sasha okay?"

"*Sasha*'s fine. She's at your neighbor's house."

Emma absorbed the words. "Oh," she said, her voice barely there. "In the apartment?"

Hester nodded. "But I shouldn't say much more. I'm Libby's friend, or I was." *Friend* was a stretch, but Emma didn't need to know that. "Did you know Barret?"

"That guy who comes over. Or girl. Or whatever."

"Guy would be my guess," Hester said.

"He doesn't even come in through the front door. He climbs the side of the house and comes in her window. I told her — I told Libby — that I don't want her leaving the window open, that if Barret could climb in, so could someone else. And they got in a huge fight the other night. It woke me up. I went into the hallway and pretended to use the bathroom, then Barret stormed out."

"Was Libby upset?"

"I don't know. Maybe. She seemed more relieved than anything else, but she talked and talked after he was gone. She broke up with him because she was dating someone else." Emma pointed to her finger. "Some old guy. Married."

"Do you know his name?"

"It was the first I'd heard of him."

"Wait here," Hester said, stepping away and calling Angela.

"What?" Angela said.

"I have a present for you," Hester said, and a moment later the sergeant had found them.

"We've been looking for you," Angela said to Emma. "Are you okay?"

"Kind of numb," Emma said.

Angela made a call, and a moment later the other roommate ran outside. "Oh, my God. Oh, my God. Oh, my God," she screamed, as the two women walked away, arms wrapped around each other.

"You should check the windows in Libby's

bedroom to be sure they're locked," Hester said.

"Do I tell you how to use the Dewey Decimal System?" Angela asked.

She held up a finger to keep Hester from responding, and then called someone. "Check the windows. Are they locked?" She listened and said, "Thanks," before clicking off. "Guess what? They already checked, and they were all locked."

"Trying to help."

Angela sighed, burying her hands in her pockets. "I know," she said. "Things are tense here. For more reasons than one."

"Is it about last night, our conversation with Bob O'Duggan?"

"You should forget that ever happened." Angela sighed. "Stan still smokes. There's no one at home to tell him not to. And I'd light up right now if Cary wouldn't kill me later."

Angela dug in her pocket for a pack of gum. "Want one?"

Hester took a stick and waited.

"I'm pondering," Angela said.

"Ponder this, then," Hester said. "Emma told me that Libby had another boyfriend."

"We know that already," Angela said. "Pregnancy stick. Remember?"

"She said he was old and married. To

someone that age, old could mean anything north of thirty."

Angela blew a bubble with the gum. "Like Gavin Dean."

"There were three students on that list," Hester said. "One's dead and two are missing. I bet Libby wanted nothing in the world more than for that video to disappear forever."

"That's a fair guess," Angela said.

"Naomi Dwyer has a secret too. She was one of those kids whose parents paid to have their SAT tests taken for them. That seems like a pretty big coincidence."

Angela wadded her gum into a piece of paper and handed it to Hester. "Find a trash can for that," she said. Then she searched the crowd of officers by the house. "Zane," she shouted. "Get over here. We need to find someone." She turned to Hester, adding, "I hate it when you're right."

MAXINE

The evening with Vanessa was winding
down. Maxine hadn't stopped thinking
about the inevitable, not once. She was on
her fifth Manhattan, her tongue loose, that
truth simmering beneath the surface.

"What's wrong?" Vanessa asked.

"I love you so much," Maxine said.

"You're veering toward maudlin," Vanessa
said. "But I love you too. Like a second
mother. It's nice here, away from the world.
It's good to forget for a while. I wish we
could stay here forever."

"You'll see, when your baby comes. You
don't even realize how much you can love
someone."

Vanessa rested her head on Maxine's
shoulder. Even now, when Maxine closed
her eyes and smelled Vanessa's skin and
hair, she saw that little girl, the one who'd
clung to her, the one that wasn't quite hers
to claim, but that she'd claimed as her own

anyway, like a discarded doll. She remembered sitting in the apartment, the cardboard boxes stacked around her, her phone ringing as Stan tried to reach her, Vanessa sleeping against her shoulder.

"What would you do if someone you loved betrayed you?" Maxine asked.

Vanessa turned to Maxine, who couldn't bring herself to meet her eyes.

For years now, Maxine had cast herself as Vanessa's savior, as the woman who'd ridden in and shepherded this girl into adulthood, but the story had other perspectives, ones that Maxine tried her best to ignore, ones that dismissed her as the whore, the adulterer, the mistress. Words Maxine had rejected long ago. Didn't mistresses secretly hope for a ring and submit to plastic surgery? Didn't adulterers yearn for a different life? Maxine hadn't asked for any other life than the one she had, but she supposed that Jennifer hadn't asked to have her life usurped, either.

And the only way to take charge of this situation, the only way Maxine could save her relationship with Vanessa, was to get in front of it and take the power from Gavin.

"Your father . . ." Maxine began. "He and I. We . . ."

Vanessa pulled away, her face expressionless.

"For a long time now," Maxine began again. "Your father and I . . ."

"I should go," Vanessa said, checking the time and reaching for her wallet.

Maxine stopped her. "My treat," she said. "And I have to say this. I have to tell you before someone else does. It's important."

"Don't," Vanessa said, taking Maxine's cocktail and drinking down the last of it.

"We've been . . ." Maxine continued.

"I don't want to hear it!" Vanessa snapped, standing and struggling into her coat. She grabbed the tab and motioned the bartender over. "Can you run this?" she asked. "Now."

"I said I would get it," Maxine said.

"I don't care."

"Gavin knows," Maxine said. "And he wants to use it."

Vanessa put her hands over her ears. "Gavin is the least of my worries," she said, as the bartender returned the bill. "He's having an affair."

Maxine reached out, but Vanessa shrugged her off.

"I bet you already knew that he's been fucking students," she said. "I bet you've been trying to protect me."

"I didn't," Maxine said.

"And I don't want to have this conversation, whatever it is you're trying to tell me. Not tonight. Not ever. Whatever happens tonight, remember that we were here. That's all I need." She signed the bill and grabbed her bag. "Tonight . . . it wasn't the night for true confessions."

Vanessa left, hurrying into the rain. Maxine stared after her and then into her empty glass and imagined the lonely years stretching in front of her. The days and hours. The Friday nights by herself. The secret was out. Or enough of it was. Enough so that they wouldn't be able to pretend anymore. And as much danger as secrets held, Maxine still wished she had kept this one to herself. This would force Tucker to choose now, and, in truth, she couldn't imagine Tucker choosing her.

She swirled the ice at the bottom of her glass, unable to bring herself to leave the restaurant and face the rest of the night. To face Jennifer or their shared truth.

Over the bar, a TV played, images flashing by.

"Another?" the bartender asked.

"Absolutely," Maxine said.

"That's what the noise has been about," the bartender said, nodding toward the evening news, where a reporter huddled under an umbrella outside a ramshackle house. "That's about two blocks from here."

The camera left the reporter and panned across the building, across the yellow tape, to where a group of uniformed police officers stood in a group. The ticker beneath the image read, *Local Woman Murdered.*

Homicide.

Stan would probably be there by now. Angela too. Maxine could use a brother right now. Even a bossy one.

The bartender finished mixing the drink.

"What'll you have?" Maxine asked her.

"I'm on the job."

"It's late. The restaurant's empty. Except for me."

The bartender poured a half shot of bourbon and toasted.

"Have you ever made a choice?" Maxine asked. "One that you regretted?"

"I don't know anyone who hasn't. We usually recover. And you'll survive whatever this is. You seem the type."

"Like a cockroach?"

"More like a phoenix."

Maxine rolled her eyes. "You've pulled that one out before," she said.

Still, she folded a hundred-dollar bill and left it under her glass. "Time heals all wounds, right?"

On the screen, the camera panned to the reporter. The sound was down, but the ticker had changed to read *Victim Identified as Prescott University Student.*

"Oh, Jesus," Maxine said, sobering up in an instant.

She downed the last of her Manhattan and punched, Call me. Now. 911, into her phone and sent it to Tucker.

Outside, Maxine hurried to the crime scene. Neighbors had gathered at the perimeter, as the news trucks had begun to pack it in for the evening. She searched the police officers' faces till she spotted Stan conferring with a uniformed cop. She sent him a text, and he glanced at the screen and put the phone away. She called his name, but he didn't seem to hear her.

"Maxine?"

Maxine nearly collided with Hester Thursby.

"What are you doing here?" Hester asked.

Maxine could have asked her the same thing. "I've had a long night. Is Angela here?"

"She's following up on a lead."

Maxine turned toward the house, to where rainwater poured from a broken downspout. "One of my students was killed."

"It was Libby Thomas," Hester said. "From the list you've been having me research. Maybe it's time you told me what's going on."

ANGELA

Zane pulled up to a two-family house and double-parked as Angela ended her call. "That was the ME," she said. "He confirmed it. Libby Thomas was six weeks pregnant."

"The sooner we find the father, the sooner we find the killer," Zane said.

As guesses went, it was a pretty good one. When it came to murder, the obvious won out nine times out of ten. "We know he's married," Angela said. "And probably didn't relish the idea of a baby. My theory is that she surprised him with the news, and something went wrong. You'll see the more you work this job that people make stupid mistakes. Now we follow the evidence to see if that's true."

"Any suspects?" Zane asked.

Angela opted against sharing Hester's theory about Gavin Dean. She needed more evidence before she'd bring it to her colleagues. Right now, all she had was a librarian's gut feeling and a touch of hearsay. They got out of the car and walked to the house. A brand-new-looking label on the second-floor mail slot read David Sawyer.

"Want me to lead?" Zane asked.

"I want you to follow."

Angela rang the bell, and when no one answered, she pounded on the door. Finally, a man answered wearing nothing but boxers and a T-shirt. Angela showed him her badge.

"Yeah?" he said.

"Let us in, or we'll break down the door," Angela said.

"You're not allowed to do that."

"Don't test me."

He led them to the second-floor apartment, where the air hung with enough pot smoke that Angela worried about a contact high. A pizza box sat open on the kitchen counter, and she couldn't help but notice the cold, half-eaten pie with orange pepperoni fat glistening under the fluorescent lights. She hadn't eaten since lunch.

"Dude!" Zane said.

"Quit it," Angela said.

David Sawyer was all arms, legs, and hair. Through the open bedroom doorway, a woman struggled into a pair of jeans.

"Naomi?" Angela asked.

"You told me you broke up with her," the woman said, tying her hair into a ponytail and stuffing clothing into a bag.

"We did," David said. "I promise."

"When exactly did you break up?" Angela asked.

David took a split second too long to answer. "Two weeks ago."

"Try again," Angela said.

The woman shot him a glare. "See you around," she said.

"Before you dump him," Angela said, pulling up the photo of Libby, "do you know her?"

The woman turned on David. "Are you sleeping with her too?"

"I wouldn't do that to you," he said.

"Take a closer look," Angela said.

The woman studied the image. "Haven't seen her. Can I go now?"

"Get her name and number," Angela said to Zane. "We'll be in touch if we need anything."

David tried to give the woman a hug, but she brushed past him and onto the landing.

"How stoned are you?" Angela asked.

"It's legal," David said, and when Angela waited, he laughed and said, "Pretty stoned."

"You know what isn't legal? Lying to a cop. Especially when we show up in the middle of the night. Got it? Answer every question without attitude and maybe — maybe — you'll make it out of this."

"My dad's a lawyer."

"Great. You can call him from the station. Let's go," Angela said, taking out her cuffs.

"Okay, okay," David said. "Ask."

"When did Naomi move out?"

"This morning. I've been trying to break it off for a while."

"I'm not your therapist," Angela said. "But I need to know where she is."

"Some other woman came looking for her today."

"Black hair, glasses?" Angela asked, and when David nodded, she added, "I know about that already. And anything you told her, she told me. Tell me why you broke up with Naomi today of all days. Tell me where she is. Or, you can come to the station in handcuffs and face an obstruction charge at best, or, if you like, a murder charge. Am I getting through to you?"

The gravity of the situation — of having two detectives show up at his door at nearly midnight — seemed to finally make its way through David's stoned brain. "She left her phone on. I saw some things I shouldn't have."

Angela waited for him to fill in the details.

"Sexts," David finally said.

"Who did she send them to?"

"I'm not sure." David caught himself and laughed. "She called him Goopy. I got dumped for someone called Goopy."

Angela let him have that one. She even cracked her own smile. "That's sad," she said.

David covered his face. "It's pathetic. But I had Tiff waiting around, so it wasn't that bad."

Angela had played fast and loose with plenty of hearts in her time. Who was she to judge?

"Are you sure Goopy is a he?" Zane asked, joining from outside the apartment "Sounds like Gwyneth Paltrow to me."

"Yeah . . . He sent some photos too. But let's say he didn't send the right headshot for me to recognize."

"Any chance you forwarded any of those photos to yourself?" Angela asked.

"It's not that I liked looking at them," David said.

"But if you do have them," Angela said, "I need you to send them to me. And while you're at it, send me Naomi's new address."

David pulled up a text and forwarded it to Angela. He also showed her the daylong back and forth between a couple parting ways. Nothing in the messages suggested Naomi was in any danger from this man.

"Send her a text," Angela said. "Tell her to call you."

"She won't answer," David said. "She turns her phone off when she goes to bed."

Angela had to find the one college student on Earth who didn't keep her phone on twenty-four hours a day. "If she writes, tell her to stay put and don't tell her one thing about this conversation. Understood?"

Angela added Naomi's number to her phone and pulled up the photo of Libby again.

"I don't sleep around," David said, when she showed it to him.

"I don't care if you have a dozen girl-friends," Angela said.

"I saw her at school once or twice, but I don't know her name."

"What's your major?"

"User interface design. UI/UX. I have four job offers."

And they all probably paid more than Angela made after nearly twenty years on the force. "How about a woman named

Brittany Hardenne? Or a guy named Barret?"

"Sure. They're the same person. He's a street artist. Kind of cool. Hangs out at Dreamscapes."

"Is he friends with Naomi?"

"Not that I know, but maybe."

"Don't go anywhere," Angela said, motioning to Zane that it was time to leave, before doubling back to where the pizza sat on the counter. "Are you gonna eat this?" she asked.

"I lost my appetite," David said. "Have at it."

Angela took the box with her.

In the car, she called Stan as she wolfed down one of the slices. "Have you gotten into Libby's phone yet? Anyone called Goopy in her contacts?"

"Yeah," Stan said. "And he has an enormous schlong."

Angela peeked at the photo David had forwarded. "We may have our man," she said.

BARRET

Jennifer had made tea and taken a box of cannoli from the refrigerator. Now, she paced the kitchen floor. She wore a loose, patterned dress that floated with her nervous energy, until she loaded a tray and carried it toward the sitting room. "Come," she said, waving Barret after her. "We have to catch up."

He sat on a sofa and eyed the cannoli.

"Go ahead. I know you're hungry," she said as she took a seat across from him.

He put one on a napkin, and Adele leapt onto the sofa beside him.

"She likes you almost as much as she likes food. Fred is the same."

As if on cue, Fred leapt to his other side. The dogs tried to snatch the cannoli, and Barret gave up on appearances and ate the whole thing in two bites. Across from him, Jennifer's eyes darted toward the windows.

"I need to talk to Gavin," Barret said.

Jennifer sighed. "I don't know if he'll be back," she said. "At least not tonight. Maybe not ever."

"Where is he?" Barret asked.

"You painted that mural, didn't you?" Jennifer said. "The one on the house. My friend showed me a photo. It's of Gavin. He used us. Our history. He played it against us." She rested a hand on Barret's. "Can you remember that? You might add something like my eyes flashed with anger when I said it."

Jennifer was making Barret uncomfortable. He sat up to leave, but she passed him tea, the cup rattling against the saucer. "Stay," she said. "Please. Tonight, I may have finally gone off the deep end."

Barret glanced toward the French doors, toward that poker leaning against the wall.

" *'She thought she'd gone off the deep end.'* Those are the words you should use," Jennifer said. "Can you do that?"

Barret took the tea and sipped it, the warm sweetness spreading through him. "Why?" he asked.

"You'll know. And you're too young, I think, to know what it's like to be close to the edge. You haven't made enough mistakes yet."

All Barret did was make mistakes. "I probably got fired today," he said. "I left my job without telling anyone, halfway through my shift."

"Getting fired can be a blessing," Jennifer said. "When I was your age, I got fired from a Ben & Jerry's for eating too much ice cream. I put on ten pounds in about three weeks. But then I met Tucker, and it wouldn't have happened otherwise because I would have been working. Vanessa came soon, and then . . ." Jennifer's voice trailed off. When she spoke again, her eyes didn't quite meet Barret's. "Vanessa was here, earlier. I told her to go out with Maxine. They go out every Friday night, have for years, and it's for the best, I think, to keep things the same. She doesn't know that she can trust me, or how much I've looked out for her. Part of that's because of me, but part is because of Maxine. She's the best friend you could ever have. And the worst. She puts herself last, except when she doesn't."

Jennifer leaned toward Barret so suddenly that he sat back with a start, the tea spilling into his saucer. But she lifted Fred onto her lap, and then ran her fingers through his fur.

"Do you have friends?" she asked.

"Some," Barret said.

"Show me."

He scrolled through his phone till he found an image of Rusty that he liked. It was from a few years ago, when Rusty still followed him down the cornrows. "He's beautiful," Jennifer said, lifting Fred over her head, and kissing his furry nose. "Dogs don't discriminate. But surely you have a human friend."

"I thought I did."

He found an image of Libby where she stood on the edge of the pond, her curls blowing across her face. "I took this across the water. By the boathouse," he said.

"She's lovely," Jennifer said. "You must be popular with the . . ." She paused. "With the girls?"

"Yes, the girls."

"I thought so!" Jennifer said. "People don't think I know the world, but I know more than they realize. None of these things are new anyway."

"We were supposed to meet tonight, but she didn't show up," he said.

Jennifer joined him on the sofa and wrapped an arm around his shoulders. Barret resisted, but then gave in to being wanted. "Where's your own mother?" Jennifer asked. "She should be here for you."

Barret's vision blurred, suddenly.

"There's nothing like a broken heart," Jennifer said. "You shouldn't face one alone. I've had mine broken over and over again. Maxine and Tucker think I don't know, but I do. I'd be blind if I didn't. Then, there's Rachel, of course, but that's more than a broken heart. That's a heart that's been shattered and stomped on and put through the meat grinder. You remind me of her. Of Rachel. My daughter. My other daughter. I worry . . ." Jennifer's eyes shone in the light. "All the time, I worry."

Barret wiped his eyes, embarrassed. "Where does Rachel live?" he asked.

Jennifer took a moment to answer. "She's traveling," she said. "She'll be home one of these days. When she left, it . . . I fell into a deep depression. It's hard to be away from your own child. It's hard when you have no one to talk to, no one you can confide in, but I imagine her. She's twenty-six now, and so confident. That's the important part. She believes in herself. I imagine her living in the city, London, maybe, or Shanghai. Somewhere in the center of it all, with amazing friends. She wouldn't think of settling down, not yet. Maybe not ever . . ."

Jennifer's voice trailed off. Barret took her hand in his. It was cold, the bones brittle beneath a gossamer skin. "Maybe she'll come for a visit," he said.

"What do you remember," she asked, "from when you were four? What do you remember seeing?"

Barret remembered Rusty, who'd come home that year. He remembered the puppy's fat belly and stubby tail, the joy seared forever on his memory.

"You remember flashes," Jennifer said. "Nothing more. Nothing specific."

Barret thought to his childhood, to the farm. "We used to have the whole family over in the summer," he said. "It would be hot, but we'd play games anyway. Everyone wanted me on their team, because I was a good hitter."

"But not when you were four. You couldn't hit when you were four."

"It all runs together," Barret said. "Unless it's important. Unless it stands out."

"That's the way memory works," Jennifer said. "Because they'll ask. They'll want to know what you remember, and all you have to say is *She went off the deep end.* You can do that, right? It's the only way to get through tonight. Say it with me. *She went off the deep end.*"

Barret's tongue wouldn't move.

Jennifer touched her sleeve, her fingers playing with torn fabric. "See, my dress is torn," she said. *"Her dress was torn. She went off the deep end. Her eyes flashed with anger.* You can remember it all."

Behind her, through the windows, the lights of Jamaica Plain shone. They seemed close, and yet so far away. Far beyond reach.

"She went off the deep end," Barret said.

"That's perfect," Jennifer said. "Just like that."

HESTER

"I'll ask you again," Hester said to Maxine. "Why did you want me to find those students?"

Maxine turned toward the house. "I didn't realize Libby Thomas was on that list till you told me right now. I'm here because I heard a Prescott University student had been killed. This'll be a PR nightmare."

"The police haven't been able to find the other two on the list," Hester said. "Naomi Dwyer and Brittany Hardenne. Or Barret Hardenne, which is what Brittany goes by now. Do you know them?"

Maxine tapped a search into her phone. A moment later she nodded. "I don't think I've met Naomi, but here's an appointment in my calendar from January. I met with Brittany Hardenne. My note says *Talented,* whatever that means."

"Do you ever look into a student's background before admitting them? Do you check their references?"

"God, no," Maxine said. "We'll take anyone who's willing to pay. Gavin manages student information."

"Gavin Dean gave you this list," Hester said.

"He gave me the original, flawed data," Maxine said. "We have retention issues. Sometimes, we have students enroll and pay the registration fee, and then never bother to show up, especially in our online programs, so I keep records of my own. When I washed what he gave me against my own records, I saw that he hadn't reported on a subset of students."

"Do you know why?"

"Some of them."

Hester waved toward the crime scene. "I don't mean to make this into a big deal," she said. "But I can help you if you let me."

"You can't help. Everything I know, everything I care about is about to blow up, and I honestly don't know if this woman's death is part of it or not."

Maxine walked away. Hester ran after her. "Did you know about this video? This one with Libby in it?" she asked, pulling it up and showing it to Maxine.

"So, she got cancelled," Maxine said. "Big deal. I'm about to get cancelled myself. It doesn't feel good, I can tell you that much. And I bet she'd have done anything in the world to keep it from happening again."

"I have a friend," Hester said, "who insists on doing jigsaw puzzles without looking at the picture, so at first all you're doing is blindly trying to match like with like and form some sort of image. That's what this feels like. Everything fits together in some way, but I have no idea what the final image will look like."

"Your friend sounds like an idiot," Maxine said. "Take any advantage you can get in life. You don't know when you'll lose it."

"I'll tell Morgan you said that."

"Dr. Maguire? That boy is hardly your 'friend.' Here's some unsolicited advice: Treat things that are important like they're important, otherwise you lose them."

Hester had deflected more pointed jabs at her relationship than this one, but something about Maxine's words spoke to experience. And that experience hit home.

She grasped at one last straw. "Do you remember Bob?" she asked. "Bob O'Duggan."

And as soon as the name passed her lips, she knew she'd hit on something. The blood drained from Maxine's face. "How could I forget Charming Bob? He worked with my brother. He used to hit on me every time I saw him."

"I talked to him last night. He worked Rachel's drowning. How come he didn't interview you?"

"Leave it alone," Maxine said. "I went out of town. By the time I got back, the investigation was closed. It was an accident. An awful, awful accident. One that we've been trying to put behind us ever since."

"Have you?" Hester asked. "What about the book from the other night?"

"Jennifer left that book for herself."

"I figured that out on my own."

"Then you're smarter than you look. Jen gets bored and wants attention, and I thought dragging a detective to the house would get her to finally stop. That's the whole story."

"That book is about infanticide," Hester said, slowly. "It's about a woman who leaves a baby in a field to be taken by the elements. Jennifer's implicating herself in the murder of her own daughter. Why?"

Maxine threw her hands up, as all the fight seemed to drain out of her. "People deal with grief in different ways," she said. "She lost track of her daughter, and her daughter wandered out of the house and drowned. Guess what? She blames herself. Show me one mother who wouldn't. Sometimes the answer's not as complicated as you want to make it."

Maxine stalked away from the crime scene and was halfway down the block before Hester caught up and grabbed her arm. "How is Libby connected to Rachel's death?"

Maxine shook her off. "I doubt Libby Thomas was even born in 1997."

She stopped at a rusted-out Trans Am parked halfway on the curb. Rain had plastered an orange parking ticket to the windshield, which she took from the glass and tossed into the back seat with a dozen other tickets. Before she could drive off, Hester yanked at the passenger's side door and slid in. "Nice collection there," she said.

"My brother'll get those fixed."

"What else does he fix for you?"

"You don't give up, do you?" Maxine said, pulling away from the curb, and then screeching to a stop at a red light.

"Your brake pads sound bald," Hester said.

"Get out of my car."

Behind them, someone honked a split second after the light turned green. Maxine inched forward and slammed on the brakes again, and then gave the driver the finger before peeling away. "You can ask whatever you want, but I'm not answering. The problem is a lot bigger than missing student data."

Hester knew almost nothing about this woman, where she'd grown up, what scars she carried from her fifty years on the planet, but the two of them had more in common than maybe even Maxine knew. They both were raising another person's child. Hester looked at the contours of Maxine's face, her bone structure, her hair, and imagined her as a young woman, before the stress of running an organization and caring for someone else's family.

"I'll start with what I know," Hester said. "Then you can have a turn. Your brother responded to a drowning at Ward's Pond on August 30, 1997. The other detective on duty was Bob O'Duggan. The investigation was brief, and Bob took the lead, at Stan's request. The death was ruled an accidental drowning by the coroner, everyone signed off, and the family was left to grieve in peace. Have I gotten most of that right?"

"There was nothing to investigate. It was a terrible, terrible accident."

"That's problem number one," Hester said. "Because from what I've heard, Bob was a dirty cop, one with his hand in a lot of cookie jars, and one not that focused on the law. He liked cases to close easily, so that he could hit the bar or work his connections. But this should have been important to you. Those girls are important to you. You've played surrogate mother to Vanessa for most of her life, and I suspect you played a similar role with Rachel. Do you remember my niece Kate? You met her at the party. Five years old. Bossy. I keep asking myself what I'd do in your situation, if something like this happened to Kate. It makes me sick to my stomach to imagine it, even for one second, but I know this: If someone ever hurts Kate, in any way, there will be nothing that can possibly stop me from digging and digging and digging until I know every single person responsible has been held to account, even if I have to buy a gun and shoot them in the head myself. And in your case, if my brother was a detective in the police force, I'd have made damn sure Rachel's death got the attention it deserved. You should have been at the center of this whole thing. And that leads to problem number two: I saw the police file. Or at least I heard enough about it. Bob only talked to Tucker, who claimed he found Rachel's body in the pond. Why didn't he speak to anyone else?"

"Jennifer was in the hospital," Maxine said.

"But where were you?"

"I was away," Maxine said. "It was Labor Day weekend, and I'd taken Vanessa with me on a trip. We used to do that, the two of us. It was to help Jennifer out."

"Did she need that kind of help?"

"Anyone with kids need some kind of support."

"So, where were you?"

"In the Berkshires."

"And when did you find out what happened?"

"Not till later, after everything was over." Maxine came to another stoplight and turned to face Hester. "Most people didn't have cell phones. We weren't expected to be available at every moment, and Tucker, he had other things to worry about. It was easier for him to tell me when I returned."

"By other things, you mean Jennifer."

"Mostly."

"Didn't you call Jennifer to check in?"

"And I got voice mail," Maxine said. "I left a message and didn't think anything of it. You forget that 1997 was a completely different world. We could still disconnect. When I took Vanessa, Jennifer didn't *want* to hear from me. She wanted peace."

"And you didn't hear anything till when?"

"Tuesday morning, when I drove home."

"But there's the third problem," Hester said. "This should have been all over the news. I mean, didn't Jon-Benét Ramsey die around this time, and we still see her in the tabloids. I searched in all the local news archives and the only press coverage I found was the obituary. I'm surprised a case like this didn't make national news, let alone local news."

The light turned green. The driver behind them leaned on his horn and then gunned his engine as he sped around them. "I wrote that obituary," Maxine said. "I kept it sparse, which felt like a crime. It still does, but I didn't want to give anyone an excuse to pick up on it. Tucker and Jennifer used to be in the papers all the time. They'd bought Pinebank and been on *This Old House* for the renovation. They were local celebrities."

"And not the types who would escape media scrutiny."

Maxine drove through the light. "Rachel died a few hours before Princess Diana. That was the only news item for a week, and by the time the news cycle reset, Rachel's story was old, and the case had been resolved. It was nothing but luck."

"That's a strange word choice."

Maxine turned off the main road and onto a narrow, one-way street and cut the engine. When she spoke again, the fight was gone. "We were lucky in that the worst thing that ever happened to any of us somehow stayed ours and ours alone. For that one thing, I've been grateful ever since. No one likes for-profit colleges. We're the joke of the academic world, which is something I'm acutely aware of. I work for an industry that the media likes to tear down and destroy, even as I try to make good every day. Rachel's death is still a story that could have legs. Back then, Tucker and Jennifer seemed like people who had everything. Enrollments at the school doubled every year, and we didn't talk about job placement or endless student debt. We didn't care about retention. Thankfully, we grieved in private — like you'd hope anyone would be able to do — and then went on with our lives."

"Except Jennifer," Hester said. "She hasn't gone anywhere."

"Except any of us. Somehow, I shielded Vanessa from most of the crazy, and it hasn't been easy, not by any stretch, but she's happy and successful, and that's all I can hope for now."

Hester followed as Maxine got out of the car.

"Rachel was a wonderful girl," Maxine said. "She'd begun forming sentences, though she didn't put most of the words in the right place. Talking to her was like working the Jumble in the newspaper. I used to think there'd be a day when she'd figure that all out, and then I'd miss trying to piece it together. It didn't happen that way."

Kate had taken forever to use pronouns; now Hester would give anything to hear that little voice one last time.

Maxine took a deep breath and sighed. "Here's the bad part. They wandered out of the house, and Tucker found them by the pond. End of story. Not a day goes by that I don't think about Rachel and wonder if I could have done more."

"Like what?"

"I don't know."

There was always more to do. Hester knew that, and she suspected that Maxine did too. "You said *them*. You said that Tucker found *them* by the pond. Who else was there?"

Maxine walked away, stopping at the bottom of a long staircase, and craning her neck to where the lights blazed in the third-floor unit. "The dog," she said. "Shadow.

They had a Newfoundland. They're famous for rescuing drowning people. She was there, trying her best. But it was too late."

She took the stairs slowly, not looking back once.

MAXINE

Maxine felt Hester watching as she climbed the stairs to the house. She absorbed the judgment, from Hester, but mostly from herself. She'd made her choices. She'd made them years ago, but how could she have spoken about Rachel like that? How could she have made the child sound as though she didn't matter?

Her hands shook as she searched for her keys. The door swung open, and Derek rammed the baby carriage into her shin. One of the babies screamed.

"Could I get out?" he asked.

Exhaustion had taken over every part of him — his eyes, his skin, his every move. It was the same exhaustion Maxine had seen in Jennifer.

"Sorry," she said.

Derek moved around her and didn't bother to say thank you. She stepped inside and closed the door, bumping her hip into the wood to be sure it latched. She could smell Rachel now. She could feel her little hand.

Watch her. Don't let her out of your sight.

Maxine had taken Vanessa from Tucker and held the girl against her shoulder while she listened to him retreat down the stairs. She hadn't known the rest of the story, not that night, though when her kitchen phone began to ring again, she sensed without looking that it wasn't Jennifer calling anymore. It was Stan. And she knew she couldn't speak with him. She left the apartment without packing, bundling Vanessa into her car as that phone in her apartment rang, as Stan tried to call her from the crime scene.

Stan was a good cop. He was a great cop, and not one who ignored suspicions or gut feelings. Maxine had spent the afternoon with him. She had a rock-solid alibi, but he wanted to learn anything he could about Tucker and Jennifer, and he couldn't find a better source than Maxine. He'd have asked about Jennifer's tired eyes and the messages she'd left on Maxine's voice mail. He'd have asked why Tucker brought his older daughter to a friend's house before reporting the drowning.

He'd have asked about the bruises on

Vanessa's arms.

Maxine made her choice. She chose to protect Jennifer. And, if she was being completely honest, she'd chosen to protect herself, her job, her life. The school wouldn't have survived a month once the scandal hit. And the one thing she couldn't say to Stan, the one thing she couldn't admit to herself, was that she knew all along that Stan would choose her over anything else, including his integrity.

Behind her, Derek struggled up the stairs again. "I'll help," she said, conjuring a smile from somewhere.

Something in Derek awoke. "Thanks," he said, as he took the front of the carriage and Maxine took the back. On the second floor, he added, "Sorry I made you fall. The bruise is fading, at least."

Maxine had forgotten the bruise. "Those things happen," she said, and nearly asked him if he wanted to have a glass of wine one of these days but stopped herself. Derek would be moving soon. He wasn't worth the time.

"See you around," she said.

Upstairs, the door to her apartment was ajar. In the kitchen, Tucker waited, drinks already mixed. She went to him, folding into his arms. "I was hoping you'd be here," she said.

"I got your text," he said. "And I came. What happened?"

She didn't tell him that everything was falling apart, that Vanessa knew about them, and Gavin had ruined the school, and some woman she'd hired to do a tiny little data mining project had uncovered their darkest secret. She didn't tell him that everything was coming down around them. Because she feared that it was.

"I just needed to see you," she said.

Later, in bed, Maxine lay in the crook of Tucker's arm.

"You're off somewhere," he said.

She should tell him, about Gavin, about what Vanessa knew, about what Jennifer would know soon enough, but Tucker wanted a world where good happened. She didn't trust that he could handle what was to come. "A student died tonight," she said.

Tucker swung out of bed and kissed her forehead. "That's terrible."

"She was murdered. Libby Thomas."

"Libby?" Tucker said. "Jesus. Are you serious? What happened?"

"I'm not sure."

"Can your brother tell you anything?"

"Did you know her?"

"I worked with her this spring. She was talented. I helped her get an internship with an architect. I even took her to Craigie one night for dinner."

"You took that girl to Craigie on Main?"

"I've been bored," Tucker said.

"With me?"

"With life. And it felt good to help someone out. But that's all that happened between us, if that's what you're asking."

Maxine reached out to him. "I'm so sorry," she said. "I didn't know you knew her. Stay for a while."

"Jennifer will miss me," he said, distracted.

Maxine sat up, feeling her nakedness as he dressed. Every decision they made came back to Jennifer, and for once, Maxine wanted tonight to be about her. Tucker sat on the side of the bed and slipped his feet into his shoes.

"Why did you bring Vanessa here?" Maxine asked.

"Was Vanessa here?" Tucker asked.

"Not tonight. Then. That night."

Tucker's hands froze as he tied his laces. "I trusted you," he said. "I still trust you. I needed someone to do the right thing."

For years, a question had niggled Maxine, one she'd wanted to ask but hadn't. "Why didn't you call the police?"

"I did. After I brought Vanessa to you. I wanted her out of harm's way, and away from scrutiny. We're lucky now that she doesn't remember much. Imagine what would have happened if the police had gotten hold of her. They weren't careful, not like now. They'd probably have planted a repressed memory. They'd have pinned the whole thing on me."

Maxine lifted the sheets to cover her breasts and pushed herself against the headboard. "I don't mean then," she said. "I meant before. When Rachel went missing. How long were you searching before you found her?"

Tucker went back to tying his shoes. "An hour," he said. "Maybe a bit less."

"But you live right next to a park. You have people walking through your yard all day. And your two-year-old daughter went missing. Why wouldn't you have called the police right then, as soon as she was gone?"

"I don't remember," Tucker said. "I guess you can question all sorts of actions, afterward. Why did you disappear with Vanessa?"

"Because you asked me to."

"I didn't. I asked you to watch her. That's it."

"I was protecting Jennifer."

"Jennifer's half-gone. No one can protect her."

"I'm not asking about Jennifer," Maxine said. "I'm asking about you."

Tucker put on his coat and left without another word. Maxine listened as he crossed the living room and headed down the stairs. On the second floor, one of the twins cried, followed by the other.

All these years, Maxine had thought she'd known whom she'd been protecting. Maybe she'd gotten it wrong all along.

ANGELA

Angela radioed in their location as Zane pulled in front of a Prescott University dormitory, an old art deco hotel in Roxbury that had somehow survived the city's wrecking ball in the sixties and seventies. Inside a still-ornate lobby, a student security guard sat at a desk trying to keep himself awake while working on homework.

Angela showed him her badge, "Would you tell me where Naomi Dwyer lives?" she asked.

He checked the computer. "She ain't here," he said. "At least according to this."

"Do you know if anyone moved in today?"

"Not on my shift, but I didn't start till midnight."

Angela conferred with Zane for a moment. It worried her that she hadn't found this woman, the kind of worry that any good detective paid attention to.

"Maybe she's in an empty room," Zane

said. "There have to be a few."

And maybe this kid would make it as a detective after all. "Nice one," Angela said, returning to the security guard and asking him if there was a way to find the empty rooms in the building.

"Not without a search warrant," he said. "That'll get me fired."

Angela wasn't in the mood. "I have one dead body," she said. "And evidence linking that body to this building, which, to me, sounds like probable cause. That means I can search every room and wake every student in the building. I'll get started right now."

The guard hit a few keys on the keyboard. "We need this for fire alarms," he said. "There are four empty rooms in the building."

"Keys?" Angela asked.

The guard handed them over.

"Don't call anyone," Angela said. "Not till we're done."

The elevator was small and rickety. Angela opted for the stairs, and on the second floor turned the key in the first of the four rooms while Zane flanked the other side. She kicked the door open. The room was empty. So was the second room they opened. On the third floor, they found two young men sitting in the hallway. Angela flashed her badge and told them to go to their rooms. "Dude," one of them said.

"What's going on?" the other asked.

"Let's hope nothing, but keep quiet," Angela said.

And when they checked the room on that floor, it was empty too.

Finally, on the fourth floor, Angela could tell that someone was inside the last of the rooms, even without opening it. The smell of incense and scented candles poured from under the door. "Christmas Cookie," Zane whispered. "From Yankee Candle Company. It's my favorite."

"You never cease to surprise," Angela whispered. She turned the key, and Zane toed open the door. Inside, Chinese food containers littered a kitchenette. "We won't starve tonight," Angela whispered. And then she added, a bit louder, "Boston Police. Who's here?"

A thump came from the bedroom, followed by swearing. Angela's hand hovered over her holster. The bedroom door opened, and a woman came out wearing an oversized T-shirt. Unless Naomi Dwyer had a twin sister, this was her.

"Do you have a search warrant?" she asked. "I have a right to be here."

"What's with the procedure tonight?" Angela said. "You're breaking and entering. You don't have any rights."

"Squatter's rights," Naomi said.

"No such thing. But I'm happy you're not dead. It's the best news I've had all night."

Angela went to show her the photo of Libby, when a crash rang out from the bedroom. "Don't move," she said to Naomi. "Not one inch."

Naomi was big, like a linebacker, not someone who seemed like she'd shy away from a confrontation. She tried to block the door, but Angela swatted her aside. In the bedroom, lit candles covered every surface, and a gauzy red shawl had been draped over a lamp.

And the window was open.

Outside, the sound of shoes clomping on metal echoed up the side of the building.

"He's running," she shouted to Zane. "Take the front."

Angela spoke into her radio, calling for backup, then she ducked out the window and onto the fire escape. Her stomach churned at the height, but she shoved that aside and pounded down the slick metal stairway. Below, the ladder released and crashed to the ground.

"Police!" she shouted. "Stop!"

She reached the ladder and slid down it to a cobblestone-lined alley. Ahead, in the dark, someone ran. As she took off after him, she wished she'd made it to the gym this winter, that she'd trained for that marathon Annette had bugged her to run. Hell, she wished she could run for forty-five seconds on the treadmill.

The perp turned a corner. Angela shouted the location into her radio, barely able to form the words through gasps. And then her foot caught on a loose cobblestone and she hurtled forward, ducking in time to roll as she slammed into a brick wall. She lay on the damp ground wondering if she'd broken every bone in her body. Off in the distance, a siren approached. Zane sped past her, his feet pounding the cobblestones. "I got him," Zane said, as though he were strolling through the woods.

Angela hauled herself to her feet and took off too, but Zane outpaced her, turning out of sight fifty yards in front of her.

A gun went off.

Angela tore around the corner.

Ahead, Zane lay on the ground, blood pooling between cobblestones. The calm of crisis took over Angela's every move, her every emotion. She ripped her coat off and tore at her sweater, wadding it up and holding it to the wound. "He got away," Zane said, his words slurred.

"Not a problem," Angela said, softly. "Listen to me. Stay awake, and I'll fill your apartment with Christmas Cookie candles. Hell, I'll buy out the entire Yankee Candle Company." She hit her radio, keeping her voice as calm as she could. "Officer down," she said, giving their location. "Get a bus here. Now."

Fifteen minutes later, Angela let her hand rest on the ambulance as it pulled away, with Zane inside. The paramedics had managed to stop the worst of the bleeding, and Zane, thankfully, was still breathing, though he'd lost consciousness. And Angela blamed herself. She'd thought of him as annoying, a pain to deal with. And it didn't matter that she could have easily been the one lying on that gurney fighting for her own life. It never did.

Her phone rang. It was Stan.

"They're taking him to Mass General, and then we wait," Angela said.

"Go home," Stan said. "You need to debrief on the shooting."

"I want to get this guy," Angela said.

"We'll have an APB out on the whole city," Stan said. "We'll get him. But I don't want an angry sergeant doing anything stupid because she's pissed off at herself."

Angela took a deep breath. Stan was right, of course, but Naomi Dwyer waited upstairs in that dorm room, a uniformed cop hovering over her, and Angela would be damned if she'd leave without finding out what the woman knew. "I'll talk to Naomi. Then I'm out of here."

Stan sighed. "Okay," he said. "This body here isn't getting any deader. We can finish this up in the morning, after we deal with what happened tonight."

Angela rang off. They'd already cordoned off this crime scene where Zane had been shot. She'd been through this before, the guilt of surviving, the insufferable waiting. She didn't know a thing about Zane, or who would be at the hospital tonight for him? Tomorrow, she hoped that she'd be telling him he was a hero. And in ten years, she hoped she'd be able to rib him about being a hotshot young detective.

She spoke to the uniformed cops and then headed inside the building, past the security guard, and up the elevator to the fourth floor. By now, most of the students in the dorm were awake, either wandering the hallway or clustered in groups. "We'll be at this for a while," Angela said to one group.

"But there's nothing to worry about, so go to bed. If we need to speak to any of you, we'll let you know."

She waved one of the uniforms over, and then stepped into the apartment. Naomi sat on a plastic chair, a handcuff on one wrist.

"This is false arrest," she said. "I'll have your badge."

"Someone's been watching TV," Angela said, swinging a chair over and straddling it. Still, she nodded, and a uniformed officer unlocked the cuffs. "Thanks," she said to the officer. "And would you mind blowing those candles out. The ones in the bedroom. They're a fire hazard. And they kind of stink."

The uniform went into the bedroom, while Naomi rubbed her wrists. She had soft blond curls that hung around strong shoulders. Angela spoke softly. "My partner thinks those candles are Christmas Cookie, from Yankee Candle. Are they?"

"Some of them."

"He told me Christmas Cookie was his favorite. That was before he got shot in an alley. He's at the hospital by now, and let's see if he makes it to the morning."

Naomi swallowed, her eyes wide. "Am I under arrest?" she asked.

"Not yet," Angela said. "But you might be soon."

"I'm leaving. I know my rights."

"Then you are under arrest," Angela said. "For trespassing. Oh, and also for abetting in the assault of a police officer. And possibly murdering one. We'll find out soon." Angela had learned to compartmentalize her rage years ago. It was how she worked with the terrible people she encountered every day. Tonight, she wouldn't bother with that. "I'll make sure to let everyone know. So that you can get the right reception at the station. The kind you're used to. If you watch TV, you know what happens to cop killers."

"I didn't . . . I didn't know that. I didn't know any of that."

"Why do you think there are a dozen police cruisers in the street outside? Why do you think everyone in this building is awake, wondering if they're safe? But let's start with what you do know. Who was in your room?"

"Okay, okay," Naomi said. "It was Gavin Dean. From the college."

Angela got on the phone with Stan. "It's another road straight to those people, straight to that house, that school," she said.

Stan didn't take the bait. "We'll have his

photo with every cop in the city," he said. "He'll have nowhere to hide."

"You and I, we need to talk," Angela said. "I'll come over there when I finish here."

There was silence on the other end of the phone, till Stan said, "I'll see you when you get here."

Angela hung up and turned to Naomi. "Did you know Gavin had a gun? Tell me the truth, or I'll find a way to arrest you."

"I didn't know," Naomi said. "I wouldn't have let him in if I had. It was his idea to meet. But he was . . . he was acting weird when he got here. He closed the blinds and told me not to check my phone. Like he was hiding something."

Angela flashed the photo of Libby. "What do you know about this woman?" she asked.

"Not much."

"Not much is still something. Tell me what it is."

"Gavin had a thing with her, too. But he broke it off, like, yesterday or something."

"You people should figure out who's sleeping with whom. When did your other boyfriend discover this whole thing? David, right?"

"I screwed that up," Naomi said.

This wasn't going anywhere. "Let me start again," Angela said. "This woman in this photo is named Libby Thomas, and she goes to the same school your boyfriend's wife owns, the same school you attend, the same school where you're squatting in an empty dorm room. Or, I should say, she went to the school, because today, she turned up dead, and when we came here, instead of sticking around and chatting with us like someone with nothing to hide, your boyfriend grabbed a gun — a gun you apparently knew nothing about — climbed out a window, and shot a cop. So, now we have one dead woman and another who was lying beside a concealed weapon."

Angela had seen her share of Oscar-worthy performances, but, to her eyes, Naomi seemed genuinely shocked as she covered her mouth and gasped.

"Tell me about the admissions scandal," Angela said. "You were part of it?"

"I don't want to talk about that," Naomi said.

"Sweetie, you don't have a choice. What's it got to do with all of this?"

Naomi slouched forward and waved a hand toward the bedroom. "That's how this all began. The relationship. Everything. Gavin asked me to come to his office a few months ago. He had the articles about my mother on his computer screen." Naomi wiped at her eyes with a fist and nodded. "I didn't want people to know," she said. "It would have started all over again."

Angela pulled a chair up to Naomi and sat with her for a moment. "He did the same thing with Libby?"

Naomi nodded.

"Anyone else?"

"I don't know. Probably."

"There's a special place for people who do things like this," Angela said. "But we have our guy now. And you can help us bring him down."

Naomi looked out the window, to where lights still flashed on the street below. "When was she killed?" she asked. "What was the time of death?"

Angela didn't answer, but the killing had happened sometime after six o'clock when Libby's roommates left for dinner and before 9:30, when Sasha came home and found the body.

Naomi turned to her. "Unless she was killed before five-thirty this afternoon, you might get him on being a stupid asshole who shoots cops, but you won't get him on murder. He's been here with me since then. And it's on videotape. I can show you."

"I'll take your word for it," Angela said. "But give me the tape anyway."

BARRET

Adele woke, turned in a circle and snuggled in against Fred as Jennifer stroked the dog's fur gently. "Imagine," she said, "having someone travel through life with you. These two haven't been apart. Not once, in their whole lives."

There'd been a time when Barret had believed Alice would be with him forever, but she'd told him she couldn't see how a life together with him could work. "It was an infatuation," she'd insisted, retreating up the stairs to the choir at the back of the church. "A mistake. Something I've out-grown."

Barret followed her, to where she slipped into one of the pews. Below, the church, with its cavernous interior, was empty for once. Sunlight streamed through the windows and lit the altar where Alice's father stood on Sunday, where she joined him when he took out his guitar for a song. Alice stared ahead, her face serene. "You can call yourself whatever you want," she said. "But you're not a boy, and you're not a man. You won't ever be."

She got onto her knees, lifting her hands in prayer. Barret didn't have the sense, not then, to hear her words as ugly, or to take them as anything but truth.

"Pray with me," Alice said, her eyes closed, "Brittany."

He resisted, and then gave in, kneeling beside her, watching as her lips moved over words only she knew. He remembered a time when this church, when Father Todd, when the congregation had brought him peace, and he added his own prayer, asking God for the strength to find that peace again, somewhere.

Alice touched his arm. "Feel better?" she asked.

"I do," Barret had said.

That conversation had broken Barret in a way that had made him wonder if he'd ever recover, but in the end, he'd healed.

"I thought I'd travel through life with my girls," Jennifer said. "I lost some of it with Vanessa. Maxine took it for herself, and I probably didn't put up enough of a fight. But she never asked, either. And Rachel . . .

I get confused sometimes. I think Rachel's here. That she's come home. I'll see Shadow trotting through the house, even though Shadow's been gone for twenty years. It's not that I really believe Rachel's here. She's traveling, right? It's more like I'm having a dream that I know is a dream, and yet I can't wake from it no matter how hard I try."

"Why don't you call her?" Barret asked.

"She won't answer."

"Leave a message."

"You call your mother first."

"What if she doesn't want me anymore . . . like this?"

"That won't happen," Jennifer said, taking his hand. "And my guess is that your mother already knows. We usually do. I can almost guarantee it."

It was the "almost" that Barret feared most. It was that same fear he'd faced since the day he realized he'd been born in the wrong body. "I should find Libby," he said.

Jennifer's grip tightened. "Libby," she said.

"The woman. In the photo. My girl-friend."

Jennifer stood suddenly, her teacup shattering on the floor. The dogs leapt from the sofa, dancing at her feet, while Barret picked up the broken china to keep the dogs from cutting their paws. Outside, headlights flashed through the trees. Jennifer spun toward the window. Rain lashed against the glass. "That's Vanessa," she whispered. "She's back."

"She won't want me here," Barret said.

Jennifer crossed the room in a few swift steps.

"I did something terrible," she said. "You'll want to hate me, and you should. Despise me with every ounce of your being. And the story won't end tonight. It'll keep going and going, and they'll say things, afterward, about me. Horrible things. And there'll be cameras and shouting and there might be a time when you remember meeting me, when you remember talking and that I gave you a cannoli and listened to you, and you'll want to say something good, something to make it end. But don't." She shook her head, as though trying to clear her thoughts. And when she opened her eyes, she seemed lucid, more lucid than she'd seemed since the moment they'd met. "Maxine will look after Vanessa. She thinks she loves the girls as much as I do. I let her believe it. But she doesn't. She couldn't. That's the part I've kept for myself."

The front door slammed open, and a gust of wind swept through the house. Jennifer's hair swirled across her face. The dogs charged toward the foyer.

"Whatever they say, in your heart, remember that I loved Rachel as much as Vanessa. Maybe more. I loved her with all my being. Can you do that?"

Barret nodded.

"In here," Jennifer shouted, and then lowered her voice. "No one will forgive me," she said. "And they shouldn't. I deserve it. I deserve it all. Remember that too."

"I'll forgive you," Barret said, the words he owed his own mother. The words he hoped to hear from her.

"You can't," Jennifer said. "No one can. There'll be DNA. Skin cells. Fibers. It's all there. Because I killed someone tonight. Someone you love."

The tiny hairs on Barret's arms stood on end.

"Now you understand," Jennifer said. "I can see it in your face. I've done terrible things, and I'm sorry I hurt you, but she'd have destroyed everyone. She had information on the school, on my family. She would have used the pregnancy. And she had to be stopped. *I* had to stop her."

"Who?" Even as Barret asked, he read the answer in Jennifer's face.

She reached toward him, but he slapped

411

her hands away.

"That's good," Jennifer said. "Be afraid. You should be afraid."

Vanessa hurried into the room. She paused when she saw Barret, but ran to her mother, embracing her. Barret backed against the wall. His hand gripped the cold brass handle of the fireplace poker.

Jennifer put her fingers to Vanessa's lips. "Don't say anything."

The French doors flew open. Gavin stumbled in from the rain, his thick hair plastered to his scalp, his eyes wild. He pointed a gun at Jennifer and Vanessa while Barret shrank away, trying to make himself disappear.

"I know what you did," Gavin said. "I know everything."

HESTER

The ride app showed a car sitting at the same intersection where it had sat for the last twenty minutes and not moving. Soaked through from the rain, Hester hit Cancel and had nearly requested another, when the door to Maxine's house opened and Tucker Matson headed down the stairs.

Tucker and Maxine. That was new information.

When he reached the sidewalk, Tucker took a deep breath and leaned over his knees, shaking. From where she stood, Hester couldn't tell if he was laughing or crying, but when he approached, his eyes were red and swollen. He paused at the sight of her, straightening to his full height, a mask quickly descending. "You were at the house the other night," he said. "The book . . ."

Hester saluted with two fingers. "You read it yet? It's a classic."

"Maybe when I get home."

"Come here often?"

Tucker took her in again and walked toward a Lexus parked a few spots down the street.

"Who else was by the pond when you found Rachel?" Hester asked. "How did you even know to look there?"

The lights on Tucker's car flashed. He put a hand on the door handle. "Because it was one of Rachel's favorite places to go," he said. "And do me a favor? Get lost. If you keep harassing me or my family, I'll call the police."

"I have the cops on speed dial," Hester said.

Tucker stepped toward her, his fingers twitching beneath his coat sleeves. "What do you want?" he asked. "How much?"

Someone approached Hester from behind. Maxine passed by and touched Tucker's arm. "Head home," she said. "Or head somewhere. Leave this to me."

Tucker went to say something.

"Don't," Maxine said.

"You should let people mourn in peace," he said to Hester, before getting into the car.

Maxine faced away from Hester as the car sped around the corner and out of sight.

"How long has this been going on?" Hester asked.

"Oh, forever now," Maxine said. "It'll be out for all the world to see soon anyway, if Gavin has his way. Every family has secrets. Tucker and I, we're one of the secrets."

Every family did have secrets. Hester knew that better than most. She followed Maxine to her car. "You're like herpes," Maxine said. "You keep coming back. I assume you'll throw yourself on the hood unless I let you come with me."

"Where are we going?"

"To find Vanessa."

"Where is she?"

"Wherever she thinks I won't look."

"Then she should be easy enough to find," Hester said, sliding into the passenger's seat.

"I guess we're going to Pinebank," Maxine said. "She'll be there. With her mother."

Mothers and daughters. It's what this whole story had been about, from the start. Barret with his mother. Vanessa and Rachel with theirs. Even Hester, with Kate, and her own mother. Her own truth.

"Where's your mother?" she asked Maxine. "Do you get along?"

"She's dead. We get along great," Maxine said. "But yeah, mostly. And now that she's gone, I wish I'd tried harder. She didn't like all the choices I made, even if they were mine to make. And she didn't like Tucker one bit. She thought I should have stayed in Stoughton and married Nate." Maxine snapped her fingers. "I've been trying to remember that guy's name all day. Nathan! Nate. Five decades in and he's my sole ex."

"Do *you* wish you'd married him?" Hester asked.

"Not on your life," Maxine said. "He was clinically dull. When I moved into town, I had every intention of living it up and leaving a trail of broken hearts behind me, like your friend Angela."

"Angela?" Hester said. "She's as settled as they get."

"Not when I met her," Maxine said. "She was quite the heartbreaker! I think she and Stan may have had a thing, not that he'd ever admit it to me. They both got divorced around the same time."

Hester had no idea Angela had been married before, or, frankly, had had a sex life away from her home in Dorchester, but everyone had their own histories. She'd have to work harder to learn Angela's.

"How about you?" Maxine asked. "Do you get along with your mother?"

"She's my best friend," Hester said. The lie came easily.

Maxine turned off the road and into the trees. Lights from the mansion blazed through the darkness and rain lashed at the windshield. "They're all up," Maxine said. "Waiting. They've probably sharpened their claws." She pulled to a stop and cut the engine. "I don't want to go in there," she said.

"We could leave," Hester said. "Walk away from the whole thing."

"Could you walk away from Kate?" Maxine asked.

Hester didn't bother to answer. "Whatever happens, remember that you'll have Stan. Maybe you'll have Angela. Heck, maybe you'll even have me as a friend. Lately, I've been collecting people faster than Morgan collects strays. And sometimes it's not bad to start over."

"It is when you're fifty years old and no one wants you anymore. You're a pup. How old are you, anyway? Thirty?"

"I'm far north of thirty," Hester said. "But thanks for the compliment."

"That non-husband of yours is a keeper," Maxine said. "Make sure you don't lose him by being an asshole."

"We have our own thing going," Hester said. "People don't understand it, but we like it."

"Does he?"

"As far as I know," Hester said, though she knew the real answer, one that she pretended wasn't true. Morgan wanted something else, something more, something she hadn't been able to give him.

Maxine glanced toward the house. "One day you'll ask why you didn't say yes to whatever came your way, why you didn't put happiness in front of all else. That's the day you know you're old. Don't let yourself get there."

She opened the door. Rain pelted the inside of the window and armrest. "Sit tight. I'll take you home after they boot me out."

Maxine dashed through the rain to the front door as Hester settled into the car seat and took out her phone. You up? she wrote to Morgan.

Her phone rang, like she'd hoped it would.

"Jamie left and went to bed," Morgan said. "It's me and the dogs now."

"Ian, too."

"Can't forget Ian."

"He's part of the gang now," Hester said, her eyes growing heavy as she listened to Morgan's voice.

"I finished the puzzle," he said. "All but the last piece."

"Where does it go?"

"You can figure it out when you get home, but I won't see you tonight, will I?"

"It's not tonight," Hester said. "It's tomorrow. Ask me why I left home."

"Okay," Morgan said. "Why did you leave?"

Hester took a deep breath and sighed.

"You don't have to tell me unless you want to," Morgan said.

But it was her own question. Hester needed the answer for herself, more than anyone. She remembered the way Mrs. Connor had pinched her lips together when Hester's mother had shown up in the yard, her T-shirt too tight, her hair too big, her makeup too heavy. "You won't want to be like your mother," Mrs. Connor said one day when Hester arrived to babysit wearing lipstick she'd bought at the CVS.

Hester should have taken the comment for what it was, a repudiation. She should have seen Mrs. Connor as a grown-up version of the mean girls who prowled the halls of the high school, but instead, she took the warning to heart, removing the lipstick with the back of her hand in a conspiratorial swipe. Even later, when the babysitting ended, and Mrs. Connor used those same pinched lips on Hester, she still yearned for acceptance. She wanted to be what Mrs.

Connor wanted, what she thought the world expected. Her mother was a lot of things — she drank, she slept around, she ruined marriages, she wrestled with bouts of unbridled energy that had her baking hundreds of cookies into the night and flinging flour across the kitchen while Hester scurried behind her, trying to keep order. But she also offered an arm to lean into while the two of them watched *General Hospital* after school. She took out a chess set and taught Hester how to play. She yearned for another life.

Hester could tell Morgan about the times when her mother claimed people watched her through the television. She could tell him that her mother called her a slut and asked why she'd taken Mr. Connor from her, or how her mother had run through the streets, her bathrobe trailing behind her, as she tossed the pages from Hester's senior thesis into the air. She could say that she'd left to save herself.

Or she could tell the truth. Hester had left to escape shame, and she'd been running ever since. It was something she had in common with Libby Thomas and Naomi Dwyer. And she suspected that she had it in common with the Matsons too.

"My mother's sadness would have swallowed me whole," she said to Morgan. "Or, that's how I saw it then. It's how I've seen it ever since, but lately I've wondered if my perspective has changed. I could try being more forgiving."

"Why not try?" Morgan asked.

Because she'd lived a lifetime without her mother, and admitting her own faults, her own mistakes, scared her. "What if I've been wrong?" she said. "The whole time. What if I've held on to this anger for no reason?"

"You'll have a whole lifetime to make up for it," Morgan said. "That's not bad."

Hester settled into the seat and closed her eyes. She could call. She remembered her mother's phone number. It was her PIN number at the bank.

"Your turn," Morgan said.

Hester listened to the rain drumming on the roof of the car, steady, assuring, like Morgan. Compromise meant giving in sometimes, and compromise wasn't about making things easier, but about working toward something better. It was about knowing when to fight, and when to offer kindness. "Do you want to get married?" she asked.

A part of her wanted to believe that the words formed on their own and surprised her, but they were her choice. Hers alone.

"You're asking me on the phone?" Morgan said.

"Maybe Ian will give you a kiss for me," Hester said.

Morgan had put up with compromise for so long now that for the first time since an inkling of a yes had grown in her heart, Hester wondered if she'd missed her opportunity.

"Big wedding," he said. "Four hundred guests."

"I'm not wearing a dress."

"I may not wear pants, but I'll show up, nonetheless."

It was as close to a yes as she'd get. "I'll see you when I see you," she said.

"I love you too," Morgan said.

After she hung up, she couldn't stop grinning. She hadn't realized how much lightness letting go could bring. She also hadn't realized how much she'd wanted to be generous and selfless, or the joy it would bring.

Her phone rang. "Second thoughts?" she asked.

"Where are you?"

It was Angela, not Morgan.

"Maybe I'm in bed, pissed off at you for waking me up."

"I mean it. Where are you?"

Hester heard a siren in the distance. "I'm at Pinebank," she said. "Outside, in Maxine's car."

"Can you get out of there?"

"She took the keys."

"Lock the doors," Angela said. "Block any light. And don't move. Gavin Dean is armed. He's dangerous. And my guess is he's headed that way."

Hester peered over the dashboard. "Maxine's in the house," she said.

"Do *not* get out of the car. Do you understand me? I am five minutes out, and there's a squad car on the way. Please, for once in your life, do what I ask."

"I will," Hester whispered.

She ended the call and turned the phone off, searching the darkness, and then crouching beneath the dashboard.

A pop echoed from inside the house, followed by another. A moment later, someone ran through the woods, not five yards away. This time, the sound of a gun firing was clear. With the fourth gunshot, the rear window of the car shattered.

Hester cupped her hand over the phone to block the light and dialed nine-one-one. She doused the car's interior light, kicked the door open, and rolled to the muddy ground, crab walking across the gravel driveway and into the woods. A nine-one-one operator answered.

"Gunshots," Hester said, her voice barely a murmur.

Feet pounded across the ground a few feet from where she hid. She clicked off the call, rolled on top of the phone to block the light, and tried to disappear.

ANGELA

Angela flipped on her siren and pushed the pedal to the floor as she sped through narrow streets, rain splattering against her windshield. Her phone rang. It was her sister Audrey, who was probably getting off work at her restaurant. "Can't talk," Angela said.

"Bye!" Audrey said.

Almost no one was out as the few cars on the road pulled to the side to give way. She careened around a corner and into the woods, radioing her location in to Dispatch, finally skidding to a stop beside Maxine's car, which had a shattered rear window.

Angela was the first on the scene.

She went into automatic, pushing away any fear and analyzing her last conversation with Hester for pertinent information. Hester had said that she was in the car, and that Maxine had taken the keys, presumably into the house. Angela put her hand to her firearm, grabbed a heavy flashlight, and scanned the environs. Most of the lights on the ground floor of the mansion were ablaze, giving off enough light to see within the wall of fog.

Angela opened the window a crack and listened but couldn't hear much beyond the pounding of rain on the roof of the sedan. She whispered Hester's name. No response.

She slid out, keeping herself low and between the two vehicles for cover. She peered over the window of the Trans Am. Shattered glass covered the back seat, but Hester was gone, with no sign of blood or injury.

Another car pulled in through the trees. Angela's radio crackled with Stan's voice as he called in his location. "There's at least one gunman," she reported when he joined her. "He shot out your sister's car. I think Maxine's inside the house. Hester Thursby is here too, location unknown."

"Do you have an ID on the gunman?"

"Not confirmed, but for now, I'm assuming it's Gavin Dean."

"Let's get this guy," Stan said. "I'll cover you to the house. Go around left. I'll take the right."

Angela nodded. "Keep a clear head," she said. "I know you're worried about Maxine, but don't do anything stupid."

"Same to you," Stan said.

Angela kept low and dashed across the driveway. When she reached the house, she motioned to Stan, who ran in the opposite direction. She edged along the brick foundation. The storm swirled around her, wind blasting at trees, rain pelting the ground.

"Boston Police," she shouted.

On the other side of the house, Stan mirrored her identification.

To Angela's left, someone scrambled in the bushes. She dropped to the ground and leveled the barrel of her firearm toward the noise. It took every ounce of her willpower not to shoot blindly.

"Hands up," she shouted, shining the flashlight into the thick underbrush. "And come out where I can see you. Slowly."

Someone crawled out of the bushes and into the light. The beam of the flashlight showed black hair and a slight build. "Don't move," Angela said, crossing the lawn. "Name?" she asked, as she felt for weapons.

"Barret. Barret Hardenne."

Angela let the firearm fall to her side and pulled him toward the house. His clothes were soaked and flecked with what looked like blood. "We've been looking for you all night. Are you hurt?" Angela asked.

Barret shook his head.

"Which way did he go?"

"He?"

"Gavin."

"Gavin's in the trees over there. He's been shot."

"Is he dead?"

"I don't know."

Behind them, two squad cars sped into the driveway, sirens screaming. Uniformed officers ran around the house, guns drawn. "Don't move," Angela said to Barret.

She left one of the officers with Barret, briefed the other, and then led him into the trees, where they found Gavin lying facedown, blood pooling around him in the mud. She checked his pulse. "He's still breathing," she said, radioing in for an ambulance. "Weak pulse."

"Angela," Stan shouted. "Over here."

"Stay with him," Angela said to the officer. At the house, she motioned to Barret and the officer to follow. She hugged the foundation till she peered around the corner. On the veranda, Stan crouched beside Maxine, who cradled Vanessa Matson's head in her arms.

"She's been shot," Stan said.

"It's her leg," Maxine said. "She's lost a lot of blood."

"Ambulance is on the way," Angela said.

As Stan hovered over Vanessa administering first aid, Angela waved Barret in behind Maxine and Vanessa and then stood, facing the trees. "There's an active shooter in the area," she radioed. "Proceed with caution. Identity to come." She flipped off the radio and spoke over her shoulder. "What happened here?"

"It's Jennifer Matson," Maxine said. "She shot Gavin."

Angela turned to Barret. "Is that what happened?"

Barret swallowed. "She went off the deep end," he said, his voice flat.

"I'm shocked it's taken this long," Stan said.

"Don't," Maxine said, glaring at him.

"Jennifer told me she killed Libby," Barret said. He sat suddenly, as if hearing the words for the first time, burying his face in his hands.

Angela turned to Maxine.

"Gavin had a gun," Maxine said. "He shot Vanessa, and then Jennifer managed to get it from him. It went off. She chased him into the storm."

"Tucker?" Angela asked. "Where's he?"

"Not here."

"And what about Hester?" Angela said,

429

her voice even. Emotion would only get in the way.

"I left her in the car," Maxine said.

"Get an APB out on Jennifer Matson," Angela said into her radio. "She's armed and dangerous." Her voice broke. "We may also have a hostage situation on our hands. Stand by for a photo."

She clicked off. "Send me one. A good one. Now!" she said to Maxine.

When the photo popped into her phone, Angela pulled up an image of a slender woman, white hair cascading around her shoulders, two cocker spaniels on her lap. "Photo's on its way," she said, into her radio, and then sent her own photo of Hester.

Angela turned in the yard, taking in the woods and the pond and the lights from Jamaica Plain. Jennifer Matson could have gone anywhere. She could be hiding in someone's backyard. She could be in the city with a gun and not a care in the world.

By now, sirens screamed from all directions as squad cars descended upon the house. Angela worked with the uniforms to begin securing the perimeter, so that when an ambulance arrived moments later, the paramedics could approach safely. They loaded Gavin onto a gurney and Vanessa onto another. When Maxine went to follow, Angela put a hand on the woman's arm.

"I need to go with her," Maxine said. "I need to make sure she's safe."

Angela could have asked about Rachel, demanded the truth. Maxine knew, or at least she knew parts of it, but then, so did Stan. "We'll talk later," she said.

After the ambulance drove away, Angela found Stan, took his arm, and led him to a stone stoop on the side of the house, with an overhang that shielded them from the rain. They sat side by side and looked out over the pond. Angela had to do her job. She had to be Sergeant White. Here, silence should have been her best tool, but Stan knew that. He knew all her tricks, because he'd taught her most of them. One trick he'd offered up long ago was to recognize the time to strike. "Let me be crystal clear," she said. "If something happens to my friend tonight and you could have prevented it, I'll take you down. And I'll make it as messy as I can."

Stan sighed.

"From the beginning," Angela said.

"Maxine moved into her apartment the day that Rachel Matson drowned," Stan said. "I helped her lug the boxes up those stairs, all of them, and when it was over, I got called to a shooting by the Ruggles T stop. That was around sunset. Later that same night, I got called to the Matsons' house. I knew the family through Maxine, I'd even met the girls once or twice. When Bob O'Duggan was assigned to the case, I nearly asked to have him removed because I wanted this to get the focus it deserved, the focus that Maxine would want it to."

"And you didn't take yourself off the investigation either."

"I called Maxine at her apartment. She didn't answer the phone. I went over there, and the front door to the building was ajar. She'd left. In the middle of the night. And the little girl was missing too. All Maxine had talked about for days was her first night in that apartment, and how much it would mean to her to be on her own. But she was gone, and I had no way to contact her."

He stopped, as though hearing his words for the first time. As though fully realizing what his actions could mean to him, and to his sister. "I panicked," he said.

"You panicked," Angela said, mirroring his words.

Stan knew that trick too, but it didn't matter. He didn't want these secrets anymore. "I let Bob take the lead on the case," he said. "I made sure nothing pointed to my sister. And I let the case close early and easily. By the time Maxine showed up that Tuesday, the ME had already signed off on an accidental death. And we were lucky that the local media didn't pick up on any of it. That would have been a different story."

"Was it an accident?" Angela asked.

Stan turned to her, his face drained of all color. "I couldn't prove otherwise, not after all this time. But maybe it doesn't matter now."

"Tell me what you think happened then."

"Jennifer Matson drowned her daughter," Stan said. "And I helped cover it up. If I hadn't, maybe none of this would have happened tonight."

Angela's final emotions drained away. "Hypotheticals don't help," she said.

"Sometimes they're impossible to avoid."

One of the cops by the house shouted to them. "We may have a lead. There's been a sighting."

Angela stood, and then relented and offered Stan a hand.

He considered her outstretched palm before giving in and letting her pull him to his feet.

"Don't think this is over," Angela said.

"It never is," Stan said.

MAXINE

The ambulance took less than five minutes to reach Faulkner Hospital, but to Maxine, it seemed like an eternity. She watched Vanessa the whole time, stroking her cheek, touching her hair, listening for any signs of lucidity, but Vanessa stayed unconscious. Behind her, Gavin's breathing was strained as the paramedics tried to stop his bleeding.

At the hospital, Maxine got out of the way as they unloaded both gurneys. She lost track of Gavin as she followed the paramedics wheeling Vanessa through the bay, and into the building where someone slipped an oxygen mask over Vanessa's face. Someone else checked her vitals. All of them looked prepubescent. A nurse stopped Maxine from continuing on to an elevator.

"They're taking her to surgery," the nurse said.

"She's pregnant," Maxine said. "Twelve weeks in."

He nodded and made a note.

"Will she wake up?" Maxine asked. "Will she be able to speak?"

"It's unlikely."

"I need to be with her when she wakes," Maxine said.

"If it works out," the nurse said in a quiet, measured voice Maxine was sure he'd perfected on people much nicer than she was.

Still, Maxine held her tongue and let him get her coffee and lead her to a waiting room filled with long rows of empty chairs. She'd have to trust the doctors to do their jobs. To stop the bleeding. To extract the bullet. Maxine collapsed into one of the chairs. The nurse stood by quietly, and Maxine wondered what it must be like to take on such grief, all day and every day. What it must be like to see death as routine.

"I'm fine," she said. "I'll sit here for a while."

"Let us know if you need anything," he said. "I'll give you updates on your daughter when I have more information."

Maxine was too numb to correct him, or to do anything but stare after him as he left, but she was thankful to be away from the house, away from the police, and away from Angela White in particular. If Angela had found her at this moment, if she'd poked in the right way, in a way that any detective would, in a way that Stan should have long ago, the whole truth would have come out in a torrent.

"Watch her," Tucker had said. *"Don't let her out of your sight."*

Maxine had tried. She'd given her life to watching over Vanessa, and it couldn't come to this. It couldn't possibly end with a bullet. With a few ill-spoken words.

She remembered sitting in the car with Hester, knowing that what waited for her inside Pinebank would somehow change her forever. She remembered being grateful to have a friend to greet her when she re-emerged. "I'll take you home after they boot me out," she'd said, before dashing into the rain.

At the door, she almost retreated. But she found her resolve and stepped inside. Voices echoed from the back of the house as Fred and Adele tore around the corner, jumping up, resting their paws on Maxine's knees in a way they were absolutely not supposed to do and in a way she was thrilled to see. She broke a treat in half, and made them sit, and then followed the voices. Right before she turned the corner, right before she faced what she had to face, she stopped, desperate to keep the before from forever becoming the after. Desperate to hold off her own future.

"Ma'am?"

It was the nurse. His face was long, the practiced mask of someone used to dealing with tragedy. But surely the doctor would be the one to deliver the worst news. And they couldn't have news like that, not yet.

"I need you to sign some consent forms," he said, thrusting a clipboard toward her.

Maxine held it on her lap, unsure what to do. Even the simplest tasks seemed insurmountable.

"I can explain the forms," the nurse said a moment later. "Or give you some time to read them through."

What did he want her to do? "Her husband's in surgery," she said.

"I know. That's why you need to sign them. Next of kin."

"I'm not her mother," Maxine said, and it felt as if she'd torn her own heart out.

"Who are you then?"

"A friend. Her mother can't be here."

The nurse took the clipboards away. "We'll need someone with authorization to sign these."

An orderly pushed a bed through the halls

carrying an older woman in a hospital gown. She'd taken her teeth out, and slept, her mouth agape, her gums bright and pink, her hollow cheeks sinking in around her face. All vanities forgotten.

"You'll have to find someone else," Maxine said to the nurse.

She closed her eyes and listened as the nurse shuffled away. The images from the night flooded through her again.

At Pinebank, she'd finally turned that corner, but it had taken a moment for the scene in front of her to make sense. The French doors were open to the storm, and Gavin stood on the threshold, rain lashing behind him, the drapes swirling in the wind. His hair was plastered to his scalp, and his white shirt clung to his skin. And he held a gun. A young man Maxine recognized from school crouched against the wall. Vanessa faced away from Maxine on the opposite side of the room. And Jennifer hovered between them. None of them noticed her, even as the dogs ran into the room and barked.

"What did you do?" Gavin said. "Why were the police looking for me?"

"I told you to lay low," Vanessa said. "I told you I'd take care of it."

Gavin swung the gun toward her. "You

planned this. From the start."

Vanessa's eyes flashed with anger. "You're the one with the plans," she said. "Preying on those women. Those girls. Even me."

"You didn't complain," Gavin said.

"He used our secrets," Vanessa said, turning to her mother. "Your secrets. How the hell do you think he got into this house, into my bed? He used Rachel. He told me I was smart, that he could help me become someone. Then he told me I was beautiful but that I shouldn't tell. That no one would understand. Then he asked about Rachel, about what happened that night. And the more he asked, the more I knew we had to keep it secret."

Jennifer reached toward Vanessa. "I've watched you, in every way I could."

"You've never been anything but a drunk."

"Both of you shut up," Gavin said, tightening his grip on the gun, his finger twitching at the trigger.

"Put that down," Maxine heard herself say.

Gavin turned on her. "Saint Maxine," he said.

"Nothing can be worth this," she said. "Whatever you did tonight, we can work it out."

"You have no idea who these people are,"

439

Gavin said. "Or what they can do."

"Shut up," Vanessa said.

Maxine stepped toward him, reaching for the gun, her eyes focused on Gavin's face, on his rage. Then everything slowed. The dogs ran from the room, their tails between their legs. Jennifer's hands flew to her face. Across the room, Vanessa buckled over, clutching at her leg, red seeping around her palm.

It was only then that Maxine finally heard the gun blast. And the world sped up again.

Gavin took a step backward, staring at the gun in his own hand, as though he couldn't believe he'd pulled the trigger himself. Then he cried out. The young man, the boy, had smashed a fireplace poker on Gavin's arm. The gun fell to the floor, spinning across the rug.

Maxine found herself at Vanessa's side, pressing a cloth against the wound as blood pooled beneath it. "It's okay," she said, as Vanessa struggled to stay awake.

Behind her, Gavin said, "There's no way you'll pin this on me."

"Don't move."

Jennifer had the gun. She aimed it at Gavin. The boy cowered by the French doors. "Go," she said to him, and he ran outside, into the storm.

"You treated Vanessa like those other girls," Jennifer said. "Using her. Using what you thought you knew."

"I know about that baby," Gavin said. "The one who drowned. I know that someone killed her."

This time there was no mistaking the gunfire as glass behind Gavin shattered. "What the hell?" he said.

Jennifer fired again. Red burst from Gavin's chest. He looked down as though he couldn't quite fathom what had happened, and then spun and fled into the darkness. Jennifer followed, pausing at the threshold as though daring herself to leap into the night. "Take care of her," she said to Maxine, before diving forward and fading into the murky night.

Someone sat beside Maxine. Without having to look, she knew it was Tucker, that he'd mostly come for Vanessa, but that he'd come for her, too. She leaned against him, her eyes closed, and he wrapped his arm around her and kissed the top of her head as they propped each other up. They looked like any couple in any waiting room, hoping for the best and dreading the worst. They looked like they belonged together.

"Where'd you go?" she asked.

"To a bar. I couldn't face going home."

Tucker never liked confrontation. Why would tonight have been different? But he'd have to face this news. "Jen shot Gavin," Maxine said. "And she says she killed that girl, the one from school, Libby Thomas. Vanessa's in surgery, and I'm sitting here hoping. That's all I know."

She folded into him. He kissed her again, and here, in this public moment, it felt right.

HESTER

Hester stumbled through the trees, the barrel of a gun digging into her shoulder. Ahead, lights from a streetlamp shone, and police cruisers sped by.

"They're looking for us," Jennifer whispered.

Her wet hair hung around her face, but, to Hester, it seemed as though every molecule of night air had infused the woman with new life. "We're almost there," Jennifer said.

Earlier, Hester had lain flat, trying to disappear into the mud. Footsteps pounded toward her. She held in a cry as a foot caught her in the ribs, and someone sprawled forward, tumbling across the ground. She scrambled away, pressing herself against a tree trunk. Gavin Dean moaned as he tried to stand, and then slumped forward.

Behind her, a twig snapped. Hester swung

around to see Jennifer Matson standing over her with a gun. Slowly, Hester raised her hands. She swiveled onto a hip, ready to fight. Jennifer aimed the gun at Gavin and then turned the barrel toward Hester. "Did you call your mother?" she asked.

Hester wriggled away. "Not yet."

"Is he dead?" Jennifer asked.

"I hope not."

"I should shoot him again."

"Or let him be."

Gavin tried to stand. He groaned again and collapsed.

"I didn't think you left the house," Hester said.

Jennifer looked around, as though seeing where she was for the first time. "I don't usually," she said. "And I probably won't again."

Slowly, Hester stood, her hands still raised. A siren approached as a car sped into the driveway and skidded to a stop.

"You shouldn't have come here," Jennifer said.

"Don't I know it," Hester said.

Out in the driveway, Angela whispered Hester's name.

Jennifer waved the gun away from the house, and Hester took a few steps into the trees. "Don't try anything," Jennifer said.

■ ■ ■ ■

Now, they crouched in the shadows by the edge of the road. When the last of the police cruisers sped by, Hester went first as they dashed across the street and down a steep embankment into the wooded area surrounding Ward's Pond. Jennifer paused as they reached the bank, staring out over the dark surface. "It hasn't changed. Not after all this time."

She nudged the gun into Hester's ribs, shoving her forward as they skirted the pond to the opposite shore. Above them, traffic sped along the Jamaicaway, so close, and yet too far away.

"We used to come and sit right here," Jennifer said, wading into the water, the hem of her dress trailing behind her. "Me. Vanessa and Rachel. Shadow too. Vanessa would play with her dolls. She could be jealous. Protective. But Rachel, even when she was a baby, she'd crawl toward the water. It was like it called to her."

"A little Esther Williams."

Jennifer's eyes snapped up at the sound of Hester's voice. "That's exactly what I used to say. I told Tucker to watch Rachel, whatever you do. She'll try to swim."

445

Hester held her palms out. "I won't leave," she said. "I promise. But don't point that gun at me. It scares me."

Jennifer looked at the gun, and then at Hester and let the gun fall to her side. "I wanted to come here, one last time."

Jennifer was two yards away, and Hester could fight. She'd proven it before. But the gun made fighting too risky. "I'm playing a game with my husband," she said. "My non-husband. We ask each other questions, one a day, and we have to answer, no matter how much we don't want to."

"Do you ever lie?" Jennifer asked.

"Is that your question?"

"It's my first one."

"Sometimes I don't tell him everything," Hester said. "I'll tell him a piece of the truth but leave out the most important parts. The parts that hurt. He knows I left home when I was eighteen. He knows that my mother drank and was erratic, but he doesn't know how much of her I see in myself. He doesn't know that I'm afraid of what I might become."

Above them, a siren blared.

"That sounded like an ambulance," Jennifer said. "Vanessa's probably in it, with Maxine. Maxine will take care of her tonight, like she always has."

"More than you?"

"Is that your question?"

Hester shook her head. "Why the book? Why *Adam Bede*?"

Jennifer stepped out of the water and sat on the bank. She lay the gun beside her. "Maxine was an English major," she said. "She wrote her thesis on George Eliot. She knew that the book was about a mother who kills her own child."

"It was for Maxine?"

"In a way," Jennifer said. "You can shape memory. You can make people remember what you want them to. That's what I did with Vanessa. Anytime she seemed to remember something she shouldn't, I'd find a way to squelch out the truth. I knew the baby was coming. The new baby. And I knew it would surface memories. Four-year-olds remember more than you know. It was important that they talk about me, focus on me, on my truth."

"What would she have remembered?" Hester asked.

"That's a second question. Or the part you're leaving out. The part that hurts."

Jennifer lifted her face to the rain. "This is nice," she said. "Being outside. It's the first time I've felt the rain on my face in years." She turned to Hester. "Are you frightened?"

447

"Of you?"

"That's my next question. What frightens you?"

Hester waved a hand around the darkened forest. "I've survived worse than this."

"You didn't answer the question."

"I'm getting married," Hester said.

"You're afraid?" Jennifer asked.

"I'm afraid of losing myself. I don't want to be part of the patriarchy." Hester heard her own words and laughed at them. "That sounded so stupid and pretentious, and it's not what I mean, anyway. Not at all. But sometimes, it feels like I'm being forced into this box, and I'm not sure if it's the right box."

"You want to choose your own path."

"That, and I want to not choose any path. I want options. All the options."

"You have no idea how lucky you are. It's when you lose those choices that you see what you've missed the whole time."

"Morgan's put up with a lot already," Hester said. "He'll be there for me. We'll be there for each other."

"That sounds like your truth."

It did. "I'm getting married," Hester said, again, and this time it sounded less foreign. "But I'm not letting anyone call me his fiancée, and if one bride magazine shows up at my house, I'm calling the whole thing off."

Through the trees, above them, a police cruiser screeched to a stop, followed by another. Hester let her feet dangle above the surface of the water. She wrapped an arm around Jennifer's sodden waist. "They'll be here soon," Hester said. "Tell me about Rachel."

Flashlight beams dotted the night as a corps of cops descended into the woods.

"You have a child," Jennifer said.

"In a way," Hester said.

"You either have children or you don't. There's no halfway."

"Then you're right. I have a child."

"You protect your children at any cost," Jennifer said. "I protected mine. I let people see what they wanted to believe."

Hester stared at the misty surface of the water as the final pieces of the puzzle began to fall into place. "They all think you killed Rachel. Or that's what Tucker and Maxine believe. And you leave little clues, books like *Adam Bede,* to make sure they keep believing it."

Jennifer turned to Hester. "I found them. I found both my girls by the pond. Vanessa was sitting right here, right where we are now. Her arms were covered with bruises."

The cold seeped through Hester's coat, into her skin.

"It was an accident," Jennifer said. "That's the only option because the alternative . . . it was too terrible to face. It *is* too terrible to face. It's the only thing I can believe. I've looked for signs, for anything that would tell me she was dangerous, to herself, to others. Vanessa's a wonderful person . . . no matter . . . it *was* an accident, no matter what happened tonight."

On the other side of the pond, someone shouted, "I see them!"

Hester turned to Jennifer. "You took the blame and let them protect you while you watched Vanessa."

Jennifer put a hand up as a floodlight shone across the water. "I won't say that," she said. "Not to you. Not to anyone."

"But it's the truth."

"Maybe it's yours. I have my own."

"Did Gavin know?"

"He knew enough. Enough to manipulate Vanessa. Now, I hope he's dead."

A voice came over a megaphone. "Come toward us with your hands up."

It was Angela.

Jennifer raised her hands and stood slowly. "I did it," she said. "And it won't matter if you try to tell Sergeant White something else, because that's the truth. I killed Rachel. I shot Gavin. And I killed that girl, too. Libby. I killed them all. That's the only truth anyone will believe."

Jennifer smiled down one last time, and then walked away, toward the light. Halfway around the pond, she fell to her knees, and then lay on her stomach while two cops, guns drawn, cuffed her. After they led her away, Angela detached herself from the group and trudged through the mud. She lay a blanket over Hester's shoulders and then joined her, scooting in as close as she could and pulling the blanket over them both. Hester rested her head against her friend's shoulder and closed her eyes. "We should go into business together," she said a moment later. "Start a PI firm. Thursby and White."

"White and Thursby," Angela said. "And you're delirious. You don't want to see the ugliness that I do. It wears you down. Stay at the library."

Angela dropped the gun into an evidence bag and hauled Hester to her feet. As they picked their way through the trees and then along the path and up to the street, Hester had to lean on her friend more than she expected.

"What'll happen to Jennifer?" Hester asked.

"She shot Gavin. She says she killed Libby Thomas. She'll go to jail. Or a psychiatric hospital."

"She didn't kill Libby."

"She did, though. We found one of her hairs on the scene."

"It was Vanessa," Hester said. "Vanessa Matson."

"You sound like you have Stockholm syndrome. Two witnesses saw Jennifer shoot Gavin with the gun in this bag, and we have a confession. Jennifer told Barret Hardenne that Libby was going to come forward with a sexual harassment case against the school, and from what you uncovered these last few days, my guess is it would have snowballed."

Hester stopped, thinking through her conversation, grasping for anything that might get Angela to listen. "Jennifer told me how much she liked the fresh air," Hester said, closing her eyes, searching for Jennifer's exact words. "She told me that she was feeling the rain on her face for the first time in years. But it rained all day. If she left the house earlier, she'd have felt the rain then."

A car pulled to the side of the road twenty yards away. Stan stepped out, and Angela caught his eye. "When you're in Homicide," she said, "you take the wins. This isn't a win, it's a shutout. Here's the truth. Jennifer Matson killed an innocent woman to protect her family's business and then she shot her son-in-law."

"Because she didn't want him to talk," Hester said. "Listen to me. None of this makes sense."

Angela cut her off. "Sometimes, the truth is right there, ready to be plucked. In all likelihood, Jennifer Matson drowned her two-year-old daughter and has been wandering this earth without suffering the consequences for over twenty years. Now it's time for her to pay."

"She told me that she found *both* girls by the water. She found Vanessa there too."

Angela dragged Hester to a squad car and yanked open the back door. Jennifer sat, her face a mask of serenity. "Did you shoot Gavin Dean?" Angela asked.

Jennifer looked at Hester as she answered. "I did," she said.

"And what about Libby Thomas?"

"I went to her apartment this evening to talk some sense into her," Jennifer said. "She wanted to destroy everything my husband and daughter have built. We argued, and I shoved her. She hit her head on

453

the kitchen counter."

"And your daughter. Rachel Matson."

"I drowned her."

"That's not what you told me," Hester said.

"I didn't tell you anything," Jennifer said.

As Angela went to close the door, Jennifer stopped her.

"I liked you," she said to Hester. "From the first time we met. I thought we could be friends, in another lifetime."

Hester looked at the woman, hands cuffed behind her back, her dress clinging to her skin. She seemed tiny. And alone, but not helpless. And not someone who'd budge. An image of Jennifer, the young Jennifer, flashed through Hester's mind. She imagined that woman, the one with the confidence, the one with the easy laugh, running from Pinebank, calling to her children, fighting her way through trees and shrubs, a black Newfoundland galloping at her side. At the pond, she ran as though she could walk on water, plunging beneath the surface even as she pulled herself forward. Shadow dove into the pond beside her, swimming with assured strokes to where Rachel floated, facedown. But it was too late.

Vanessa sat on the banks of the pond.

Jennifer took the girl in her arms, holding

her close, ignoring the bruises. It was too late for one child. But she could still save the other. She could protect her. She could be sure that all eyes turned to her. So, she waited until Tucker found her. She let him fill in his own truth, and she let that truth spread like a virus to Maxine.

She'd have let it spread to the world, if she'd needed to. And it probably would now.

"You seem like someone I can trust," Jennifer said.

"It's the height," Hester said.

"It's more than that. We have a lot in common. We'd have understood each other."

Would Hester have made Jennifer's choices for Kate? Maybe?

Probably.

But she prayed she'd never have to find out.

"You done?" Angela asked, and when Jennifer nodded, she closed the door and tapped the roof. The cruiser pulled away. "There's the truth," Angela said. "Straight from her own mouth. There isn't another one, even if you want there to be."

Angela waved over one of the uniformed cops. "Take Ms. Thursby home," she said. "Walk her into her apartment. Don't leave till she's changed into her pajamas and gone to bed. Understand?"

Hester tried to argue one last time. "Enough," Angela said, as Stan approached. "I'll talk to you when I talk to you."

Hester glanced at Stan. "You're choosing him," she said, and when Angela didn't respond, Hester let the officer lead her to a car and help her into the passenger's side. As the cruiser pulled away, Angela and Stan both watched Hester watching them, till the car turned a corner, and they disappeared.

■ ■ ■ ■

SATURDAY, APRIL 3

■ ■ ■ ■

MAXINE

Eighty-seven steps. They were all still there. Every one of them. And Maxine had never wanted to face them less.

But she did. With Fred tucked under one arm, and Adele under the other.

The surgery had been successful, and Vanessa lay in recovery, sedated. The baby had survived too. The doctors had assured Maxine that it was safe to leave, that Vanessa would be out for another few hours. The police had come and questioned her, and Stan had recused himself from the investigation this time around. They'd taken Tucker to the station, to see Jennifer.

Maxine would have to go there later too.

No one had mentioned Rachel. Somehow, that had stayed in the family for now.

Already out of breath, Maxine paused on the front deck to hold the door for Derek — or whatever his name was — as he maneuvered the baby carriage out the door.

She'd nearly headed inside when she asked, "What're their names?"

"Henry and Elizabeth," Derek said.

"Regal," Maxine said.

"I've heard."

"They're cute."

"Not at four in the morning. I hope they didn't keep you up."

"I haven't been home."

In another lifetime, Derek would have assumed Maxine was taking the walk of shame. Now, she doubted Derek saw her as sexual in any way. "I'm Maxine," she said.

"Dan," Derek said. "My wife is Danielle."

Not Derek. Dan. And Danielle. "Easy to remember," Maxine said. "I'll have a nephew or niece in a few months. There'll be plenty of screaming coming from my apartment then. Maybe we can have a play date."

"As long as you bring the wine," Dan said.

"In the meantime, if you need someone . . ."

Dan cut her off. "Danielle's mother takes them when we go out."

Too familiar, Maxine reminded herself. Baby steps.

He maneuvered the carriage to the street below. By the time Vanessa gave birth, Dan and Danielle and their royal babies would probably be gone anyway.

Inside, Maxine put the dogs down. They trotted up the remaining stairs, and she hauled herself after them to the landing outside her apartment, where she paused, the key in the lock, her hand on the door-knob.

Had Tucker finished with the police? Would he be waiting inside?

Would he have coffee brewing? Coffee they'd forgo. Would she give her heart to him? And afterward, in her white bed with its white sheets and her beautiful white blinds, would she still feel the same? Would it still be her perfect little place? Everything they'd done, every thought, every action, had had Jennifer at the center. Rachel too. Who would they be without them?

Maxine had spent so many years wishing for a do-over, that she'd lost track of her hopes. She didn't know if she dreamed of what was, or whether those dreams meant moving on and becoming someone new. She opened the door. It was time to find out.

ANGELA

As the sun came up over Boston Harbor, Angela sat in her driveway, wondering if it would be easier to curl up here and ignore the demands of her day. Whether she could give in to exhaustion for once. But, somehow, she rallied and got out of the car. All around her, birds chirped, announcing spring, announcing the end of the torrential rain and the pending arrival of the sun.

George met her at the front door, his tail taking the lead in a whole-body wag, his mouth turned up into a grin. He pressed himself against Angela's leg, and she crouched to pet him, scratching that spot on his side that made him kick his hind leg. The stress of the night, the anger, the lies, all flowed into him. Angela lay beside him as he curled into her, his tail beating a slow and steady rhythm.

"Your breath stinks," she whispered.

He licked her face.

No matter her complaints, no matter how much she blamed Morgan for bringing this creature into her life, she loved George. It was their secret. She loved George in a way she hadn't loved another human. Sometimes, in moments like this one, a profound sadness came over her as she imagined the days, not far from now, when he'd no longer be with her. By then, her whole world would be different: Isaiah would be a teenager; Stan would be retired; Angela would be in her fifties; and Cary, well who knew where Cary would be? And no matter what, Brenda would find a way into her life.

Angela had to anticipate, she had to worry — it was how she'd survived as a cop — but still, she sometimes wished she could appreciate the moment for what it was.

"Best boy," she whispered.

George stood. He pressed his nose to her face till she opened her eyes and sat up. It was time for a walk.

Down by the bay, she let the cool, spring air clear her head as she tossed a ball down the sand. She checked her phone for news of Zane, but none had come in. She nodded at the other dog walkers and kept to herself.

At home, she fed George breakfast and finally gave in to exhaustion. It was already after six. Isaiah would be up soon, and the day would begin again. She had to face the mess she'd helped create and find a way to move forward. There was truth, and it was made up of pieces, and Hester didn't have enough of those pieces to *know,* but she knew enough. Most of all she knew that Angela had chosen to protect Stan over anything else. He'd covered up that child's murder. Angela believed Jennifer's confessions, no matter what Hester claimed Jennifer had shared. Stan had let Jennifer Matson go free all these years, and he'd done it out of loyalty to his sister, as Angela had chosen loyalty to Stan, and Hester — she trusted — would choose loyalty to her. They would guard all these secrets and hope they wouldn't fester.

She left George in the kitchen and crept up the stairs to her bedroom, with its slanted ceilings and tiny closets. She peeked in on Isaiah, who slept soundly. Then she eased the bedroom door open. Cary slept with her body sprawled diagonally across the mattress. Angela wondered if she liked it better that way, whether she liked the space to spread out.

Cary stirred. "Come to bed," she said, her eyes barely open. "We can find five minutes."

Angela didn't bother to get undressed. She toed off her shoes and slid beneath the comforter, letting her eyes close and her body relax. "I'm here to shower and change," she said. "Then I have to head to the station."

"Did you find the bad guys?" Cary asked.

"Most of them found us."

"It's all you can ask for."

How many bad guys were there in a city the size of Boston? A thousand, maybe? Ten thousand? Every now and then, Angela made sure one of them didn't do more harm. Every now and then, she did some good. At the very least, Jennifer Matson was off the streets. That, she was convinced, was for the best. The new baby could be safe. And Angela had done the right thing, or she hoped she could convince herself she had. Eventually. "The world's an ugly place," she said.

"But this house is warm," Cary said.

A thump came from the hallway as Isaiah leapt from bed. George woofed at the foot of the stairs.

"I'll take care of them," Cary said.

"Stay," Angela said. "Two more minutes."

Now it was Cary's turn to tense up before relaxing into the decision.

"What'll happen to Isaiah?" Angela asked.

"What are you yammering about, now?" Cary asked, rolling toward her.

"I mean if we break up. Where'll I be?"

"Are you planning to dump me? I expect alimony, you know. And half your pension."

"He has you," Angela said. "He has Brenda."

"Think how lucky he is," Cary said. "Most people have one mother. He has three. Each of us watching over him and guiding him through this world. Each of us fending off evil. It's like a fairy tale."

"Like the three of us standing in a circle, holding hands? The ABCs?"

"Why not!"

"It stinks of eternity, and that's too much Brenda for me."

"She likes you!" Cary said. "She tells me that all the time. But you're kind to put up with her."

"I'm less kind than you know," Angela said.

"You know what we'll do," Cary said. "We'll write up a plan, and we'll all sign it. Even Brenda. Then you won't have to worry."

"I always worry."

Cary kissed her. "Family always comes first. When you remember that, it's one less thing to keep track of. One less thing to worry about."

Family came first.

Always.

Cary, Isaiah, George, Angela's parents, her sisters, Hester, Morgan, Kate, Jamie, Waffles, O'Keefe, Butch, Ian. Even Brenda.

And Stan.

What would come from taking Stan down? He was a good cop, a good friend, one who'd kept the world safer, one who'd made sure his own share of bad guys came off the streets.

"Family first," Angela said.

Her phone beeped. Zane's out of surgery, Stan wrote. Things are looking okay.

Downstairs, something shattered. It sounded like glass.

And the day began.

BARRET

Barret dozed in the hospital lobby. At noon, he swung by Information and then took the elevator to the sixth floor and waited for clear corridors before scurrying down a wide hall to room 6-21. He glanced through the open door to where Maxine sat by the bed, staring at a magazine. Barret found a set of chairs thirty yards away and waited for her to leave.

He'd already gone through a police interrogation in the wee hours of the morning with Angela White. Sergeant White. She'd asked how he knew Jennifer, why he'd come to the house. He tried to answer as truthfully as he could. When she slid a photo of Libby across the table and asked where he'd been yesterday afternoon, the dams finally broke. He lay his head on the table and sobbed till he couldn't cry anymore. And when he looked up, Sergeant White waited. Patiently.

"When was the last time you'd heard from her?" she asked, her voice as soft and kind as the most loving mother.

He showed her the text. The one Libby sent. "I knew there was something wrong when she didn't meet me," he said. The words sounded as if someone else had spoken. "Who killed her?"

"Jennifer Matson says she did."

"Why would she?" Barret asked.

"I'll ask you the same thing?"

"I couldn't tell you."

"Let me ask you about Gavin Dean."

Barret told her all about the meeting in Gavin's office. How his breath had smelled of coffee. "Men hit on women all the time," he said. "They use their power. But my mother taught me how to deal with that."

"Good mother," Angela said. "I have one too. He gathered secrets and used them against other women. Did he have something on you?"

"Probably that I'm trans," Barret said. "But that's not a secret. Not one I needed to hide. I don't think he knew that."

"He used one of Libby's secrets to manipulate her," Angela said. "But she threatened to go to the press with her pregnancy. At least that's what Jennifer Matson claims."

"What happened to Gavin?"

"He's dead. He died in surgery."

Good, Barret thought. "I'm glad," he said.

Angela hovered on that one, but Barret let the silence fill the room. He didn't have anything to add. When she asked more questions, he answered without thinking them through. At the end of the interview, she seemed done, if not satisfied. "We'll be in touch if we need anything else," she'd said.

Down the hallway, Maxine left Vanessa's hospital room and turned the corner. Barret waited a few moments, and then walked like someone who belonged, right into Vanessa Matson's room. She lay in the bed, her eyes closed, her mouth slightly open. Nurses entered the room periodically to check on her, and an hour later, she stirred, eyeing him dreamily. "It's you," she said.

"How are you feeling?"

"Like I'm sitting on a cloud," Vanessa said.

"You must be in a good mood, then," he said, taking out his portfolio.

"Bold." Vanessa grimaced as she reached for the book. "I like bold."

He sat on the edge of the bed and held the book for her. When he came to a photo of a mural he'd painted near campus, she stopped him.

"I saw this the other day," Vanessa said, tapping the page. "It's good work."

Barret sat back in his chair as she paged through the book. He thought about Libby, imagining her last moments. He liked to hope that she'd been putting on her coat to come meet him at the boathouse when the doorbell rang. He imagined her stopping and touching her belly. The swelling hadn't begun yet, but she knew already. The home test had confirmed it, and she'd sent a photo of the stick to Gavin, making sure to focus on the plus sign. The police had that piece of evidence. Sergeant White had shown it to him. Libby ran down the stairs, but it couldn't have been Gavin standing there, waiting. He had an alibi. Tucker Matson had an alibi, too. Barret had learned that from Sergeant White. He'd been at a bar with fifty other people. It couldn't have been Jennifer, either. She hadn't left that house that day, or any day, for that matter.

That left Vanessa.

Barret wondered how Vanessa convinced Libby to let her into the house. Maybe Libby believed she could negotiate. Maybe Vanessa told her that Gavin had used her too. Barret wanted to give Vanessa the benefit of the doubt, especially here, now, as she reviewed his portfolio. Maybe Libby threatened her first, and they struggled, and Libby slipped, and the whole thing had been an accident. Or maybe Vanessa had shoved Libby on purpose, happy to see her head crack open against the marble counter. Only Vanessa would ever know for sure.

"This is good too," Vanessa said, pointing to a mural called *Chicken Day.* "So much blood."

She winced as she said the word.

"That's of my family," Barret said. "We slaughter chickens in the spring. It's a big party."

"And the dog?"

"That's Rusty."

Vanessa closed the portfolio. "What do you want, anyway? You could sue us over everything that happened last night."

"A show," Barret said. "At the gallery."

She turned to the portfolio and nodded. "I bet there's some scholarship money too."

"And no boxed wine at the reception."

"That's pushing it," Vanessa said.

Barret had come here to lay out the case of what had happened to Libby — to coerce, to blackmail — but Vanessa had given him what he needed, even if it meant betraying Libby, in a way. He thought about the way Libby had put her art above anything else in life, the way she'd focused on success. She'd understand his choice. She'd forgive him.

He'd save this secret for another day.

JUNE

Hester

The spring rain had begun to fall as Morgan parked the truck. "Ready?" he asked Hester.

"Can't wait. A night to remember."

"It's not night," Kate said, from the rear cab, where she sat with Jamie and Waffles.

"You're right," Hester said. They were approaching the solstice. Outside, the air was warm, and the sun still high in the sky, even at seven o'clock. "But you remember it when you do something special for a friend."

It didn't even occur to Hester to help Kate from the truck. Those days had ended. The girl ripped off her seat belt and ran along the sidewalk with Morgan, Jamie, and Waffles right behind her. Down the street, Angela's car turned the corner, and Hester retreated to the gallery.

"I'll meet you inside," Morgan called to her.

He hadn't taken sides. He hadn't even

taken Hester's side, but Hester didn't know if he knew there were sides to take. Angela still came to the house for baseball games. She still drank PBR, but these days Hester excused herself and left Morgan and Angela to themselves. Hester understood loyalty and what it meant to choose. She understood that Angela had chosen to protect Stan over all else. But it didn't feel right.

From inside the Matson Gallery, she watched. Cary kissed Morgan's cheek. Kate and Isaiah held hands and jumped up and down. George and Waffles wrestled. Angela said something to Jamie, and even from here Hester could guess that she'd asked after her. Jamie pointed toward the gallery, and Hester tried to melt into the crowd.

Barret's art hung from every wall, and people from all over the city had come out tonight to see Vanessa Matson's latest discovery. Vanessa moved through the room, her ever-expanding belly leading her. Even from ten feet away, Hester could hear the constant refrain of "marvelous" and "brilliant." She approached, meeting Vanessa's eyes and trying to see the other woman's secrets, but Vanessa's face was a mask of hospitality. "So good of you to come," she said as if they hadn't met, gently pulling Hester along and moving to the next guest.

Maxine Pawlikowski lurked in a corner, her mouth turned down in a scowl, the two cocker spaniels sitting at her feet. Across the room, Tucker Matson drank wine from a plastic cup. Even now, Hester wondered if their charade had ended, or if they'd simply perfected their lie.

And at the center of it all, Barret held court, describing one of his murals, a sea of yellow and red and green. "It's called *Chicken Day,*" he said. "It's about family."

A few feet away, Elaine Hardenne looked on with Rusty curled up at her feet. Elaine had driven here all the way from Illinois so that Rusty could come to the show, and then Barret had insisted that all the dogs come too.

"I'm proud of her," Elaine said.

"He's talented," Hester said.

"Him," Elaine said, catching herself. "I'm not used to it yet, but I'll get there."

"Why *Chicken Day*?"

"It's a day in the spring. Bloody but fun. Well, not for the chickens. I'll tell you about it when we get home."

Barret had moved into Hester's aerie. When she'd offered it to him, she'd told him he could stay for three months, that she'd need the space again or else she'd go crazy, but two months had gone by and she knew he'd stay as long as he needed and that she'd hate the day when he moved out. Like Jamie, Barret came to dinner most nights. He babysat Kate when Hester needed help. He liked to play chess, hated NASCAR, and had taken a shining to Ian the iguana, who spent most of his time in the aerie now, too. Hester needed allies. In the end, she didn't need the apartment as much as she thought she did. She didn't need half the walls she'd built over the years. And besides, she'd finished all nine seasons of *The Waltons.*

"I'm glad you came," Maxine said, offering a cup of wine.

"I won't say no," Hester said. "The finest box around."

"We're using bottles tonight," Maxine said, taking a long sip. "Angela's over there," she added.

"I didn't know."

"Go over and start talking. You'll be surprised. It'll be like nothing happened, and for a while you can pretend it's true. Then, when you're ready, you can have that talk. Whatever talk you need to have."

"How are things with Stan?"

"We're fine," Maxine said. "We'll always be fine."

The school and the gallery were in the

news. The attorney general had brought charges against them for admission irregularity, and while most of the fraud charges had been levied at Gavin, Maxine still faced possible jail time for refusing to cooperate with the federal investigation.

"How about Vanessa?" Hester asked. "Things good with her?"

"It's easier in the end to forgive," Maxine said. "For both of us. Jen too. I see her every week. I visit for lunch, bring the dogs. She's . . . happy. That's all I can hope for."

Jennifer had taken a plea deal and was in a psychiatric ward, where she'd stay for at least ten years.

"And Tucker?" Hester asked. "I was hoping for a happy-ever-after for the two of you."

Maxine's eyes smiled. "Tucker? Why would I care?"

"Always a secret with you two."

"You should talk."

"I don't have secrets," Hester said, even if, a week earlier, she and Morgan had slipped away to City Hall and said, "I do," to each other. Except for the justice of the peace, no one else knew. Not even Kate.

Across the room, Morgan swung Kate around, nearly toppling a tray of wine. He put her down, and she chased Isaiah through the crowd. Cary chatted with Jamie. And Angela.

Hester caught Angela looking at her, and when she raised a hand, Angela waved too. Maybe Maxine was right. It was easier to let anger go.

Maybe it was time to forgive.

Outside, Hester tapped a number into her phone, one of the few phone numbers she still knew by heart. She wondered if it still worked, whether it had been reassigned or disconnected. As she dared herself to hit Send, the door opened. It was Angela. "I forgot to pick Isaiah up at swim practice yesterday," she said. "He was waiting for almost two hours before Brenda came."

"I let Kate watch *Law and Order,*" Hester said. "It helps her sleep."

"Like mother, like daughter."

Hester traced the number on the screen. She took a long quaff of wine. "Maybe we can go on another stakeout."

"Don't tell Stan."

"I need to do something," Hester said. "By myself."

"You know where I am," Angela said, and headed inside.

Hester hit Send. The phone rang four times.

"Hello?"

She could have said hello too, or "It's me, Hester."

Instead, she listened to the sound of that voice, one she'd recognize anywhere, any day. "Who's there?"

Hester let the voice pull her to another time, to being young, to being lost, to wanting to escape. She let it pull her one step closer toward forgiveness. And when her mother hung up, Hester stared at the phone as Kate's photo appeared.

She'd made a gesture. She'd make another soon.

Maybe tomorrow.

ACKNOWLEDGMENTS

I am writing these acknowledgments in May of 2020, right in the middle of the COVID-19 pandemic. When you read this book, I hope this strange time is a distant memory for all of us. Like many authors, I struggled with how to address the pandemic in a contemporary novel, but I ultimately decided to leave much of the manuscript as it was originally written (though careful readers will notice that no one shakes hands in these pages!) Right now, I yearn for a world with passed hors d'oeuvres and caviar stations, one where students go to college and live in dorms, and where friends meet at restaurants for dinner. Let's hope that the simple pleasures of the recent past will soon be part of our future.

In such a sad and tumultuous year, saying thank you seems especially important.

First, thank you to the many booksellers who play a vital role in communities all around the world. Authors can't do what we love without you, and I look forward to working together for many years to come.

Thank you to the bloggers, bookstagrammers, and reviewers who help promote writers: Dru Ann; Kristopher; Ann, Tracey, and Kathy; Daniel, Dave, and Sean; cofounder of His Girl Thursby, Jackie Shephard, as well as Linda Zagon, Book Gypsy, and the other members of the group; and many, many others.

I am indebted to Bruce Robert Coffin, former detective sergeant with the Portland Police and current author, for helping me with the details of police procedure. If you like expertly plotted police procedurals, check out his fantastic Detective Byron series (www.brucecoffin.com). Also, many thanks to Odile Harter of the Harry Elkins Widener Memorial Library for giving me an inside view of this fascinating institution and the day-to-day life of a research librarian. *Widener: Biography of a Library* by Matthew Battles also provided important details. As always, any and all errors are my own.

When I returned to Boston from San Francisco in the early 2000s, I lived a few blocks away from Jamaica Pond and went running there most mornings, right by a ruined, burned-out mansion that sat behind an imposing chain-link fence. This was Pinebank Mansion. Most of the details about the house in this book are true — it sat on a hill overlooking the pond; it was the only existing house on the pond that Frederick Olmsted worked into the design for the Emerald Necklace; and it was severely damaged by two fires in the seventies. What isn't true is that it was saved. After many attempts to preserve the house, the structure was deemed too damaged to restore, and it was razed. I bet I wasn't the only morning jogger who imagined what it might be like to live in the beautiful house and to wake up each morning beside the pond, so I decided to resurrect Pinebank for this novel. Many thanks to the Jamaica Plain Historical Society (www.jphs.org) for helping me research the history of Pinebank. If you would like to learn more about it, or Jamaica Plain, they are a terrific resource.

Thanks to my early readers, who help save me from myself: Katherine Bates, Daniel Ford, Shawn Reilly Simmons, and Alicia Young.

Maxine, Tucker, and Jennifer began as characters in a short story called "White Tights and Mary Janes" published as part of the Department of First Stories in the

January/February 2018 issue of *Ellery Queen Mystery Magazine.* I will forever be grateful to Janet Hutchings and Jackie Sherbow for giving me my first big break.

Many thanks to Ron for Chicken Day, to Will for hiding that box top; to Ann and Michael for Fred and Adele, and to Katherine and Ben for the many memories on Sherwood Street.

To my agent, Robert Guinsler, thank you for your friendship and support. And to the incredible team at Kensington, starting with editor extraordinaire John Scognamiglio; the whole publicity team, including Vida Engstrand, Larissa Ackerman, and Lauren Jerningan; Darla Freeman and the whole sales team; Lou Malcangi, for his stunning cover designs; and Steve Zacharius, Lynn Cully, Tracy Marx, Robin Cook, and everyone else behind the scenes. I couldn't ask for a better publishing team.

To Betty, Jack, Christine, and Chester; to all of the Hills and the Rowells; to the Starrs, Maroldas and Sullivans (and especially to Bob and Christine) thank you for your continued support.

To Edith Ann for putting up with endless walks and belly rubs during the pandemic (follow her on Instagram! @edithannlab).

I wrote this novel as a love letter to

Hester's ever-patient partner, the kind and compassionate Morgan Maguire. I hope he got his due. And I offer a special shout-out to my own patient partner, Michael, to whom I dedicate this book. None of this happens without your continued love and support. Thank you!

Finally, to anyone who takes a chance on this book, thank you a million times over. I can't tell you how much it means to me. Please be in touch!

Web: www.edwin-hill.com.

Facebook, Twitter, and Instagram: @ed winhillauthor.

ABOUT THE AUTHOR

Edwin Hill is the author of the critically acclaimed Hester Thursby mystery series, the first of which, *Little Comfort,* was an Agatha Award finalist, a selection of the Mysterious Press First Mystery Club and a Publishers Marketplace *Buzz Books* selection. The second installment, *The Missing Ones,* was also an Agatha Award finalist and a Sue Grafton Memorial Award nominee. Formerly the vice president and editorial director for Bedford/St. Martin's (Macmillan), he now teaches at Emerson College and has written for the *LA Review of Books, The Life Sentence, Publishers Weekly,* and *Ellery Queen Mystery Magazine.*

He lives in Roslindale, Massachusetts with his partner Michael and their Labrador, Edith Ann. Visit him online at Edwin-Hill .com.